I0776663

The
Blind
Trust

a 509 Crime Story

by Colin Conway

The Blind Trust

Copyright © 2019, 2023 Colin Conway

Original Cover Design by Zach McCain
Updated Cover Design by Rob Williams

First Edition – 2019, Second Edition – 2023

ISBN: 978-1-961030-07-7

Original Ink Press, an imprint of High Speed Creative, LLC
1521 N. Argonne Road, #C-205
Spokane Valley, WA 99212

Visit the author's website at www.colinconway.com

What is the 509?

Separated by the Cascade Range, Washington State is divided into two distinctly different climates and cultures.

The western side of the Cascades is home to Seattle, its 34 inches of annual rainfall, and the incredibly weird and smelly Gum Wall. Most of the state's wealth and political power are concentrated in and around this enormous city. The residents of this area know the prosperity that has come from being the home of Microsoft, Amazon, Boeing, and Starbucks.

To the east of the Cascade Mountains lies nearly two-thirds of the entire state, a lot of which is used for agriculture. Washington State leads the nation in producing apples, it is the second-largest potato grower, and it's the fourth for providing wheat.

This eastern part of the state can enjoy more than 170 days of sunshine each year, which is important when there are more than 200 lakes nearby. However, the beautiful summers are offset by harsh winters, with average snowfall reaching 47 inches and the average high hovering around 37°.

While five telephone area codes provide service to the westside, only 509 covers everything east of the Cascades, a staggering twenty-one counties.

Of these, Spokane County is the largest with an estimated population of 506,000.

For Jason.
Gone too early.

*And if a house be divided against itself,
that house cannot stand.*

\-   Mark 3:25, King James Version

The
Blind
Trust

PART I

Chapter 1

Whitman County Sheriff Tom Jessup turned off US-195 at the small town of Steptoe to head eastbound onto WA-23. Earlier in the day, light snow had fallen. Only a smattering remained alongside the shoulder of the road. The pavement itself was wet but clear. As the miles passed, his mind wandered.

The bottom of his fist lightly tapped the steering wheel.

Yesterday had been Valentine's Day—a holiday Jessup hadn't celebrated for eight years, not since Mia's death. Her diagnosis had been a surprise. How quickly it took her was an even bigger shock.

Mia passed during their son's sophomore year of high school. With each passing day, it seemed William pulled further away from Jessup. Whenever he reached out for his son, Will pulled away faster. If Jessup gave him space, he continued to slip away, albeit slower. He ran away for three days when Jessup suggested they go to a counselor. He didn't suggest that again.

What should have brought them closer only drove them further apart. He knew Will blamed him for his mother's death. It was irrational and immature, but the boy's mother had died. Jessup didn't know how to reach his son, so he kept quiet, hoping that someday Will would come around and realize his anger was misdirected.

They had developed an uneasy peace until Will graduated and went to Washington State University, twenty minutes south of their hometown. Although they had continued to reside together in the same house, they rarely spoke to each other.

When he finished college, Will moved to New York and had yet to return to Colfax. Jessup's only contact with his son was the occasional stilted phone call, and an annual Christmas card signed only *Love, Will.*

A couple of miles from the town of St. John, Jessup cleared his mind and focused on the reason he was there. His office had been notified of a dead body. He wasn't usually the first to respond to these types of calls. However, his deputies were busy, so he accepted the responsibility this morning. Truth be told, Jessup liked taking calls and getting out of the office. Being sheriff was a great responsibility that he still enjoyed, but he missed the day-to-day life of a deputy.

He drove through the small, picturesque town and made a left turn on Park Street. He continued southbound through the neighborhoods until he arrived at the last house on the block. St. John had less than six hundred residents, so it only took a few minutes to get where he was headed.

Even though it sat on a couple of acres, the house was located only a hundred feet from the street. The property abutted neighboring farmland.

A dented blue Chevy truck was in the driveway, light exhaust pumping from its tailpipe. Jessup pulled in behind the truck, blocking it in. He climbed out and walked up to the driver's window.

An older man was asleep behind the wheel.

With the back of his bare knuckles, Jessup rapped lightly on the window.

The man started, then studied Jessup. He blinked several times until he nodded and rolled down his window. "Mornin', Sheriff."

"You call this in?"

"Yes, sir."

"What's your name?"

"Bernie Henderson, but my mother and the church call me Bernard."

Jessup jotted the name in his notebook. "Mr. Henderson, how did you discover the deceased?"

"Oh, me and Renny, we been friends for ages. We meet every mornin' at the St. John Inn. For coffee and whatnot. Have been for years. When he didn't show today and didn't call, well, I figured somethin' mighta been wrong."

"You went inside?"

Henderson nodded. "We walk into each other's places all the time. Nobody locks their houses around here, Sheriff. You know how it is."

"Touch anything?"

"Only him. I shook him to see if I could wake him. When I realized he was… well, I called you."

"Did you use a cell phone or the house phone?"

"The house phone. Don't have a cell."

"Is the house still unlocked?"

"Yes."

"Wait here," Jessup said and patted the side of the truck.

He walked to the house, pausing near the door to let his eyes sweep over the exterior of the light blue home. It was large, one of the biggest he remembered seeing in his previous times through St. John. However, it would be considered rather ordinary in a city like Spokane.

He opened the house and stepped in. The sheriff paused again, letting his eyes scan the living room. He then proceeded slowly through each room, deliberately taking care to notice anything that might be out of place. When he made it to the rear bedroom, he moved inside.

Renard Andrew Smith lay alone in a queen-size bed. Sixty-six years old, according to the information Jessup had pulled from the DMV before leaving his office.

The sheriff leaned over the man and carefully examined his face and eyes. He looked for signs of an assault around his face and neck. He didn't notice anything that would indicate foul play.

He stood and walked through the house again. Nothing seemed out of place. He slowly examined each room, looking for anything that might lead one to suspect unnatural causes. Twenty minutes later, Jessup stepped back on the small concrete porch.

Bernie Henderson stood outside his truck, smoking a cigarette. Jessup walked over to him.

"Was Smith married?"

"*Was*, but he hadn't been for more than a decade. She got her divorce and ran off to Hawaii. Can you believe that? She wanted a life that Renny had no interest in living." He thought for a moment. "Actually, I think she just wanted a life without Renny."

"How about a girlfriend?"

"Me?"

Jessup stared at him.

Henderson shook his head. "Well, of course, not me. Sorry, don't know what I was thinking, Sheriff. No, Renny didn't have a woman. He became quite sore toward the opposite sex. Who can blame him after what his wife did? He sort of figured all women would do the same thing to him. Renny was an acquired taste anyway, the kind most women ain't going to stick around to develop."

"Acquired taste, how?"

"He was quiet. Didn't talk much. Kept to hisself."

"What about children?"

"He had a son. Died in a boatin' accident while in high school out on Rock Lake. Real tragedy. That's what eventually did in his marriage, you ask me."

A quick thought of his son, William, flashed through Jessup's mind. He pushed it away and asked, "What about parents? They still alive? Or siblings?"

"Parents are long dead. I know that as Renny talked about it once around Christmas. He never said much beyond that. As for siblings, I don't think so, at least he never mentioned any. Renny wasn't the type of man you pried into, understand? We never tried the cards, but I'm bettin' he would have been a helluva poker player."

"Health issues?"

"He had a heart attack a few years back. He tried to take care of hisself after that. Go for daily walks. Eat right, mostly. That sort of thing. He even worked out every day with those ladies on the videotapes. You know what I'm talkin' about? I'd come into the house, and he'd be gruntin' and groanin' on the floor, just to keep the ticker in shape. I guess it didn't do him a whole lotta good in the end, huh?"

Jessup glanced back to the house and was quiet for a minute.

Henderson interrupted his thoughts to ask, "Want me to hang out here some more, Sheriff?"

Jessup turned back to him and said, "I think I've got what I need."

He shook Henderson's hand and then walked to his truck. He backed it out of the way so the older man could remove his vehicle from the driveway. Jessup then picked up the radio microphone and keyed it.

"Autumn," he said. They didn't have the formality that he had observed while a member of the Spokane Police Department.

A moment later, a female voice came over the radio. "Hey, Sheriff."

The snow began to fall lightly again.

"I'm in St. John," he said. "Call the medical examiner. Ask him to head this direction."

Chapter 2

A couple of hours later when he returned to Colfax, Jessup parked his truck outside the sheriff's office, which was housed in the same building as the county jail. The Colfax Police Department sat kitty-corner to their building.

Along with protecting the county, the sheriff's office was responsible for overseeing the jail. On most days, the jail population was in the low thirties, but some days it could climb to over fifty. He had a staff of deputies and supervisors who ran the jail, for which he was thankful. That was not where his heart lay, though. He had been a patrol officer with the Spokane Police Department before returning to his childhood home to join their department. He had moved to a smaller department for Mia. It wasn't his dream, but he was happy to do it. Everything was worth it when done for her.

"Morning, boss."

Deputy Rodney Howard held the door for him as he entered the sheriff's office. Howard and Jessup were the same age and had attended high school together. It made Jessup happy to be working with his high school friend.

Outside of the jail staff, the sheriff's office was a small team, made up of him and several deputies like Howard. He patted his deputy's shoulder as he walked past him into the office.

The furniture was dated, some of it as far back as the 1960s. It could all use replacing, but money was a perpetual issue, and the limited budget for equipment always needed to be spent on keeping up with the latest upgrades in technology, not the latest in fashion. Therefore, the gray gunmetal desks would last well past Jessup's tenure, however long that would be.

"Good morning, kiddo," Jessup said as he approached Autumn Summers.

Autumn was the department's go-to problem solver—receptionist, administrative assistant, social media expert, and web page manager. For Jessup, she was also his primary connection to William. The two had been friends in school, and she still kept tabs on him. How she did it, he never really knew, but she was always good for a recent update from him that let Jessup feel like he still had some understanding of his son's life.

"It's almost noon, Sheriff."

"Then technically, it's still morning," he said, walking into his own office. He dropped into his chair and looked up just as Rodney Howard walked in.

"Was it bad?"

"What?"

"The DB?"

"The dead body?"

"Yeah, the DB."

"You're watching too much TV again."

"You knew what I meant."

Jessup shook his head. "Might have been a heart attack. Won't know for sure until after the autopsy."

"I would have taken it, you know?"

"I know," the sheriff said. "It wasn't a big deal."

"The Fables' garage had been burglarized, and they wanted someone to come out to take pictures."

"It's okay, Rod. You were busy, so I took it."

"But you're the sheriff."

"I'm still a duly commissioned peace officer in the State of Washington."

"Yeah, but you're… the sheriff."

"Do I look old and frail?"

"Can I answer that?" Autumn yelled from outside his office.

Jessup ignored her and stared at his deputy. He still liked handling cases. That's why he became a police officer and then a deputy. He wasn't going to stop just because he had the political and administrative responsibilities of being the sheriff.

Finally, Howard said, "I get it," and wandered back to his desk.

Jessup turned his attention to the papers in front of him.

Chapter 3

After work, Jessup remained in his uniform and drove over to his childhood home to visit his parents. They lived on South Lake Street with a view of the main drag through town.

It never occurred to Jessup while growing up that there was no lake to be found nearby. The street was only eight blocks long, so someone would think a city founder could have picked a more creative name for the road. There wasn't even a lake within the city limits. The Palouse River flowed through town and forked off, creating a smaller cousin, the South Fork Palouse River, but there was no lake.

He bounded the steps and opened the door. His mother, Vera, was in the kitchen chopping carrots on a white cutting board. She looked over her shoulder as he entered.

"You're in time for dinner," she said with a smile.

"Not staying, Mom. Wanted to check in on you guys, then go home and shower."

"I can make a plate of something for you."

Jessup kissed her on the cheek as she continued to work through the last of the carrots. "I'm fine, Mom. Truly. Where's Pop?

"In the back, fiddling with something."

Jessup found his father, Dwight, near the woodpile. "What are you doing?"

"Hmm?" Dwight said and turned to him.

"What are you doing, Pop?"

"Came out for some wood."

"Then, you decided to stay out in the chill?"

"I didn't forget what I was doin' if that's what you're thinkin'."

"I just came out to see you."

"Uh-huh," his father mumbled.

"So, what were you doing?"

"Thinkin'."

"About?"

"Can't a man have a private thought without his family always buzzin' around his beeswax?"

Jessup smiled and put his hand on his father's shoulder. "Okay, Pop. I'll leave you to your thoughts."

Dwight's face relaxed then. "I guess I was thinkin' about time."

"Time?"

"Yeah, time. I'm seventy-two, you know?"

"I know."

"Yesterday, I was twenty-one. How the hell did this happen?"

Jessup furrowed his brow and studied his father.

"Don't look at me like that. I know I was seventy-two yesterday as well, dummy, I was speakin' metaphorically. At least, I think that's what I was doin'. That's the right word, right? Metaphorically?"

"I'm not tracking," Jessup said.

"This is what I was thinkin'. Yesterday, I went to bed. I was twenty-one years old. I was freshly married. We didn't know we were going to have a baby yet. That's you, by the way. We had just bought this house. My whole life was ahead of me. The world was my oyster. I wake up today and find myself standin' in front of this woodpile, wondering how many years I got left— wondering where my whole life went. How did it happen so fast? How did it happen without me realizing it was happenin'?"

"That's how life goes, Pop. To each of us."

"I remember twenty-one so vividly, the sights, the smells. I remember painting each of those rooms with your mother. Your mother. Oh, Tommy, she was a sight. I love her so much. Even to this day, I would be lost without her, but back then, your mother could enter a room and take my breath away. Sophia Loren couldn't hold a candle to her."

His father fell silent then and stared off into the distance. Jessup watched him. He'd never seen his father this way before.

"Where did all the time go?" he asked as his eyes dropped to the woodpile.

Jessup put his arm around his father's shoulders and said, "I love you, Pop."

The older man nodded and softly said, "I love you, too, bub." He wrapped an arm around his son's waist and patted him. "Let's get this wood inside. Your mother's probably gettin' cold by now."

Chapter 4

A couple of days later, Lawrence Inklebarger walked into Sheriff Jessup's office and dropped a manila folder on his desk. The heavy-set man wore a slightly wrinkled gray suit with a freshly pressed white shirt. He lowered himself into the seat across from Jessup.

"You all right, Larry?"

Inklebarger rubbed his legs. "My knees are killing me, Sheriff."

"What's this?" Jessup asked, putting a finger on the manila folder.

The gray-haired man lifted his chin and said, "The autopsy for Renard Smith."

Jessup picked it up and fanned the pages of it.

"I'll give you the *Reader's Digest* version," Inklebarger said. "He had a history of heart disease. I confirmed with his doctor that he'd had a heart attack ten years ago. However, again according to his doctor, he'd been working on his health ever since. He wasn't perfect but pretty good for a man of his age."

"Cause of death?"

"Same as always. His heart stopped."

Jessup dropped the folder on his desk and watched the medical examiner.

The older man shrugged. "Was trying for levity."

"Yeah."

"Hmm. Anyway, the only thing slightly out of the ordinary was some ocular petechial hemorrhaging."

Jessup's eyes narrowed in concern. "Suffocation?"

"That is a sign of suffocation, yes, but it's also consistent with a heart attack."

"He was on his back," the sheriff said. "Pretty difficult to accidentally suffocate in that position."

"True. But a pretty normal position to find a heart attack victim."

"Did he aspirate at all?"

Inklebarger shook his head, his jowls swaying. "Nope. Mouth and throat were clear." He gave Jessup a half shrug. "If it wasn't natural, maybe someone covered his face with something."

Jessup picked up the report and started to read it carefully. Inklebarger took that as his cue for dismissal.

When the examiner left, Jessup turned to his computer and called up the folder of photos from Renard Smith's bedroom. He'd taken them before the removal of the body.

He looked at the pillow next to Smith. It was smooth. That didn't mean anything, Jessup reminded himself. Maybe he didn't disturb it while he slept.

Even so, he wanted to take a closer look at it.

If this wasn't a heart attack, and it was suffocation, why did it have to be that pillow? Couldn't it have been something else, anything else?

Chapter 5

Jessup pulled into town and was about to pass the St. John Inn when he noticed a familiar pickup parked in front. He slammed his brakes and turned his truck into the tiny lot in front of the building.

He had planned to head to Smith's house first and examine the bedroom, but there would be time for that. He got the house key from the evidence locker, so he could let himself in whenever he arrived.

Several people were inside the café when he entered. They all turned his way with expectant faces. When they realized who he was, their looks turned to suspicion. A county sheriff coming into a small town often meant bad news for someone.

Jessup made eye contact with Bernie Henderson and nodded. He walked over and extended his hand. Henderson shook it.

"Got a minute for a few follow-up questions, Mr. Henderson?"

"O' course, Sheriff," he said and motioned for him to sit at his table.

A waitress walked over. "Morning, Sheriff. Cup of coffee or something to eat?"

Jessup smiled politely. "No, thanks."

She nodded and walked away.

"Would anyone want to harm Mr. Smith?"

"Renny? Not a chance. He was salt of the earth. He kept to hisself, but people generally liked him enough to say hi to."

"He never mentioned any trouble then?"

Henderson frowned. "You suspectin' somethin'?"

Jessup tapped the table. "Not sure. Following up mostly."

Henderson sipped his coffee and watched the sheriff.

"He ever talk about a will?" Jessup asked.

"Not that I remember, no. If he had one, you'd want to talk with that legal beagle, Earl Kelly. He handled all of Renny's affairs."

"Is he in town?"

Henderson chuckled. "Everyone who matters is in this town. He's a couple blocks down the street."

Jessup left his truck parked and walked two blocks to the Law Office of Earl Kelly. When he stepped inside, he saw it was a one-room affair. A silver-haired gentleman walked out of the restroom. He wore a blue sweater, khaki pants, and brown New Balance hiking shoes. He had a ruddy complexion and a clean-shaven face. He stopped when he saw Jessup's uniform.

"Is everything okay?"

"Earl Kelly?"

"Yes," the attorney said, drawing out the word, suspicion growing on his face.

"I'd like to ask you some questions about a client of yours. Renard Smith."

Kelly breathed a sigh of relief. "I thought you were here to deliver bad news."

"Beyond Mr. Smith?"

The older man waved his hand and walked toward his desk. "Well, yes, of course, but I already knew about that. I meant personally. I have a wife and children, Sheriff. Grandchildren, too. When a man in uniform walks in, you expect the worst." Kelly sat in his swivel chair and asked, "What can I do you for?"

"Did Mr. Smith have a will?"

"He did, yes."

"Who were the beneficiaries?"

Kelly stood and moved over to a filing cabinet. He lowered himself to a knee and yanked open the bottom drawer. He flipped through several files before pulling out a folder. With some effort, he righted himself and moved back to the desk. It took him only a couple of seconds to locate the document. He didn't bother consulting it but handed it directly to the sheriff.

As he read, Jessup's eyebrows lifted. "There was only one beneficiary in the event of Mr. Smith's death?"

"That's correct. The local Catholic church, Our Lady of Perpetual Help. Renny was a devoted follower. He left everything, including his house, to the parish."

Jessup quickly scanned the Last Will and Testament of Renard Andrew Smith. Earl Kelly was named the executor of the will. "There's not much to this document."

Kelly shrugged. "Everything went to one place. Renny wasn't much of a talker. He walked in one day and said he wanted everything to go to the church. When I asked him for further details, he said that should be enough. I worked with what he gave me."

"How much was Mr. Smith worth?"

"About half a million now, I guess, if you don't count his pension, which will stop payment now that he's died. His wife got a good chunk of that when she divorced him and ran off to Hawaii."

"The ex doesn't get anything following his death?"

Kelly laughed. "Oh, God, no. He despised that woman. He admitted it wasn't a very Christian thing to feel, but she broke his heart. When she left, she made it very clear that she no longer wanted to waste her life in this town."

"What did he do for a living?"

"He was a teacher over at the high school."

"And he was worth half a million?"

Kelly shrugged. "He wasn't a flashy man and sure didn't live an opulent lifestyle. Maybe he invested wisely or got some from an inheritance. I don't know."

"He talk about his family?"

"Not really, no. Renny was a quiet man. Nice and reliable, but quiet. Kept to himself."

"That's what I've heard. Half a million, huh?"

"Yup."

"You go to the church?"

Kelly chuckled. "Me? Oh, no. At best, I'm a lukewarm Christian. At worst, I'm a tepid atheist. The town tolerates my straddling the line of agnosticism. Most of them don't like it, but they don't want to lose another resident to the big city of Colfax."

Jessup smiled. "About the will. Did any members of the church know of it?"

"Are you implying something bad happened to Renny? Word around town is he had a heart attack."

"It looks like that, yes."

"Looks like?"

"Back to my question," Jessup prompted.

"He may have told them about the will, but I highly doubt it. As I said, he kept things to himself. Besides, the church has a loyal base. It's not like they would need this windfall. It will be nice for them, of course, but it wasn't necessary."

Jessup stepped forward and extended his hand. "Thank you for your time."

Chapter 6

There was a car in the driveway of Renard Smith's house. Jessup's heart rate quickened, and he pulled his truck in behind it. For a moment, he considered calling for backup, but it could be a considerable amount of time for one to arrive. That was the reality of working in a county—you had to learn how to work alone.

He got out and quickly moved toward the front door. He tried the doorknob, and it was unlocked. He had secured it prior to leaving several days ago.

Stepping in, he loudly announced, "Sheriff's department."

There was no answer.

He listened carefully and heard running water.

"Sheriff's department," he yelled.

When there was still no answer, he pulled his gun and walked forward. He slowly moved through the living room. He peeked into the kitchen. On the counter was a bucket of cleaning supplies.

The sound of running water was louder. He could now hear a female voice softly singing.

"Sheriff's department," he said, although this time, his voice was at a natural level.

He moved down the hallway and peeked into a bathroom.

A woman was bent over the tub scrubbing the walls. She wore pink rubber gloves and worked with a blue sponge. Headphones were in her ears, and she sang with some music Jessup couldn't hear. Her voice was soft but out of tune.

He slid his gun back into his holster.

"Sheriff's department," he said, but she didn't respond.

He reached for the light switch and flicked it quickly on and off.

The woman stopped cleaning and looked up.

Jessup clicked the switch once more.

When she turned around, her eyes widened, and she screamed.

***

After she quieted, Jessup escorted the woman into the living room. She was seated on the couch.

Her name was Joyce Fuller, and she wore a dark blue sweatshirt, faded blue jeans, and white tennis shoes. Her long sandy blond hair was bunched in the back with a clip. She was in her late forties.

"He's dead?" Fuller asked. Her eyes drifted to the floor as she thought. When they returned to the sheriff, she asked, "How? When?"

"You didn't know?"

"How would I know? I come by once a week to clean his house. Same day. Same time."

"You don't talk with him when you come to clean?"

She shook her head. "He always leaves the house before I come and does something for a few hours. I send him a bill once a month, and he sends me a check. He's one of my best customers. Never hit on me once. You don't know how rare that is."

"The house was locked," Jessup said.

"I thought that was weird, but he gave me a key when he first hired me. He's locked it before when he's gone out of town. I didn't give it too much thought beyond that."

Somewhere in the house, a buzzer sounded.

"What's that?" Jessup asked.

"The dryer."

"What?"

"I do his laundry and bedding while I'm here."

Jessup turned and hurried down the hallway toward Smith's bedroom. "Crap," he said when he saw it. The bed had been stripped, and bare pillows were on the floor.

Fuller came in behind him. "What's wrong?"

"Nothing."

"I don't know about that. You look pretty mad right now."

Jessup shook his head and walked back into the living room.

Fuller followed him.

The two stood in awkward silence for several minutes.

Finally, she said, "Sheriff?"

"Hmm?"

"What should I..." she paused, looking slightly embarrassed. "What should I do now?"

"What do you mean?"

"I'm almost done cleaning, and I'm still doing his laundry. Should I finish? And am I going to get paid? I know that sounds bad, but..."

Jessup considered her question before answering. "Get your stuff and head out," he finally said. "Go see Earl Kelly downtown. He's handling Renny's estate now."

Chapter 7

Jessup sat at his desk and reviewed his notes.

Renard Smith was found dead and alone in his house. There was no sign of forced entry, but he usually left his home unlocked. Everyone in town probably knew it. Hell, outsiders probably expected this quirky behavior from small-town residents.

Smith had a history of heart disease and at least one heart attack. However, his doctor had reported improvement.

Just because there was petechial hemorrhaging didn't mean he died from suffocation. The indicator was common in victims of heart attacks.

The house had been cleaned, so there was no further evidence to garner.

Did I make a mistake? Jessup wondered.

Should he have locked down the house and taken prints, swabs, and the like? The evidence did not initially point in that direction. To do so would have been a misuse of resources. Natural deaths happened too frequently county-wide to throw that kind of analysis at a scene with nothing suspicious about it.

Should he have secured the house better? He had locked it, and there was no way of knowing a housecleaner would show up later.

He also didn't know that he would soon be second-guessing himself on whether this was a natural death or something completely different.

Perhaps I'm jumping to a conclusion, Jessup thought.

Maybe it was simply a heart attack, and he should let the damn thing go. He read the report once more before setting it in the *File* basket. He clicked his tongue several

times against the roof of his mouth before deciding there
was nothing more to do.

PART II

Chapter 8

It was St. Patrick's Day, and Quinn Delaney was alone.

He hadn't gone out to celebrate his Irish heritage or to watch the city's parade. Instead, he spent the day alone in his new apartment. Delaney had recently sold his home and was still getting things settled in the apartment. He was surprised at how high rents had risen since the last time he'd lived in an apartment.

Regardless, the unit was new with shiny appliances, and the community had a pool and a workout room. It was still about half of what he was paying in mortgage and escrow fees on the house he had once purchased with his now ex-wife, Barbara. Getting free of the home removed a huge weight from his shoulders.

He carried a box into the kitchen. He unloaded various pots and pans, putting them where he wanted. It felt strange to set up a kitchen by himself. He hadn't arranged the previous one. It was Barbara who did. She made the decision where things went. Truth be told, she chose where just about everything went in the house. Now, he was making those choices, and he had a feeling of both satisfaction and regret.

He missed her.

Moving into the apartment was another reminder of the things he had done wrong in that relationship. He had loved her the best he could, but he had failed to grow and change as she had. In the end, she continued her personal journey and left him behind. When he finally realized she was right, that he needed to change, it was too late. The marriage had long been over.

He broke down the cardboard box and added it to the recycle pile.

The clock on the stove said it was almost a quarter till midnight. Quinn grabbed the light beer bottle from the counter and sipped from it.

As he relaxed, a wave of exhaustion rolled over him. He had hoped to get all the boxes done today so he could take it easy on Sunday. Unfortunately, he counted seven small boxes still stacked in the living room.

"Tomorrow," he said and took another sip of beer.

His cell phone buzzed, its screen identifying the caller. For a moment, he thought about ignoring it, but he knew he couldn't do that. They would have called his partner before him, or they would call her afterward. Unless they both ignored the call simultaneously, one of them would be screwed. If they both ignored it, there would be hell to pay on Monday morning in front of the brass.

When he answered, a voice said, "Quinn?"

"Yeah."

"It's Debbie at dispatch. You okay?"

"Yeah, I'm good."

"Are you sober?"

"Why do you ask?"

"Well…"

"I'm fine," Quinn said.

"I didn't mean to suppose. It's St. Patty's Day and all."

"I know."

"There's a double homicide, and you're up."

"Did you already call Marci?"

"Yeah."

"How did she sound?

"Fine, except I woke her up."

"She'll be pleasant then."

"That's your problem," Debbie said.

"Text me the address. I'm on my way."

Quinn put the nearly empty beer back on the counter. He stared at it and the empty bottle next to it. He finally shook his head, then picked them up, and threw them into the recycle bin.

It was 11:47 p.m.

I know better than to push my luck, Quinn thought.

Chapter 9

After a cold shower, Quinn snapped a dark roast module into the Keurig coffeemaker. While it brewed, he got dressed. When he first became a Homicide detective, he would rush to a crime scene after getting called. He quickly learned it didn't matter how fast he got there. The victim would still be dead, and the other officers were still going to get paid. It was better to take his time and make sure his head was right when he arrived.

He took the coffee with him as he drove to the crime scene.

The house was located on the edge of West Central along Summit Boulevard. For several decades that area of town had been considered a high crime area, except for the houses along that street.

Those homes overlooked the Spokane River. They were big and held their value while the neighborhood behind them went into decline. Most of the homeowners along this strip of real estate were older citizens who had been there for decades, long before the deterioration of the surrounding area.

With a recent wave of gentrification, though, the houses had become sought after by the city's new rich.

Times change, and people die. It's something most people try to deny, but every cop knows too well.

A three-foot-high rock wall bordered the edge of the property, breaking only where the driveway entered.

Patrol cars were parked along the street. The forensic unit was already on the scene.

After parking his car, Quinn finished the last of his coffee and got out. It was cold, barely above freezing. He wrapped his coat tighter around his body and shoved his hands into his pockets.

Turning around, he surveyed the neighborhood. There were a couple of streetlights at opposite ends of the property that lit up the road. Across the street, though, there was nothing but blackness. He knew an edge of the cliff was there that would drop down to the river.

Quinn reached back into his car and pulled out his Maglite. He turned it on and headed toward the house.

An inner and outer perimeter had already been set up. The inner perimeter was at the front of the house. The outer was set about halfway up the length of the driveway. Several officers huddled around Geri Utley from the forensic unit. They were chatting her up with big grins and puffed chests. She was an attractive woman who politely smiled back. The lieutenant in charge of the scene approached Quinn to stop him before he ducked under the outer perimeter line.

"Damn, Delaney," Lieutenant Weller said. "What took you so long?"

"Traffic," he said.

"At one in the morning?"

"It's called sarcasm, Lieutenant."

"I know what it is. My guys are tied up on this call while you took your time getting here."

Quinn turned away from the lieutenant to watch the other officers chat with Geri. When he refocused his attention on Weller, Quinn said, "It definitely looks like your guys are put out by my response time."

Weller rolled his eyes.

"Who called it in?" Quinn asked.

"Neighbor to the west," Weller said, thumbing toward the house he described. "Said she heard a couple of shots, ran to the window in time to see a car drive away. She then called 911. Cappellano arrived and found the front door open. Called for backup. They went in, found the bodies, and secured the residence."

"Quinn!"

He turned to see Marci Burkett walking up the driveway. She had a 7-Eleven cup in her hand. Quinn looked back over his shoulder to see a couple of the officers now watching Marci.

A black scarf was wrapped around her neck and tucked into a black, knee-length wool coat. A red beanie was pulled down on her head, which allowed some of her dark hair to appear underneath.

"Burkett, your response time is even worse than his," Weller said.

She shrugged, sipped her coffee, then said, "The party doesn't start until we arrive."

"You may have your lieutenant fooled, Burkett, but you better hope I never end up your commanding officer."

"You think they'll put *you* in charge of Major Crimes?"

Weller scowled at her. "You're insubordinate, Burkett."

Marci ignored him, took the final swig of her coffee, and set the empty cup down on the driveway.

The lieutenant eyed the action with irritation. "You're going to get that on the way out, right?"

"Unless you want me to take it into the crime scene and leave it there? Is that why you never became a detective?"

Weller's jaw flexed.

Marci moved toward the outer perimeter tape. "Let the grown-ups handle the heavy lifting now."

The lieutenant opened his mouth to comment, but Marci was already under the tape and headed toward the house.

When Weller turned to Quinn, the detective started to say something in support of his partner, thought better of it, and followed her under the tape.

Chapter 10

They stood on the front porch, each tugging on a pair of latex gloves, followed by a pair of covers over their shoes.

"You trying to piss off the lieutenant?" Quinn asked.

"He's a turd. He needs to be brought back down a peg."

"How do you figure?"

"He's forgotten where he came from. He was a worker bee like the rest of us once. Then he put some brass on his collar and shoved his head up his butt. We do a disservice to the newly minted upper echelon when we bow to them and treat them with respect. We ought to do the opposite. We should kick them in the nuts to remind them they're not any better than they were the day before they got that hunk of metal. Maybe then they'd treat the line-level and detectives like they remember what it was like to be one."

"That just come to you?"

"It's been building up."

"So, you let it go tonight on Weller?"

"It has to start somewhere."

"Well, keep it pointed away from me."

Marci grinned. "What are they going to do? They can't fire me. You've seen some of the crap that others have done, and they're still around. *Maybe* I get some paper in my file *if* Weller isn't a total creampuff. Big whoop. It's not going to hurt my pension. I figure I'm going to let everyone know how I feel about them. Why pretend to get along?"

"Do me a favor and don't burn down the village while I'm still standing in it."

Marci patted Quinn's arm. "You, my lily-white friend, should voice your opinion more than anyone. You don't have a damn scratch on your record anywhere."

"I take great pride in that fact," Quinn said and shrugged her hand free.

They moved to the front door then and stood there, examining the entry point.

Quinn took a mental picture of everything. When he was ready to enter, he nodded without looking in Marci's direction. She did the same, and they silently stepped into the house. Slowly and methodically, they moved through each room.

In the kitchen, there was glass on the floor near the back door. He looked closely. It appeared someone had broken a corner of the window, stuck a hand in, and opened the deadbolt and door lock. He leaned in closer. There didn't seem to be any trace of blood.

He turned around and noticed the refrigerator was open. On the counter, next to the sink, was a crack pipe and a wallet. Quinn opened the scuffed leather billfold and removed a driver's license. *Cadillac Eldorado Jones.*

"It can't be this simple," Quinn said.

"What was that?" Marci asked from another room.

Quinn was photographing Jones's license with his cell phone when Marci walked in. "Cadillac Jones is either the world's dumbest criminal, or we're supposed to think this was left on a counter by accident."

"Some of these guys are just that stupid. Maybe it's good fortune."

"I don't buy it."

Marci studied the license for a moment. "Yeah... I don't buy it either."

Quinn tucked the license back into the wallet and put it in on the counter where he found it.

They continued moving through the house until they found Clayton and Helen Smith in the master bedroom. Quinn had gotten the homeowners' names from dispatch while driving in.

Clayton was lying half in and half out of bed, his body weight partially supported by his shoulder catching on the nightstand. His left hand touched the wooden floor. He wore a white T-shirt and pajama pants. Blood had pooled on the floor underneath him.

Helen never made it out of bed. She wore a newer blue nightgown, and a pink sleeping cap covered her head. She had a gunshot wound to the chest. Blood was everywhere.

The couple appeared to be in their seventies.

Quinn couldn't be sure with how Clayton's body was positioned, but there appeared to be two wounds—an exit wound on his back as well as an entry wound near his rib cage. It could have been made by a single round that went off course through the body, or two shots had been fired at him.

The detectives examined the bed. They found one entry point in the mattress where Clayton had rolled over.

Marci stepped away from the bodies and stood at the foot of the bed. "We're not going to be sure until forensics confirms this, but here's what I'm seeing. The intruder comes in and shoots the husband and wife. The husband rolls over and gets shot a second time. What do you think?"

"Plausible," Quinn muttered.

"Execution then?" Marci asked.

"Who does that to an older couple like this?"

"We're supposed to believe some crackhead did it, right?"

"Seems simple," Quinn said.

Marci studied the couple for another moment. She finally shook her head. "Too easy."

Quinn turned and walked out of the house with Marci close behind. They stopped on the porch and took off their gloves and footies.

"I'm not ruling out the crackhead," Marci said.

"Assuming he *is* a crackhead."

"Yeah, assuming."

"Which means we don't rule out the evidence," Quinn said. "If it's legit, it will be the quickest double homicide I've solved in my career. How about you?"

"Mine, too. But there's always a first time, right?"

They walked back toward the outer perimeter, where Lieutenant Weller was waiting with Geri Utley and her team. His face pinched as the detectives approached.

Weller asked, "Well? Get what you needed?"

Marci said, "Which neighbor called this in?"

The lieutenant pointed to the house next door, and Marci left without another word.

Weller watched her walk away with disdain.

"Geri, your team is okay to start," Quinn said. "Both vics are in the master bedroom. The point of entry looks to be the kitchen. There are a wallet and a crack pipe near the refrigerator. Photograph and bag that."

"Got it," she said and led her team into the house.

"Where's Cappellano?" Quinn asked the lieutenant.

"In his car, warming up."

The detective nodded and walked down the driveway. Cappellano's patrol car was parked along the street. He saw Quinn approaching and rolled down the passenger side window. Quinn leaned on the door and asked, "Who went in with you?"

"Murdoch."

"What did you guys see when you first got here?"

"Nothing. By the time we arrived, the shooter had fled the scene. We found the victims, exited the house, and called for a supervisor."

"Did you go into the kitchen?"

"We visually cleared it, but we didn't thoroughly search it. Please tell me someone wasn't hiding in there."

Quinn smiled. "No one was hiding. A refrigerator door was open, and evidence was on the counter."

Cappellano nodded. "I saw the open fridge, but I don't remember anything on the counter. You know how it is, though. We were focused on bigger things at that point."

"I know."

"I'll cut you an additional report," Cappellano said.

Quinn nodded his thanks. He patted the door and said, "Stay safe" before heading off to find his partner.

Chapter 11

When Monday morning arrived, the Smith murders were the top priority. A home invasion shooting was front-page news, and the chief had already been before the mayor, members of the city council, and the press several times. He promised all of them that the department would focus on this heinous crime.

The murder of an elderly couple in their sleep had a way of stirring up a community's worst fears.

Quinn's desk phone was ringing when he walked up to his cubicle. He could see the internal extension and knew who was calling before he answered.

"Delaney," he said.

"My office. If your partner's there, bring her." The phone went dead.

He stared at the receiver in his hand. If Marci had gotten that call, Quinn wondered how she would have responded. Her *pushing back on the brass* concept was starting to have some appeal.

***

Captain Gary Ackerman sat behind his desk with his head bowed over some paperwork.

Ackerman's silver hair was expertly cut and perfectly combed. He wore an expensive dark suit, with a white shirt and a light blue tie. Every day he looked as if he belonged on the cover of GQ magazine.

Quinn knocked on the open door, and Ackerman lifted his eyes. "Where's Burkett?"

"She wasn't in. By your tone, I figured you wanted a response more than you wanted both of us."

"Grab a seat."

Quinn hadn't even settled onto a chair before the captain asked, "Where are you with the home invasion murders?"

"At the starting line."

"How's the hunt for Cadillac Jones?"

"You'd know better than me. We were out yesterday. Just getting in now. We've requested an Attempt to Locate but haven't heard that he's been found."

Ackerman leaned back in his chair but left his hands on his desk. He drummed his fingers while he thought. When he stopped, he said, "This case is high profile—the highest. Every news channel is running this as its lead story. That's got the chief, mayor, and council under some pressure. We've got to deliver something, anything, to give everyone a little breathing room."

"I understand."

"Check in with me regularly on your progress."

"Sir."

Ackerman watched Quinn for a moment until the detective realized it was time to go. Quinn stood and left the captain's office without another word.

Back at his cubicle, Quinn started his computer and waited. Before it had booted up, a male voice said, "You're late, Detective."

He turned to see Lieutenant George Brand behind him. His arms were crossed over his chest, and his round glasses sat cockeyed on his face. His bald head gleamed under the fluorescent lights.

"I was called into the captain's office when I first got here."

Brand's mouth dropped slightly. A stickler for the rules, he was never happy when the chain of command was violated, either up or down. "What did he want?"

"To talk about the Smith murders."

"That's why I'm here."

"It's a popular topic."

"The chief wants extra focus on this one."

"Every homicide gets our full focus, Lieutenant."

"This one is getting pressure from the press."

"I heard."

Brand's ears turned bright red, but he remained silent.

"I'll make it a priority," Quinn said, more to get him to go away than to let himself off the hook.

The lieutenant nodded and moved deeper into the detectives' bullpen where his office was located.

"I thought he would never leave," Marci said, walking from around the corner with a cup of coffee in her hand. "What did Lieutenant Ten-Key want?"

"To make sure we knew everyone was watching the Smith murders."

Marci dropped into the chair at the cubicle next to Quinn's. "What did you tell him?"

"That we would focus on it."

"So, basically, we would do what we're trained to do?"

"Yeah."

"These lieutenants," she said, shaking her head. "They need a kick in the nuts."

***

The initial photographs and reports had arrived from the forensic team.

They had dug a single round from the mattress. The bullet had been bagged and sent to the lab for further testing.

While Marci researched the victims, Quinn used the forensic report, along with his notes and those of the other responding officers, to compile the initial case file. When that was done, he got to work on creating a history for Cadillac Jones. Patrol had already been alerted to him, but no one had found the man yet.

He pulled up Jones's record from NCIC, the National Crime Information Center.

Cadillac Eldorado Jones was a transplant from Albuquerque, New Mexico, where he'd amassed a healthy criminal record. While living there, he'd been arrested and convicted on multiple charges of drugs, burglary, and malicious mischief. Nothing ever sent him to prison, but it was enough to get him into the local jail system for short stretches.

He popped up on the Spokane radar about a year ago with an arrest for driving with a suspended license along with possession of drug paraphernalia (a crack pipe) and possession of stolen property.

There was no known gang affiliation, but he had a CI flag—a confidential informant. Quinn couldn't get that information immediately, hence the word *confidential*. It would require going further up the flagpole.

However, he had a probation officer listed, Yvette Oliver. Since he'd worked with Yvette in the past, Quinn decided to visit her.

Chapter 12

Yvette Oliver's office was in West Central in a small nondescript building. Most homeowners would tend to lash out in anger when they discovered that a Department of Corrections office was opening in their neighborhood. Therefore, it was usually done discreetly and in an out-of-the-way location.

Even without a prominent storefront, parolees and probationers would always be motivated to find where they had to report in. They needed to remain in good standing with their parole officer, or they could be "violated" and sent back to prison. Most wouldn't want that to happen, so they'd go out of their way to locate a corrections office.

Yvette greeted Quinn after he walked in. He could have gotten the information with a phone call, but the department heads were looking for action on the case. Even if it was a task he could have accomplished from his desk, it was better to have someone out *physically* doing something.

She smiled as they shook hands. "How are you, Quinn?"

"Good."

"You're grayer than I remember."

"Age has a way of doing that."

She looked uncomfortable for a moment before saying, "I'm sorry to hear about you and Barbara."

"Yeah," he said, but offered nothing more.

They stood in awkward silence until she finally said, "Who are you looking for?"

"Cadillac Jones."

"What's he done?"

"His wallet was found at the scene of a double murder."

She said, "The old couple that's been on the news?"

"Yeah."

"No way. Not Cadillac."

"I was there. I saw his license."

"I'm not saying you didn't, but Caddy's a junkie, not a killer."

"Drugs have a funny way of changing people."

"I agree, but I can't imagine him killing two people."

"Why don't you tell me about him?"

"I've always gotten a sort of sweet and sad vibe from him. He's the type who got involved with drugs and realized he was over his head but could never figure a way out. Wherever his life started, drugs were better than that. Unfortunately, I think he's destined to die in a drug house somewhere, and he knows it. That's horrible to say, isn't it?"

Quinn shrugged.

She turned, waved for him to follow, and led Quinn back to her office. She settled into her chair, and Quinn sat on a sturdy metal chair in front of her desk. The chairs weren't designed for comfort. They were probably selected to keep the visitors on short-term stays—get the probationers in, then get them out.

Yvette typed on a keyboard before consulting something on her computer screen. "He was assigned to me about nine months ago. You've seen his record, right? Burglaries, malicious mischiefs, drug possessions. Nothing physical. The guy is an addict living the junkie life."

"Where can I find him?"

"Have you tried his—"

"We have. He hasn't been there since we discovered the homicide."

Yvette picked up the phone and dialed a number. She sat quietly for a few moments then said, "Caddy, this is Yvette Oliver. I need you to call me ASAP. This is important. *Call me*." When she hung up, she said to Quinn, "That's the last number I have for him, so I hope it's still good. He's always supposed to have a way for me to stay in contact. He's been good about it so far."

"So far," Quinn said.

"Yeah, so far."

"When's the last time you inspected his place?"

"You asking for a guided tour?"

"I thought you would never ask," Quinn said.

***

Cadillac Jones lived in an apartment building half a block west of the intersection of Boone and Monroe. The police department was two blocks south.

Officers had already attempted contact at his third-floor apartment on the night of the homicide, but there had been no answer.

As his probation officer, Yvette Oliver had the right to enter his apartment at any time to search for illegal contraband. Typically, this would be done with the probationer in tow, but this wasn't a normal situation.

Officer Ken Jarvis stood at the corner of Boone and Madison while Quinn approached with Yvette. His black beanie cap was pulled down to just above his eyebrows. He stood about as tall as Yvette.

"We're attempting contact of a murder suspect?" Jarvis said.

Quinn nodded.

"We should do this with a team," Jarvis said. To him, the job was a higher calling, and he treated it as such. "The three of us aren't enough if this goes bad."

"He's my client," Yvette said. "He didn't do what your department thinks he did."

Jarvis chuckled. "Really?"

"He's a peaceful guy."

"He's a junkie and junkies do crazy things. You know that, Yvette."

"I know more than that," she said and stepped toward the apartment building.

Jarvis reached out and grabbed her arm. "Hey, hold on."

Yvette's eyes snapped to Quinn and then back to Jarvis. "Ken," she said. "Not here."

He let go of her then.

The two of them looked at each other with some unspoken communication.

"Let me lead, okay?" Jarvis said. "*Please.*" His last word was soft and almost whispered.

Yvette paused for a second, then nodded. Jarvis headed toward the apartment building. She dropped in behind him. Quinn brought up the rear. He didn't need to ask them what was going on. It was obvious.

The apartment manager met them at the front of the building. He was an overweight, balding man in a black leather jacket.

Jarvis took the key from him and sent the manager back to the opposite corner of the block.

"You want another guy?" Quinn asked.

Jarvis eyed him for a moment, then Yvette. "We need a backup?"

She shook her head. "I know him. He's not violent."

"Then let's go," Jarvis said and stepped into the apartment building. Quinn was behind him, and Yvette was now third.

Inside the building, they drew their weapons and padded up the stairs. On the third floor, they approached apartment 310.

With his left hand, Jarvis banged on the door. "Spokane Police Department," he shouted.

Yvette moved to the opposite side of the door. She knocked and yelled, "Department of Corrections. Cadillac, come to the door."

A door down the hall opened, and a small child stuck his head out. His hair was mussed, and his eyes wide with curiosity. Quinn waved him back inside.

Yvette knocked a second time and repeated her announcement.

Jarvis stuck the key in the lock. "One more time," he said. "Let him know we're coming in."

Yvette pounded on the door. "Department of Corrections. Cadillac, come to the door, or we're coming in."

It was moments like these where Quinn consciously reminded himself to breathe and remain calm. It had been years since he'd been on SWAT, and he was out of practice on how to control himself when the adrenaline surged.

Jarvis waited a couple of seconds before turning the key and pushing the door open.

When nothing happened, Jarvis peered around the corner with his gun pulled tightly back to his chest.

"Moving," he said and went into the apartment.

Quinn slipped in behind Jarvis, and he assumed Yvette moved after he did. He wasn't worried about her. His focus was on clearing the areas where Jarvis wasn't. It only took a handful of seconds for the three of them to move through the apartment.

"Clear," Jarvis said.

"Clear," Yvette joined in.

Quinn met them back in the small living room. "Clear," he said, tucking his Glock back into its holster.

The apartment was a one-bedroom dump. There was trash and clothing everywhere. Uneaten and now rotting food sat on the kitchen counter.

"Hungry?" Jarvis held up a plate with a moldy sandwich.

Yvette crinkled her nose. "Yum."

"Your boy's not here," Jarvis said. "Where else might he be?"

Yvette's eyes scanned the apartment. She flipped up a seat cushion on the couch. "Scoring drugs. Couch surfing somewhere. Who knows? One thing is for sure. He's not taking care of himself."

When they were done, they secured the apartment and huddled on the sidewalk. Jarvis left Quinn and Yvette to return the key to the building's manager.

"Has Cadillac dropped off the radar like this before?" Quinn asked.

Yvette thought about it for a moment. "I've only been looking for him for thirty minutes, so it doesn't seem very long. If he doesn't show up for a couple of days, I'll let you know. He's never taken more than forty-eight hours to get back to me."

"When you hear from him, call," Quinn said. He left her then and headed back to his car.

Chapter 13

At the station, Marci was in her cubicle with her computer pulled up to the *Spokesman-Review* archive.

"How's the research?" Quinn asked.

"Next time, *I'm* leaving the office," she said.

"It can't be that bad."

"The research is fine. It's the constant hovering from the brass that I could do without. The lieutenant and captain have both been by twice this morning. Even the chief poked his head in to see how things are progressing. If we don't get some traction on this soon, we could be exposed to brass poisoning."

"Did you tell them where they could shove it?"

Marci leaned back and glared at Quinn. "What?"

"I thought your recent attitude change was all about not taking crap from them anymore."

"Pound sand," Marci said.

Quinn smiled and dropped into his chair.

"And to think I was going to tell you what I learned."

"What did you learn?" Quinn asked.

"I forget," Marci said, standing.

"What?"

"I'm going for a walk."

"I need an update," Quinn called after his partner.

"You can wait," Marci said as she walked down the hall.

"Are you kidding me?" Quinn mumbled.

"Trouble with your partner?"

Quinn glanced over his shoulder to Detective Dallas Nash. He was leaning against the cubicle, drinking a cup of coffee. His hair was slightly messy, and his tie was askew.

"She's in a mood."

"About?"

"The brass."

Nash lifted his coffee cup for a sip but paused. "They put us all in a mood."

Quinn turned to face him.

"Any idea what's got her wound up?" Quinn asked. He knew Marci had become a confidant of Nash's since his wife of twenty-seven years died last year.

"You should talk to her about it, Quinn."

"So something is going on."

"Hey, I have no idea. I asked her, but she clammed up on me. Maybe she'll tell you. You're her partner, after all." He lifted his cup to Quinn then walked away.

***

When Marci returned to her cubicle, she dropped into her chair and faced Quinn. He heard the noise and turned to face her.

She began without preamble. "Clay and Helen Smith ran with the Spokane elite."

"What's that mean?" Quinn asked. "They're rich?"

"Not Warren Buffett rich, no."

"Who is?"

"But they had means," Marci said. "We saw their house, right?"

"Yeah."

"They were members of the Spokane Club and the Manito Country Club. She was on the board of the Rotary. He was on the board of Lilac City Credit Union. As far as I can tell, she never worked. He was an executive for Washington Mutual before the market crashed. When that occurred, he jumped ship and called it a career. I've found several write-ups on him in industry magazines and in the *Spokesman*."

"Anything that might lead us to another suspect besides Cadillac Jones?"

"No, not really."

"What about family? Kids or siblings?"

"No kids, and I haven't found any siblings listed. Nothing was ever mentioned in the articles."

"Do you remember any pictures on the walls at the house?" Quinn asked.

Marci shook her head.

So far, nobody had come forward to claim they were related, and there was no database out there for relatives. Quinn wondered if that would be a useful tool or if it would be another intrusion into our personal lives. Another step toward Big Brother.

"I've gone through both of their cell phones. No other Smiths were listed."

"Maybe there weren't any relatives on his side. We should work on tracking down her side."

"We'll find more when we go back to the house," Marci said. "And we should also talk with the neighbors again."

"Let's do that now."

Marci stood and grabbed her coat.

"Hey, Marci?"

She looked at Quinn, expectantly.

"Is there something going on? With you and the department, I mean?"

"Why?"

"I was just wondering what was going on, you know, with the recent talk about the brass."

Marci frowned as she thought. Finally, she said, "I don't know, dude."

She walked off toward the exit.

Quinn grabbed his jacket and jogged after her.

Chapter 14

The gray sky threatened late-season snow. The weather forecast had predicted a couple of inches.

Quinn stood at the edge of the street, his hands shoved in his coat, and his face lifted to the sky. He had just finished interviewing Donald and Maxine Cromwell, the next-door neighbors to the Smiths. They were the couple who had notified the police after hearing gunshots. He replayed the interview in his mind.

The Cromwells were both in their early eighties and considered themselves to be night owls. They were up reading when they heard gunfire.

"Terrible thing," Donald said as he sat in his recliner.

Maxine nodded. "Just terrible."

"Such nice people," Donald said.

"Nice," Maxine added.

"What did you see?" Quinn asked.

"Didn't see much," Donald said. "A dark car leaving the house. That was it."

"Could you see the make?"

Donald smiled apologetically. "I'm not a car guy."

"He doesn't know cars," Maxine said.

Quinn nodded. "But it was a car, right? Not a truck."

"Oh, it was a car, all right," Donald said.

"A car," Maxine agreed. She reached out and squeezed Donald's hand.

"Were there any markings on the car?"

"Markings?"

"You know? Like lettering? Maybe flames?"

"You mean like a hot rod?" the husband asked.

"Sure," Quinn said, "like a hot rod."

"No," Donald said, "it wasn't that. It was a plain dark car. Sort of boring."

"Boring," Maxine agreed. Quinn smiled at her, and she brightened.

"Basically," Quinn said to Donald, "you heard several gunshots, called 911, then saw a dark car drive away."

"Yes, sir, that about sums it up," Donald said. "Not much more than that."

"Not much," Maxine said apologetically.

"Did you know the Smiths very well?"

Donald and Maxine both nodded and made murmurs of acknowledgment.

"Did they have children?"

"No," Donald said. "They didn't have any children."

"Helen wasn't the maternal type," Maxine added.

"Siblings?"

Donald shook his head. "Clay was an only child. I think Helen was, too."

"Yes," Maxine chimed in, "only children, both of them. They gave their love to their dog."

"Dog? There was no dog there."

"They had a dog," Donald said. "Mitzie. Little ugly thing. It escaped a week ago. Never came home, though. Poor Helen was broken up about it."

"Broken up," Maxine said, nodding, a look of additional sadness on her face.

Quinn sat quietly for a moment, thinking. Then he stood and tucked his notebook into his inner coat pocket. He reached over and shook Donald's hand. "Thank you for your time."

When he reached for Maxine, she held his hand with both of hers.

"Thank you for your time, ma'am."

"Are you sure you won't stay for coffee and pie?" Maxine asked. "We have banana cream."

Quinn smiled then at the memory of the Cromwell interview.

"Why're you smiling?"

He dropped his gaze from the sky to Marci, who was walking over from the house on the other side.

"Funny couple," he said and jerked his head back toward the Cromwell house.

"I remember," she said. She had interviewed them when they were called out. "Get anything new?"

"Yeah. Missing dog."

"Missing dog? They never said anything about a missing dog."

"The Smiths had a dog. It disappeared a week ago." He shrugged. "Could be a coincidence."

Marci studied Quinn. "That's damn convenient, don't you think?"

"Convenient. Or some planning. I'll lean toward the latter. How about you? What did you get?"

"Not much. The couple to the north slept right through it. I basically confirmed what they told patrol. I had to explain why we do follow-ups. Yada, yada, yada. I don't think they heard me, though, since they were irked I interrupted *Judge Judy*."

"Retired people problems."

Marci smiled. "Yeah, I guess. Are we going to stand here all day, or are we going to walk through the house again?" She turned and headed toward the Smith residence.

Quinn hurried to her. "What's your problem?"

"I don't have one. I just wanna get the walk-through done then get something to eat."

"You sure you don't have a problem?"

Marci stopped and glared at Quinn.

"What?" Quinn asked, throwing up his hands in frustration.

She turned and walked under the yellow police tape strung around the front of the house.

"Okay, so you don't have a problem," he called after her. "I get it!"

***

They walked through the house again, neither talking to the other.

It was in moments like this Quinn wanted to add to what he already knew about the deceased. He searched for those things that were missing, or that seemed out of place.

The house was tastefully decorated with antique furniture. He tried to place the architecture of the home, believing it had been built in the early 1900s. The furniture that populated the living room, the guest rooms, and the office all seemed to be from that time. It seemed like he had traveled through a time machine.

Black-and-white photos hung on the walls throughout the house. They showed a variety of locations around Spokane and appeared to have been taken in the early twentieth century. Quinn studied them with fascination.

When Marci walked into the room, Quinn glanced at her and said, "Check this out."

She walked over and looked at the picture. It was a photo of overgrown foliage surrounding a pond.

"That's Manito Park."

"You sure?"

"That's where the duck pond is now. Crazy, isn't it? How much it's changed."

"Uh-huh."

"Find anything?"

"No family," Marci said.

Quinn's brow furrowed.

"There are no family pictures anywhere. Plenty of these," she said, pointing at the black-and-white photo, "but not one of any people anywhere. Not any of themselves either. Kind of weird, right?"

"Different, at least. Find any paperwork?"

"Nothing of value and no will, which is what I was hoping to find. Plenty of bills. Utilities and whatnot."

"What about a computer?"

Marci swung her arm wide. "In this house with a couple of geezers?"

"Probably not."

"Probably not," she repeated.

"Hey," Quinn said, "before I forget, Cadillac Jones has a CI flag."

She raised an eyebrow. "Really? Who?"

"I dunno. I haven't had a chance to request it yet. Might be nothing."

"But it might be something."

"Right. We'll have to go through the process to find who was working him."

Marci smirked. "Great. More paperwork. More brass."

She stole another glance at the photo of the pond and moved into another room. Quinn turned back to the picture and studied it further.

Chapter 15

The next morning, Quinn arrived at Holy Family at eight in the morning. Marci was already parked, her car backed up to the building. They were there to meet with Rima Sepulveda, the medical examiner. Quinn climbed out of his car and walked toward Marci's. She got out and met him at the front.

"How was your night?" Quinn asked as they walked toward the hospital entrance.

"Fine."

"Still hanging out with Kirby?"

"When it's appropriate."

Quinn's eyes slanted toward his partner.

"What?"

"Appropriate?"

"What's wrong with that? We're both adults. Who needs the pressure?"

Quinn grabbed the door and held it open. "Something's wrong," he said.

"Only with your questions."

They walked into the basement where the medical examiner's office was located. Rima was in the hallway, talking to a male nurse. She turned as the detectives approached and nodded.

She was in her late forties, her black hair showing slightly grayer with the passing year. Her olive-toned skin hinted at her Spanish and Arabic heritage. She offered her hand to Marci, who shook it. Then Rima did the same with Quinn.

"How's my favorite crime-fighting duo this morning?"

"I'm sure you say that to everyone," Quinn said.

Rima smiled. "I do try to keep positive relations. Are you here to witness the Smith autopsies?"

Marci crinkled her nose.

"Yeah," Quinn said, watching his partner. He knew from experience she hated attending these and only did so out of duty to him.

"Going to be a long morning," Rima said. "You know where the scrubs are. After you're ready, come on in, and we'll get the show on the road."

Rima pushed through a set of double doors. As they swung closed, Marci turned to Quinn, "Does she always have to be so cheerful? It's an autopsy, for crying out loud."

"You prefer she was grouchy?"

"Of course not. You know this is the thing I hate most about the job."

More than the brass? Quinn wanted to say but kept it to himself, not wanting to provoke Marci's recent mood. Instead, he said, "Take off. I'll handle it. I'll meet you at the department when it's over."

"And let you tell everyone that I can't handle my water? Never."

Marci shoved past Quinn into the equipment room.

He grinned. If there was one way to get Marci to participate in anything, it was to make her think she wasn't standing up to what most men in the department would do. At that point, she would almost always exceed everyone's expectations.

***

They were seated at Qdoba. Marci had ordered a pulled pork quesadilla, and Quinn had brought in his lunchbox.

"You embarrass me," she said.

"Because I bring my lunch?"

"Yes."

"I figured you'd be used to it by now."

"I'll never get used to that."

"No one else cares, so get over it."

Marci took a bite of her quesadilla, shaking her head while she chewed.

The autopsies for both Clayton and Helen Smith took a combined five and a half hours. Rima had offered to take a break after Helen's, but they declined, so she continued and completed Clay's immediately afterward.

She extracted two bullets, one from Helen and one from Clayton. From a visual inspection, the slugs appeared to be from either a thirty-eight or a nine-millimeter. There are plenty of differences between the two rounds, but the actual bullets are similar. It would require them to be submitted to evidence and then examined at the state lab to be conclusively determined.

The bullet that entered Helen hit her square in the heart, resulting in a traumatic aortic rupture.

"What a mess," Rima had said when she removed the organ. "Death had to be almost immediate."

The first bullet that hit Clayton missed the heart but punctured his right lung and chipped the posterior portion of the third rib before exiting out his back. When he rolled over, a second-round entered between the third and fourth ribs and passed through the heart before it traveled through his body and lodged itself in his right triceps.

Death may not have been instantaneous for Clayton Smith, but it was quick.

"So, what do we know now?" Marci asked, then took another bite of her quesadilla.

"The killer—"

"Or killers," Marci interrupted.

"Entered the house through the kitchen door. There was no dog to alert the Smiths to his presence. He walked upstairs to their room, where he found them in bed—a quick shot to each. Bang bang," Quinn said, mocking the firing of a gun with his thumb and forefinger. "Mrs. Smith dies almost immediately. Mr. Smith doesn't. He turns to get out of bed and gets a second shot, a kill shot."

Marci swallowed. "Who was shot first?"

Quinn bit into his salami sandwich and thought.

"May not matter, right?" Marci said. "But who went first?"

"If it wasn't a simple burglary, is what you're implying then? If this was something more?"

"Right. That's what I'm getting at."

"Then it would matter, *should* matter," Quinn said. "You should shoot the primary target first. That person's death would be the most important. That would be my argument."

"Mine, too. Are you thinking the missus because her shot was nice and clean? Instant death. The husband hears the shot and moves. Therefore, the first shot into him isn't clean, and the second shot has to do him in."

"Regardless, they're pretty good shots for a junkie," Quinn said.

"Well, I'm just sayin'," Marci said and took another bite of the quesadilla.

"Yeah, just sayin'."

Marci's phone dinged. It was face down on the table. She flipped it over. "Geri texted. Prints are back."

"And?"

Marci held the remaining piece of quesadilla between her teeth as she worked her phone with her hands. She put the phone on the table, grabbed the quesadilla, and finished the bite. While she read whatever was on her phone, she shook her head.

"Well?" Quinn said.

"You got the same email," she said through a mouthful of food.

Quinn clicked his tongue against the roof of his mouth and pulled out his phone. He opened the top email, which had been addressed to him, Marci, and Crime Scene Analyst Geri Utley.

His eyes scanned the text. Only two sets of prints were found in the house: Clayton and Helen Smith.

Quinn looked up. "How's that possible?"

"They didn't have visitors?"

"Everyone has visitors."

"Maybe not the Smiths."

"I suppose the killer was careful," Quinn said. "It doesn't make sense when a junkie is involved, but anything's possible."

"No, no, it's not," Marci said. "A junkie isn't careful. It goes against everything we know about them. They're messed up, their systems are out of whack, there is no normal for them, so how could they carefully plan ahead to cover every base? They got rid of the dog, right?"

"Or the dog simply ran off."

"Simply ran off?" Marci said.

"It's an option, and we need to be open to it."

"Fine," Marci said. "Maybe the damn thing ran off, but if the killer got rid of the dog, then there was planning and patience involved."

"We should check with SpokAnimal to make sure they haven't found the dog. Maybe it was chipped."

"A junkie didn't do this," Marci said.

"But a junkie's ID card was found at the scene."

"Right there, gift wrapped for us to find," Marci replied, shaking her head while she wiped her fingers on a napkin. "Someone is hoping we'd be too lazy to do our homework."

"Maybe," Quinn said. "Maybe it was supposed to be enough to throw us off the track long enough for the real killer to get away."

"I'll buy that, but why? Why kill this elderly couple? What did they have that would make someone want to kill them?"

***

When they returned to the department, Quinn stopped by the office of Lieutenant Brand. The large bearlike man was searching through a black three-ringed binder. He flipped the pages with emphasis as he turned.

"Lieutenant?"

Brand looked up, startled.

"Got a minute?"

"Not really," he said, his eyes scanning the pages as he flipped through them. Finally, he stopped on a page, placed a finger in the middle of it, and began studying it as he read. A smile spread on his face.

When he looked up, he was surprised to see Quinn still standing there.

"Yes?"

"I need a minute."

He sighed, leaned back, and crossed his arms. His round glasses remained at the edge of his nose, forcing him to tilt his head back to look at Quinn.

"The suspect in the double murder," Quinn said, "has a confidential informant flag."

Quinn knew the lieutenant was a stickler for the rules, and had he jumped over him to go to Captain Ackerman, he would get his hand slapped. This wasn't one of those moments worth getting spanked for.

Brand uncrossed an arm to push his glasses back into place. He then lowered his head to its proper position and crossed his arms again.

"I'd like to find out who was working with him." Quinn stepped forward and handed a sticky note to the lieutenant.

"It's been a couple of days. Why didn't you ask for this sooner?"

"I'm asking now."

"This sounds like important information."

"Potentially. Perhaps it's nothing. We can only do what we can do, and I need your approval."

"Revealing the CI flag needs a captain's approval."

"I know. I'm trying to follow the chain of command."

"I appreciate that, Detective." Brand smiled as he read the notes on the small piece of paper. "I'll find what you're asking for."

Chapter 16

It was raining. Just a couple days prior, it had threatened late-season snow. The early spring weather had been crazy.

Marci stood alongside the Cheney-Spokane Road in a long black raincoat and tall black Wellington boots. A red umbrella rested against her shoulder.

Patrol units lined the east side of the street. Two cars with their emergency lights whirring were positioned at opposite ends of the road. Officers stood outside those cars, directing traffic in a coordinated effort to keep the early-morning commuters on time to their destinations.

Before leaving the warmth and comfort of his car, Quinn took a final glance up into the gray sky. He quickly climbed out, slammed the door, and sprinted toward his partner. When he got near her, he ducked under the umbrella.

Marci smiled. She wore a black rain hat with a brim. Underneath, her eyes were bright. "Good morning, sunshine. Isn't this rain something?"

"You're happy today."

"Why shouldn't I be? It's a great morning."

"Not for him," Quinn said and nodded at the tarp-covered body lying in the nearby ditch.

"No, not a good morning for him. That is the truth."

"You already take a peek?"

Marci nodded. "A quick one. Now I'm standing here, listening to the rain, waiting for the lab geeks to bring out the tent."

The forensic team would bring out a large canopy and erect it over the victim. This would allow the detectives to move the body and reduce further exposure to the elements. It was standard procedure in rain and snow.

"We sure it's him?"

"It's confirmed," Marci said. "One of the uniforms knew him. Cadillac Eldorado Jones. Who names their kid after a car? Especially that one? Good Lord, that's as bad as naming your kid Beetle. Or Pinto."

Quinn studied Marci. It was good to see her happy again. It had been a few days. "You get a good night's sleep?"

"I did. Thank you for asking."

He watched her, and she smiled, knowing he was watching.

"I'll be back," he said and walked toward the body.

"Take your time," she called after him. "I'm not going anywhere."

The young black man was on his back, staring up into the rain. He was skinny with dirty dreadlocks. His blue coat was open, and blood stained his white *Run the Jewels* T-shirt. Quinn leaned over and noticed three bullet holes in the center of his chest.

He returned to where Marci was standing and ducked underneath her umbrella.

"What do you think the cause of death was?" she asked.

"You are chipper for seven a.m."

She shrugged. Her smile remained intact.

"This makes the Smith homicide even more effed up," Quinn said. "Our suspected shooter, who we didn't like for it in the first place, lies there dead. This stinks worse than a roadside Port-a-Potty."

"It definitely smells funny."

"Yet you're smiling."

She shrugged. "Can't help it."

Quinn tilted his head and asked, "You and Kirby, okay?"

"When it's convenient."

"Did you guys…? Last night, I mean."

She flashed him a look of disbelief. "No," she said, but her smile returned.

The rain continued to fall, making an out-of-rhythm drumming pattern on top of the umbrella. Other officers huddled away from them in their private conversations. The evidence van pulled up to the scene behind the other vehicles.

Quinn glanced at his partner then stared at the body.

There would be plenty of time to deal with Cadillac Jones, so he let his thoughts work on the Marci mystery. It had something to do with her occasional boyfriend. What would make her so angry that she couldn't feel she could confide in him? He listened to the rainfall as his thoughts meandered back and forth.

Finally, Quinn looked back at her. "Are you…?"

"What?"

"Pregnant?"

"Oh, God, no."

Quinn shrugged and turned to stare at the blue tarp fluttering softly in the breeze. The rain continued to fall, and each detective was left to their thoughts.

Finally, Marci said, "I found a lump."

He turned to face her.

"I was scared."

"You could have told me."

She shrugged. "It turned out okay. It's benign. Nothing to worry about now."

"I'm sorry," Quinn said.

"Why? Everything is right again in the universe."

He continued to study her. He wanted to talk with her, make sure she was okay, understand her fears.

"Don't even start with the twenty questions," she muttered.

"I wouldn't," he said.

"You would. So don't. Let's stay focused on this mess. We've got two dead elderly and a junkie down in a ditch. Somehow they intersect."

Senior Patrol Officer Leya Navarro approached the detectives. Both Quinn and Marci turned to her.

"Detectives," she said.

"Were you first on scene?" Quinn asked.

"Yes. I've already got the witness statements. I'll write a report as soon as I break from here."

"Anything earth-shattering?"

"It was for the civilian who stumbled onto your victim."

Both Quinn and Marci stared at her.

"No," the patrol officer said. "Her statement was run of the mill. She saw the body and called the police."

Navarro walked off to talk with the other officers, leaving the detectives under the umbrella to listen to the sound of the falling rain.

While they waited, Quinn pulled his phone out to check his email. Near the top was one from Lieutenant Brand. Its title was *Requested Info*.

Inside were only two words: Detective Morgan.

"Damn," Quinn said.

"What's wrong?" Marci asked.

Quinn showed her the email.

"I don't get it."

"Morgan put the CI tag on Jones," Quinn said.

They both stared at the body in the ditch.

Detective James Morgan was assigned to the department's Criminal Task Force, a specialty team that handled interrelated problems like drugs, vice, guns, and gangs. A frequent argument revolved around whether only cowboys and malcontents tended toward CTF or if the unit itself promoted that type of behavior.

Perhaps it was the nature of the offenders they contacted or the fact that they were often undercover, but the officers assigned to that unit often had a higher frequency of use-of-force complaints. Over the years, when those complaints drew too much attention, different leaders had been brought into the unit to corral those complaints. As a solution, the assigned personnel would occasionally be rotated out into other divisions, which invariably led to decreased team efficiency and an increase in crimes. The noise that ensued spurred the brass to swing the pendulum back again. Statistics won every time.

The team would be quickly reshuffled, the banished officers and detectives brought back, and the unit reassembled. The offending bureaucrats would be taught a quick and painful lesson; if you mess with the bull, you'll get its horns.

And the head bull, the one with the biggest set of horns, was James Morgan.

Quinn looked at the email once more and put his phone away.

"Well, this will be fun," he said.

Chapter 17

Detective James Morgan was in the parking lot of Molly's Diner on Third Avenue. He leaned against the front of a late-model Dodge Charger, a car that his unit had legally seized after a drug arrest.

A barrel-chested man, Morgan wore a brown, waist-length leather jacket, faded blue jeans, and brown boots. On his head was a tan baseball cap with a Glock logo. The tattered brim was curled so tight that its edges touched the sides of Morgan's eyebrows. He hadn't shaved that morning, which left a salt-and-pepper scratch on his face.

His arms were crossed, and his eyes followed their car as Quinn and Marci pulled into the parking lot.

"He looks growly," Marci said.

"That's his natural state."

They parked near Morgan's car and climbed out. A drizzle had replaced the earlier downpour.

After stifling a yawn, Morgan said, "Detectives." He dropped his arms and pushed off his car.

Quinn said, "We'd like to ask—"

Morgan brushed past him toward the front of the diner. "I'm hungry. Let's talk inside."

Marci glanced at Quinn, who shrugged in return. They followed him into the restaurant.

Morgan walked past the *Wait to be Seated* sign to a booth in the far corner. He took the seat facing the entrance. Quinn and Marci sat across from him.

A short blond waitress was immediately at their table. "The usual?" she asked Morgan.

"Yeah."

She turned to the other detectives. "And you two?"

"They're not eating," Morgan said.

Quinn and Marci stared at him.

"Not even coffee?" the waitress asked.

"Not today," Morgan said.

The waitress shrugged then walked off.

Quinn's eyes slanted. "This isn't starting very well."

"We're not friends," Morgan said, "but we don't need to be friends to both do our jobs."

Marci shook her head then glanced at her partner.

"You're here because of my CI, my *dead* CI," Morgan grumbled. "Ask your questions, then push. I'll find who did him, then bring them in. You'll be able to talk with them when I'm done."

"This is our investigation," Quinn said.

"Says you."

"Says the department," Marci said, leaning forward.

"Play it how you want, sister. I don't bother with territorial pissings."

Quinn coughed a couple of times to break the tension, then asked, "What was Cadillac doing for you?"

"What do you think Rado was doing? He was a rat."

"Rado?"

"A shortened version of Eldorado. You'd know that if you were anywhere near the street."

Quinn rubbed the bridge of his nose.

Morgan smiled. "Don't quit now, Delaney. You wanted this meet, so ask your questions."

"Who was he ratting on?"

"It's not rocket science."

"His dealer," Marci said.

"And here I thought she was the muscle."

Marci squinted at the thick-chested detective.

"Who's his dealer?" Quinn asked.

"Don't worry about it. I got that angle covered."

"We're investigating a homicide. You can't hold out on that information."

The waitress returned with a cup of black coffee. She placed it in front of Morgan.

"I tell you that and then what? You two snatch him up? Take him back to the station, interview him with some bullshit Reid techniques?"

"You know there's more to it than that," Quinn said.

"Whatever. It doesn't matter. Our team is in the middle of a bigger investigation. We're building a network of dealers to get to the main source."

Marci laughed. "Oh yeah? How long have you been doing that? As smart as you claim to be, maybe you should have knocked that down long ago. Maybe you're getting a little long in the tooth for this game."

Morgan eyed her for a moment, then ran his tongue over his teeth. "I like you."

"The feeling is not mutual."

Morgan laughed. "You got some fire, lady. You should be part of our unit."

"Not a chance."

"The dealer," Quinn said. "Who is he?"

"It wasn't him. He's been under surveillance for the last two nights. I'll show you the logs if you don't believe that."

Quinn and Marci glanced at each other.

"I'm serious. No more joking around." Morgan lifted his chin toward Marci. "On account of her. She's a keeper."

"I'm not someone's property."

Morgan laughed loudly, causing several people in the restaurant to look their way. "Damn, sister, you're the best."

"We'd appreciate the logs," Quinn said, "just to strike him off our list. How about a list of known associates so we can work backward, maybe find someone who can help? We're getting pressure from city hall on the double killings."

"Rado didn't have anything to do with those murders. I'd guarantee it. That ain't his style."

"So you'll help?" Marci said.

Morgan's grin bordered on malicious. "Oh, I'll help. I'll get you a list of who he ran with, but I'm gonna start asking around, too."

Quinn said, "Again, this is *our* investigation."

"I'm not trying to get into your mess kit, glory boy."

"Glory boy?" Quinn asked, his anger rising.

"I want to find who killed my CI."

"This is our case," Marci said.

"I'll consider myself warned. Now, unless you two want to watch me eat some oatmeal and toast, it's time for you to go."

PART III

Chapter 18

Tom Jessup pushed the eggs around his plate, letting his mind drift. He was at The Top Notch Café, enjoying his morning alone, the same routine he followed almost daily. He'd gotten used to it over the past several years. Life had taken on a certain rhythm, and it suited him.

Some of the locals wanted to fix him up, find someone for him, so he could spend his days and maybe some nights in the company of a woman. A good woman preferably, but some even tried to encourage him to take up with a bad woman, with the idea that it was better than being alone.

Jessup thought the whole thing was nonsense, for he preferred no woman, no drama, no expectations. His life was his to live.

Autumn, his dispatcher, had even tried to fix him up with her mother. He politely declined, but she frequently sang the praises of her mom whenever they were alone, and the moment presented itself. Her mother was, in fact, a lovely woman, but, like any woman, she would require Jessup to spend time with her, which was something he now found distasteful at this point in his life.

The great love of his life was gone, and he had dealt with it. He felt no need to pretend otherwise. If he found another woman to love, she could never compare to Mia. Since that was the case, why would he subject a new woman to that, let alone himself?

Especially when a plate full of breakfast will do just fine, he thought ruefully. He stabbed some eggs and pushed his musings away.

Undersheriff Alex Greenway slid into the booth across from him. Jessup froze, a forkful of eggs hovering in front of his open mouth. "By all means," Greenway said.

Jessup shoved the forkful in and chewed.

The waitress walked over with an expectant look. Greenway said, "Coffee, black. Couple pieces a toast. Heavy onna butter."

She turned without a word and walked off.

As undersheriff, Greenway oversaw the jail side of the Whitman County operation. He was a militaristic man who enjoyed the rigidity of the jail system. Greenway had been a tank gunner in the Marine Corps before coming home and joining the department as a jailer.

When Jessup became sheriff, he and Greenway quickly agreed. Jessup would run the law enforcement side, and Greenway would be given complete control of the detainment system. Each man got to do what they loved, and they supported each other whenever it came to budgetary meetings with the county commissioners. It was a good system since Greenway didn't undercut him with aspirations to be sheriff. That allowed Jessup to lead without the need to put a thumb on his right hand's ambitions.

"Sorry for buttin' in on your breakfast, Tom."

"You're always welcome. Something on your mind?"

"Just breakfast with a friend."

Jessup paused, then cut a piece of pancake free. "We never have breakfast just to have breakfast. That's what makes us so special."

Greenway shrugged.

The waitress returned and put a cup of coffee in front of the undersheriff.

He lifted it and sipped before saying, "Jill wants you over for dinner."

Jessup had stuck his fork into several bits of pancakes and was about to put it into his mouth but stopped. Suspicion clouded his eyes. "Now just a minute, Al."

"No, Tom, this is something I must do. Jill said if I didn't bring you home to dinner, that she's gonna make me do something I don't wanna do. You know how she is. If we have to, we're gonna pick up some takeout—maybe Chinese, I know how you like that stuff—and we'll sit on your front porch until you come home. Basically, we're gonna ambush you into havin' dinner with us."

"I've told you I'm not interested in her sister."

Greenway sipped his coffee, then said, "It's not her sister."

"One of the girls from the hospital?"

"Not one of them either, although if there was one to be had, I'm sure Jill would be delighted to get involved."

"Who is it, then?"

"It's—"

Jessup's cell phone rang. Both Greenway and he could see the ID screen said *Dispatch*. The sheriff picked it up and answered, "Jessup."

"Hey, Sheriff, it's Autumn."

"Yeah, kid, what's going on?" he asked, thankful for the interruption.

"A Derwood Smith called for you. He asked if you'd meet him at his property."

"Who's Derwood Smith?"

Jessup looked at Greenway, who shrugged.

"Don't know, but he lives over in Palouse."

"Smith. *Smith?* Did he say if it was related to that death up in St. John? Same last name."

"I asked him what it was regarding, but he wouldn't say. I even asked a couple of times, but he kept dancing around the reason for the meeting. He was adamant that you see him, though. The guy sounds pretty frail."

"Palouse, huh?"

"Yeah."

"Email me his address. I'll head there after breakfast."

Chapter 19

Palouse, Washington, was seventeen miles to the east and had a population of roughly a thousand people. Most people believed Jessup knew everyone in his county. It was a quaint notion, he thought, but also unrealistic. Whitman County comprised almost twenty-two hundred square miles, with a population of nearly forty-nine thousand people. There's no way any sheriff could know their entire constituency.

Derwood Smith's home was on the edge of town. A wrought-iron gate welcomed Jessup a thousand feet up the driveway. When he pulled up to it, he stopped next to a column and pushed a button under a metal speaker.

The gate was an odd bit of grandeur in this county. The fence crossed the driveway and was held in place by two large stone columns. On each side, shrubs abutted the columns, blocking the view for about ten feet. After that, it was an open field. Had Jessup wanted to, he could have driven his truck off the pavement and around the gate to continue proceeding up to the house. The gate was there only for show and to stop those who obeyed society's norms.

After a moment, the gate slowly pulled back, allowing Jessup access to an additional length of winding driveway.

The home, which wasn't visible from the roadway, was large and ornate by Whitman County standards. Compared to Southern California or Western Washington, it might have seemed reasonable or even bland. On the rolling hills of Eastern Washington, though, it stuck out like a sore thumb. Since hills and trees hid it, most residents in the county had probably never seen the house.

It was a two-story with a semicircular driveway in front. Large blue spruce trees were at opposite ends of the home. As Jessup rounded the driveway, he caught a vision of a large swimming pool in the backyard that had been closed for the winter. A pool in Eastern Washington was a rarity. Finding one in the town of Palouse was like finding a snowstorm in Las Vegas.

The grounds were brown due to the early April cold, but he imagined they would be lush green by the end of the month. It was a fantastic homestead.

An older-model Toyota Camry was parked in front of the house. The dented red car was juxtaposed near the expensive home. No other vehicle was parked out front.

As he approached the house, a Hispanic woman in her early fifties opened the door. She wore faded blue jeans, white sneakers, and a gray sweatshirt.

"Mrs. Smith?" Jessup asked.

She smiled and shook her head. "He is in the upper bedroom." Her accent was thick, but her English perfect.

Jessup nodded and stepped into the lobby. Large black-and-white tiles covered the floor. The woman pointed up the staircase and to the right before heading off into another room.

The sheriff stood there for a moment, listening to the quiet of the house. He noticed a smell then. It was the heavy aroma associated with cleaning chemicals. Jessup glanced around once more before slowly ascending the grand staircase. Thick red carpet was underfoot.

At the top of the stairs, he paused and listened again. He could hear the soft whir of machinery coming from the right. He headed that direction, passing several rooms with closed doors, before stopping at the entrance to a large room.

In its middle was a full-sized hospital bed. The head had been raised so its occupant would be in a comfortable position to read or to watch television. Wires and tubes ran from various machines on each side of the bed. A clear breathing mask covered the occupant's face.

The man noticed Jessup and waved him into the room. He removed the clear mask from his face as the sheriff approached. He held out his hand for Jessup to shake.

"Derwood Smith," he said, his voice soft and wavering.

"Tom Jessup." The sheriff gripped the man's hand lightly and gave it a gentle pump before releasing it.

"Pull up a chair, Sheriff."

Jessup slid a high-back wooden chair with a red seat cushion over to the bedside. As he sat, he noticed motion on the television. It was a twenty-four-hour news channel. The sound was muted.

"It's the only way I can stand the damn thing," Smith said, pointing a crooked finger at the monitor. "I bounce between the two big news networks, trying to find the truth. If you remove all the blathering about the other side being wrong, you can usually find it in there somewhere."

"Sounds like police work."

Smith's eyes settled on Jessup. He held the mask over his face and took a quick breath. "Thanks for coming out."

"Why am I here, Mr. Smith? You were coy with my dispatcher."

Smith reached to the opposite side of the bed to where a stack of newspapers sat on an end table. He grabbed them and plopped the stack onto his lap. He rummaged through the papers for a moment. Jessup could see various banners as Smith searched—*Spokesman-Review*, *Wall Street Journal*, and *Whitman County Gazette*. Finally, Smith tugged a folded edition of the Spokesman free and put the remaining pile back on the nightstand.

The older man put the clear plastic mask over his mouth, closed his eyes, and inhaled for a couple of seconds. When he was done, he removed the mask and opened his eyes. Smith handed the folded newspaper to Jessup.

"You read the Spokane paper, Sheriff?"

"No."

Smith clicked his tongue in disapproval. "Turn it over," he said, pointing at the newspaper.

In the lower right corner of the paper was an article with the headline HOME INVASION DOUBLE MURDER. Smith bent forward and tapped the edge of the paper.

"That was my brother and his wife."

Jessup glanced up to Smith. "I'm sorry for your loss."

Smith scrunched his lips up under his nose.

Jessup studied the man before saying, "You don't seem broken up about it."

"We haven't talked in more than forty years. Not even a Christmas card in either direction."

The sheriff's eyes drifted back to the paper, noticing the date. "This is several weeks old."

"That it is," he said with a nod. "I read the *Journal* daily except Sunday, of course. They don't publish on the Lord's day. I read almost every word, although I avoid the stuff they occasionally write about movies. I haven't seen one of those in years. Don't have the time for such foolishness anymore. On Sundays, I typically read a book, something more meaningful than the daily prattle of the world.

"The local papers, well, I used to be more diligent about them back when I really cared what was occurring around here. Not so much now. When I was younger, everything seemed a lot more important, more immediate. I still get the papers, more out of habit than anything. They'd sit for days, though, maybe weeks sometimes if I got other things going on in my head. Then I get some melancholy built up to know what's going on around the region. I usually jump to the local sections, read them, and discard the rest. I've already read the national coverage in the *Journal*, and I couldn't care less about sports and entertainment. That's what happened with that paper in your hands. I read that article last night about my brother. I had to read it a couple of times to make sure it was him."

Jessup skimmed the article. Clayton and Helen Smith had been murdered in their home in Spokane. The police had made no arrests, although they were searching for an unnamed person of interest.

"I've got two other brothers," Derwood said. "Haven't spoken with them in about the same amount of time." Smith lifted the mask to his face and inhaled deeply. "I'm hoping you can contact them and let them know about Clay. Maybe the Spokane Police already did this. Who knows? But they didn't contact me, which is why I called you. I figured you might be able to get more information from them than if I were to call up to the big city asking questions."

Jessup remained quiet for a time and watched Smith. The older man's eyes were on the news, but his attention seemed somewhere distant.

"Where are your brothers?" the sheriff finally asked.

"To be honest, I don't know. Family drama drove us away from each other. In all that time, I never tried to call them. I never thought it mattered much. They didn't want to talk to me; I didn't want to talk to them. To each their own. I went my way and made my life. It wasn't until I saw that article that I realized Clay was in Spokane. I figured he would have ended up in someplace like Seattle or San Francisco. He was always a bit of a fancy pants if you ask me. Saying it out loud after all this time, sounds sort of sad, doesn't it? Not to know where your brothers are, how they lived their lives. A man like you must think me pretty weak."

"Do you have a brother named Renard?"

Smith's eyes refocused, and he turned to the sheriff. "You know Renny?"

"No, sir."

"Then, I don't understand."

"About a month ago, he passed in his sleep. I was called out for it."

Smith stared at the sheriff. No emotions passed over his face. He slowly lifted the mask and inhaled but kept his eyes on Jessup.

When he lowered the mask, he asked, "He lived in this county?"

"St. John."

"St. John? What did he do?"

"He was a teacher."

"A teacher? What did he teach?"

"Elementary school."

"No kidding. Was he married? Did he have kids?"

"He had a son who died years ago in a boating accident. His wife left him then and moved to Hawaii."

Smith lowered his head and asked, "How far is St. John from here? An hour?"

"Forty-five minutes, more like it."

The older man nodded several times, then turned his attention to the television. He gazed at it for some time. Finally, he said, "Forty-five minutes away. Forty years. In all that time, I never once talked to him. What kind of family were we?"

Jessup stared at him as the older man remained quiet for several minutes.

Finally, the old man whispered, "I guess that's all I need, Sheriff. Thanks for coming out."

"You said you had another brother."

Derwood shrugged. "He and I didn't get along at all. Haven't thought about him the longest, not even a vile word."

"His name?"

"Leland," he said. It was then sadness overwhelmed him. "I'm tired, Sheriff. I think I need to close my eyes for a bit."

Jessup stood and watched Derwood. The older man's eyes closed, his jaws flexed, and he pursed his lips as he struggled to fight back the tears. Jessup turned and left.

On the way out of the house, Jessup stopped at the front door. He waited for the appearance of the Hispanic woman who had greeted him on the way in. When she didn't show, he went to find her. She was in the kitchen, cleaning. She stopped working when he walked in.

"I'm leaving," he said.

She nodded.

"What's wrong with him?"

"His lungs are not so good."

"What's your name?" Jessup asked, his voice kind.

She eyed him with suspicion.

"You're not in trouble," he said and handed her a business card. "My cell phone number is on there. When he wakes up, he can call me direct if he wants."

She read the card and nodded.

As he turned to leave, she said, "Lupita."

He turned around.

"My name is Lupita DeLeon."

"Lupita. Isn't that short for Guadalupe?"

"Normally, but my father liked Lupita better, so that is what my parents named me."

Jessup smiled. "If you need anything, you can call me as well."

She held the card with both hands and nodded.

Chapter 20

"Run a name for me," Jessup said into his cell phone. He'd just left Derwood Smith's property and was heading back toward Colfax.

"What is it?" Autumn asked.

"Leland Smith. He'll be in his late sixties or early seventies."

"Where does he reside?"

"No idea."

"Geez, you're giving me a lot to work with."

"Sorry, kid. It's all I've got right now, but at least it's a different-sounding first name, right? See if you can find something, anything, on a guy with that name in this region. He might be across the world for all we know."

"Why are we looking for him?"

"Because two of his brothers are dead, and a third one doesn't have long in this world."

"Also, run a Lupita DeLeon for me." He spelled her name. "Same deal. Not much to go on except she's in her late forties or early fifties."

"Who is she?"

"The housekeeper."

"You worried about her?"

"Not really, but I'd like to know who I'm dealing with."

***

Thirty minutes later, Jessup arrived in town. He parked his truck and entered the sheriff's office.

Deputy Rodney Howard was in the back at his desk with a phone pressed to his ear.

Autumn Summers turned to him as he approached her. "You want the good news or the bad news?"

Jessup stopped, thought about it for a brief second, and said, "Good news."

"Lupita DeLeon is clean. Late forties. Last known address is in California. A couple of traffic infractions, but that's it."

"So, what's the bad news?" Jessup asked.

"He's dead."

"Who?"

"Leland Adam Smith."

"You found him already?"

"Google. It's scary how quickly we can find things. It's like it knew what I was thinking."

"Show me," Jessup said.

"It was a death notice in the *Spokesman*, last November. The first to be exact." She held up the notice she'd printed, and Jessup grabbed it from her. He leaned against her desk.

"It said he lived in Spokane," Autumn continued. "That's all the info it gives. No obituary ever followed in the paper, and I searched for it."

"You couldn't find anything else?"

"Not really. He's not on any social media sites. He was seventy-two. I wouldn't expect him to be an influencer on Instagram, but I checked anyway."

The sheriff shook his head and walked toward his office.

"What?" Autumn said. "That was funny."

Jessup glanced at the clock on the wall. It was shortly after one o'clock. He hollered to Autumn, "What's the number for the Spokane Police Department's Major Crimes division?"

Autumn spun around to her desk, ran her finger down a quick call sheet she had created, and rattled off ten digits.

Jessup punched the same numbers into the phone on his desk and waited while it rang on the other end.

"Major Crimes," a female voice said.

"This is Whitman County Sheriff Tom Jessup. I'd like to speak to the detective assigned to the Clayton Smith homicide."

"Hold on, Sheriff. Let me find who's been assigned that case."

While on hold, music played.

"Autumn," he hollered.

She turned to face him.

"Find me an article in the *Spokesman-Review*. Was recent. About a murder of Clayton Smith."

"Clayton Smith," she said. "Leland Smith. Renard Smith. I'm taking it they're related."

Jessup said, "Find the article."

"Grouch."

"I heard that," he said.

The music stopped playing on the telephone. "Sheriff?"

"Yes."

"Detectives Burkett and Delaney have been assigned that case. Unfortunately, they aren't in the office right now. Would you like to leave a message?"

"Yes," he said, then hurriedly changed his mind. "No, wait."

"Sir?"

"Leland Smith."

"What?"

"Could you check to see if there was a case involving a Leland Smith? It doesn't matter whether it's open or not. It was a death, and you guys would go out and check it out. Right?"

"Usually, I believe so, yes. Is it a recent case?"

"Yes, ma'am. I'm pretty sure it was the first of November."

"Close enough. Hold for a second."

The music started playing again. Jessup couldn't place it. It sounded familiar, though. He should have asked Deputy Howard to tell him what the song was. Ever since they were in high school, Rodney could easily remember the names of songs and bands. Jessup rarely listened to music now. He struggled with naming the group until the music ended, and the receptionist came back on the phone.

"Sheriff?"

"Uh-huh."

"The detectives assigned to that case are Nash and Higgins."

A memory flashed through Jessup's mind. "Dallas Nash?"

"Yes, sir. Would you like to leave him a message?"

"No, ma'am. I'm good."

Chapter 21

Jessup woke early the next morning and made the drive to Spokane. He informed Undersheriff Alex Greenway that he would be away for the day. Greenway hated whenever Jessup left the county. He didn't like being responsible for anything outside the jail. It made him uncomfortable. Jessup understood how he felt, as he disliked the days when Greenway went on vacation or attended schools and left him with full oversight of the jail.

The drive to Spokane was a little over an hour. He arrived shortly after 8 a.m. It had been years since he walked the halls of the department as a young patrolman. Most of the guys who were with him in the academy or in the patrol car would have either promoted up or retired out. He couldn't blame them. The culture of the department was radically different from that of his own.

Jessup walked through the front door of the Public Safety Building. He stopped at the metal detector and identified himself to the deputy and the civilian employees who stood watch.

He wore a black canvas Carhartt jacket, under which he had on a black sweater, jeans, and scuffed combat boots. He had dressed down for his visit. He didn't want to be in uniform while in another jurisdiction. On his belt were his duty weapon and his badge.

The deputy inspected his identification card and asked him about the nature of his visit. Jessup told him that he was meeting a local detective in connection with a crime in his jurisdiction. The deputy smiled and handed him his ID wallet back.

"Have a nice day, Sheriff."

Jessup walked around the metal detector and proceeded to the front desk. The officer seated there, a woman with salt-and-pepper hair, looked familiar. He couldn't place her name before she asked him who he was there to visit.

"Detective Nash."

"He expecting you?"

"No, ma'am."

She eyed him with distrust until he pulled open his coat to reveal his duty weapon and badge.

"Can I get a name?"

"Tom Jessup."

"Jessup? You were on patrol here, weren't you?"

"Yes."

Her distrust melted slightly as her eyes shifted to a list of names in a protective plastic cover. She ran her finger down the page, lifted the telephone receiver, and pressed several digits.

Jessup turned around and watched the people milling about in the lobby. Many of them would be on their way to a municipal court hearing while others were there to pay a fine. A few would be making records requests. He watched them all and wondered for a moment how his life would have been different had he stayed in Spokane.

He heard the front desk officer place the phone back into the cradle. "He's on his way, Tom."

***

A couple of minutes later, the hallway doors opened, and a once-familiar face exited the hallway. His eyes scanned the lobby and landed on Jessup. Detective Dallas Nash wore dark blue slacks and a white shirt. A loosened tie hung from his neck while his gun and badge were attached to his leather belt. He hadn't shaved that morning.

He smiled as he approached Jessup, his handed extended.

"Thomas Jessup, how the hell are you?"

"I'm good, Dal, I'm good. You?"

"Getting better. How many years has it been?"

Jessup scratched the back of his neck. "Fifteen now? Is that right?"

"Gotta be, I'm thinking. What were we, power shift, when you took off? You're the only guy I know who lateralled *down* to a smaller agency. You're legendary, buddy."

Jessup laughed. "I needed a quieter life."

"Still in Colfax, then?"

"Oh, yeah."

"Still with the department, too?"

"Yup," Jessup said, showing his badge. "I'm the sheriff now."

Nash's mouth slightly opened before he said, "Shut the front door."

"Hand to God."

The detective playfully smacked the back of his hand against Jessup's chest. "Good for you, man. Good for you."

"I hear you're in Major Crimes now. Made it to the big leagues."

Nash shrugged. "What can I say?"

Jessup pointed to Nash's slightly mussed gray hair. "What happened there? It's like you got snowed on."

"That's the pot calling the kettle gray."

The sheriff laughed. "It's really good to see you, Dal. I can't believe we let so many years get by us. How's the wife? Roberta, right? No, wait, Bobbie. Yeah, Bobbie. I bet she's as pretty as ever."

A sadness moved over Nash's face. Jessup immediately knew he'd said something wrong.

"Oh, man, I'm sorry. What happened?"

"Car accident. Happened right before Thanksgiving."

Jessup looked up to the ceiling, then around the lobby, suddenly uncomfortable.

Nash forced a smile. "It's okay. You didn't know. Truly, it's okay."

Jessup looked back at his old friend and nodded.

"How's Mia?" Nash asked.

"Cancer took her over eight years ago."

Nash stared at him. They remained silent for a couple of moments until he said, "Damn it."

Jessup exhaled slowly before saying, "Listen, I'm sorry, I didn't know."

"It's life," Nash said. "We haven't seen each other in forever. Then you show up, and we kick each other in the feelings. A nice thing for academy mates to do, huh?"

Jessup put his hand on Nash's shoulder. "It's still nice to see you."

His old friend winced suddenly, and his hand lifted toward his temple but stopped. He glanced at Jessup.

"You okay?"

He forced a smile.

"Dallas?"

Nash inhaled deeply then said. "I'm fine. Headache."

"Must be some headache."

"It is. So what brings the sheriff of, what is that anyway, Whitman County, yeah? What brings Whitman County Sheriff Thomas Jessup up to see this humble detective?"

"You."

"Me?"

"I've stumbled on a series of deaths I think may be interlinked. You investigated one of them."

"I did?" Nash's eyes did little to hide his confusion.

Jessup reached into his jacket pocket and pulled out a folded copy of the printout from the Spokesman-Review's obituary page. Jessup had highlighted Leland Smith's death notice.

Nash looked at the paper and handed it back.

"I remember that. Guy died in his kitchen. Natural causes."

"You sure?"

Nash's face took on a serious tone. "I'm sure."

"This guy," Jessup said, tapping the paper, "recently had two brothers die. One of them occurred in my county of what I'm now worried wasn't natural causes. Another was murdered along with his wife in their home in Spokane."

Nash grabbed the paper to look at the name again. "Damn."

"Yeah."

"Brothers?"

"Yeah."

Nash turned and walked toward the double doors. He looked over his shoulder at Jessup, who stood in the same place. "What are you waiting for? Let's go."

Chapter 22

It took Nash only a couple of keystrokes to pull the record on Leland Smith's death. Upon completion, the report had been filed and scanned, which made its access far more convenient than the system used in Jessup's department.

They were seated at Nash's cubicle. He had stolen the chair from his partner's desk for Jessup to sit in. Nash looked through the bottom desk drawer for a notebook labeled with a date range that included the date of Leland Smith's death.

He flipped through the notebook until he got to his notes.

"Okay, here we go," Nash said and leaned forward to read the report.

Jessup did the same.

Leland Smith had been found on his kitchen floor. A cup of spilled coffee was near his body.

He was wearing a set of pajamas, both bottoms and top. No trauma was found on the body.

No forced entry was made into the house. Nothing appeared to have been stolen or moved in the house.

The person who discovered the body was Mildred Wyrick, his next-door neighbor. Mildred and Leland typically shared coffee in the mornings. When she came over to meet her friend, she discovered the body lying on the floor by looking through the window of the back door. She immediately called the police.

Responding officers verified Wyrick's claim, forced entry by breaking the window of the back door, and opened the lock. The fire department responded and called the time of death.

The scene was secured, and detectives were dispatched to ensure there was no evidence of foul play.

"You're in my seat."

Jessup looked over to a stocky, early-fifties male at the neighboring cubicle. A slight beer belly pressed against his tan shirt. His black slacks were a little too tight around the hips and a bit too long on his legs. His gun was on the left side.

"My seat," he said and pointed at the chair Jessup was sitting in.

Jessup stood and pushed the chair toward the man.

"Sheriff Thomas Jessup, meet my partner, Glenn Higgins. Glenn, Tom." Nash waved a finger between the two men but never took his eyes from the report.

Jessup stuck his hand out, and Higgins shook it.

"What are you guys working on?" Higgins asked.

"Tom's got something brewing, and it might have started with us."

"What do you mean?"

Nash waved Higgins over and pointed at the report on the screen. "Remember this guy?"

Higgins leaned toward the computer monitor. "Pajama man. Natural death."

"Right. The examiner said heart attack."

"So, what's the problem? It seemed like a nice clean report."

Nash glanced at Jessup. "Why don't you fill him in?"

Higgins sat in his chair while Jessup briefed him on what he knew so far. When he finished, Higgins glanced at his partner. "We didn't miss anything."

Nash stared at the monitor. "You're sure?"

"The examiner confirmed it was a heart attack. There was no evidence of anything foul. We did it right."

Nash nodded a couple of times, then turned away from the monitor to face Jessup.

"Was he married?" Jessup asked.

"No."

"Never?"

"He was gay," Nash said. "Marriage wasn't legal for most of his life. According to the neighbor, he hadn't been in a relationship for years. He was happy being alone."

"Did he leave a will?" Jessup asked.

"Yes."

"Who benefitted?"

Nash grabbed his notebook. Using his finger, he ran down the page until he found what he was looking for then tapped it a couple of times. "United Relief Spokane. Some organization he was involved with."

"Big amount?"

"Moderate. He was a pharmacist. He had a nice home on the South Hill. It seemed like he would have some money."

"Did you guys notify his brothers?" Jessup asked, looking to Nash then Higgins.

The two detectives looked at each other, then shrugged.

"We didn't know he had brothers," Higgins said.

"The neighbor said he was an only child," Nash said and tapped his notebook, which he showed Jessup. The words *only child* were written above *no living relatives*.

"As far as I know," Higgins said, "no memorial was held. He might have had some friends, but no one did anything for him."

Jessup leaned against Nash's cubicle.

"What kind of messed up family are you dealing with?" Higgins asked.

"Would you print off your report for me?" Jessup asked. "And give me a copy of your notes?"

"Sure," Nash said.

"Why?" Higgins asked.

"I've got a death in my jurisdiction that I'm not sure about."

"But we just told you ours was squared away," Higgins said.

"I know, and I'm not challenging that. I'm just asking for a copy of it."

Nash stood. "Relax, Glenn. Tom's good. He and I go way back. Trust me."

Higgins studied his partner. "So, he's with you?"

"Yeah, he's with me."

Higgins shrugged. "All right then. Why didn't you say so?" He slid his chair toward his computer.

Jessup's brow furrowed, and he looked toward his friend.

Nash said, "C'mon, Thomas, let's get you a copy of that report."

*****

While Jessup and Nash stood at the printer waiting for the report, a man and woman entered the detective's bullpen. They were laughing.

"Who's that?" Jessup asked.

"Quinn Delaney and Marci Burkett."

"They've got the other Smith case."

Nash pulled the report off the copier and handed it to Jessup. "Well, then, let's introduce you."

Delaney and Burkett stopped talking as the two men approached. Suspicion filled Delaney's eyes, but Burkett focused on Nash and smiled.

"Marci, Quinn, this is Sheriff Tom Jessup from Whitman County."

The three of them shook hands.

"The sheriff has a problem that might involve all of us."

Burkett's smile faded. "Problem?"

"Us?" Delaney added.

Jessup retold the story. He was getting good at laying it out, this being the third time today. When he arrived at what happened to Leland Smith, Nash jumped in and told his story. After the two of them finished talking, Delaney and Burkett looked at each other.

"Well," Delaney said.

"Yeah, well," Burkett said.

They both looked at Jessup and Nash.

"We should probably bring you up to speed on our case," Delaney said.

Chapter 23

The drive back to Colfax went faster than Jessup expected.

At first, it was due to the excitement of working a case of this magnitude. The deaths of the Smith brothers appeared to be interlinked somehow. How that could be was just outside his reach of understanding, which made it exciting. His mind continued to work the problem, flip it upside down, and look at it from different angles.

When he tired of turning the case over, he began to list the various things he had to accomplish when he returned to the station.

He needed to reopen the report on Renard Smith's death. That was priority one.

Next, he needed to go back and re-interview Derwood Smith. He would start at the beginning. What had happened to the Smith family that drove them so far apart that they wouldn't speak to each other?

He needed to stay in contact with Burkett and Delaney as they continued to track the murders of Clayton and Helen Smith as well as Cadillac Jones. It would require them to work together to discover what had occurred and why.

Jessup then thought about his old friend, Dallas Nash. He had enjoyed seeing him, even if it was only for a couple of hours. They had become close friends during the academy and had remained such while he was on the department. They grew apart after he moved to Colfax.

He was genuinely saddened that Nash had also lost his wife and was now experiencing the same misery Tom had gone through. As they spoke, he could see the sadness in Nash's eyes. It was the same pain Jessup saw when he looked in the mirror every morning.

Jessup wanted to tell Nash it would get better, that time would heal the wound, but he wouldn't lie to his friend. Time does not heal all wounds. Some remain forever there.

Occasionally, Jessup wished his sorrow would diminish to a dull melancholy, which could then be reduced to a pang of loss. That childish wish occurred on those days when the sadness of her loss overwhelmed him, making him question whether his own life was worth living.

Instead, most days, like today, he wanted the despair of her loss to remain. He didn't need for it to wrap its arms around him and embrace him in some poetic way. That also was a silly and immature wish. Instead, he only wanted the heartache to remain, to be a perpetual memorial of his love for her. It was a reminder for him never to forget what he lost; it was a way to stay connected to her memory.

When Jessup pulled into the parking lot of the police station, he parked his truck. He pressed his palms into his eyes and rubbed away the tears.

PART IV

Chapter 24

Roy Utt sprinted down the dark alley. He was fast—too fast for the average junkie. His dirty red Converse slapped the wet asphalt as he ran. When he cleared the alley, he turned left and disappeared.

Detective James Morgan followed him in pursuit. When he exited the backstreet, Morgan turned left onto Riverside Avenue, his shoulder slamming into a homeless woman, sending her spiraling to the ground, her bag of contents spilling everywhere. The detective didn't bother checking on her, though. Instead, he continued his pursuit of Utt, who was now almost a block away.

The son of a bitch, Morgan thought angrily.

He knew better than to run from the detective. When he caught the man, and Morgan knew he would catch him, then he would have to reeducate him on the rules of the street.

Utt was a known associate of Cadillac Eldorado Jones, and Morgan had been searching for him since the meeting with Delaney and Burkett. He'd put out the word that Utt needed to call him, find him, send a smoke signal. No matter what Morgan told the street, Utt was nowhere to be found. And the longer Utt had remained silent, the madder Morgan became.

The kid's adrenaline would soon wear off, Morgan knew. It always did for junkies. They might outrun him in a one-block sprint, but if it went longer than that, Morgan would eventually run them down. He just had to keep his pace constant and his own excitement under control. These were things he'd learned through years on the job.

Utt was easy to follow. He was tall and skinny with long, stringy hair that looked like it had been unwashed for many days. He wore dirty, baggy jeans and an old

Chicago Bulls jersey, the type that exposed his bare arms. The first time Morgan met Utt, he was surprised the kid wasn't covered in tattoos. It was then that Roy Utt made the mistake of admitting to Morgan that he didn't like pain, that he was even scared of the prick of a tattoo needle.

The junkie struggled to push himself harder, running past a homeless man holding on to a streetlamp for balance.

"Hey!" the man yelled as Utt ran by.

As Morgan passed a couple of seconds later, the homeless man yelled, "Hey! Hey!" with his fist waving in the air.

Morgan was living proof that old age and treachery would overcome youth and skill. When it came to junkies, though, it was an unfair fight, even for one like Utt, whose stamina now genuinely surprised Morgan and was earning him, begrudgingly, some respect. All Morgan had to do, though, was bide his time, keep running, and remain focused. Either an opportunity would present itself, or the junkie would eventually quit on himself. It was in the junkie nature to do so. They all did it. Really, they had quit on themselves the minute they started using.

Half a block ahead, Roy Utt suddenly pulled up, grabbed his side, then bent over and puked.

Morgan leaned forward and ran harder, the lessons and thrills from his days as a high school linebacker rushing back to him.

The junkie turned and looked up just in time to see the freight train barreling down on him. He reflexively straightened and yelled, "Wait!"

Morgan's shoulder hit Utt in the chest, lifted him off his feet, and sent him sprawling to the sidewalk several feet away. When the junkie rolled, the concrete scraped and tore the bare flesh on his arms and hands.

Utt squealed in pain when he came to a stop.

As he walked over to where the man lay, Morgan sucked deeply for air, his hands on his hips. The junkie rolled to his hands and knees, blood already starting to appear from the scrapes on his arms. Morgan put his foot on the junkie's ass and pushed him back to the ground.

"Stay down," the detective said amid deep gulps of air.

Utt quickly flipped over to his back and defensively put his hands in the air. "I give! I give!"

"Stop talking," Morgan said, glancing around, still breathing deeply.

No one was in this part of downtown tonight. Even though most of the city had experienced gentrification over the past two decades, this part of the business district was lagging. It was a part of the town that Morgan still loved. He wasn't one of those uppity types who loved the new Spokane—clean and presentable and looking to make a top ten list for best places to something or other. He liked the way the city had been—dirty and underachieving.

From the ground, the junkie stared up at him, waiting.

When his breathing recovered, Morgan said, "You made me run."

"I'm sorry, man."

Morgan kicked the junkie in the thigh, the toe of his boot digging into the meat.

Utt jumped in response. "I'm sorry, Morgan! I'm sorry!"

"Making me run. That's going to cost you. You understand that, right?"

Still on the ground, Utt nodded. He did not attempt to stand.

"And I mean, way past tonight, Roy. I won't forget this."

The junkie lowered his hands. "I know, Morgan, I know. I fucked up."

"You're damn right, you did."

Utt rested his hands on his chest, his eyes watching Morgan.

"I got questions for you, Roy. Things I know you know. The answers are non-negotiable, understand?"

Utt remained silent, eyeing Morgan.

"We're going to do this here or at the station. If we do it at the station, then you're going to jail, and I'm booking you for possession."

"But I ain't holding, Morgan. You know I ain't that stupid."

"I know, Roy. You ain't that stupid." Morgan pulled a small baggie of white powder from his jacket. "However, you're going to hold this one way or another. You can walk with it later, or you can go to jail with it now. Understand?"

It took him a moment, but the junkie finally nodded.

Morgan tossed the baggie to Utt, and it landed on his belly, near his hands. The junkie made no move to touch it.

"Put it in your pocket, Roy."

Utt remained still.

Morgan kicked him in the thigh again, and the junkie squeaked, yet he made no move to pick up the small baggie on his chest.

The detective said, slowly and deliberately, "Pick it up."

Utt slowly grabbed the baggie and tucked it into the front pocket of his jeans.

Morgan then bent over and grabbed the junkie, lifting him by his shirt and shoving him against the wall. Utt raised his hands slightly but did not attempt to fight back or push the detective away.

"Now, Roy, I want you to think of me as a bumblebee and this," the detective said, holding up his fist, "this is my stinger. Any time I think you're lying, I'm going to sting you. Are you allergic to bee stings, Roy?"

"Come on, Morgan, man, I don't lie to you."

He slugged Utt in the stomach.

The kid doubled over and retched.

Morgan straightened him up, holding him by the shoulder with his left hand. The kid's face had reddened, and he struggled for breath.

The detective waited for the junkie to recover before saying, "I'm gonna ask that question again. Are you allergic to bee stings?"

He nodded emphatically.

"You should be careful then. I don't want you getting stung and going into anaphylactic shock. That would be bad, right?"

Utt nodded.

"Let's get to it, Roy. You run with Rado Jones, don't you?"

The junkie started to say something, glanced at Morgan's fist, then closed his eyes. "You know I do," he said.

"That's right, I do, but when you tell the truth, you don't get stung. See how this works?"

"I told you, I don't lie to you, man."

Morgan punched him again, pinning his stomach against the brick building.

"Ugghh."

Utt wasn't able to double over because Morgan still held his shoulder against the wall.

"That's a lie, Roy. Anytime you lie, you get stung. Get it?"

The junkie retched and struggled to breathe.

"Say it."

"Anytime I lie, I get stung," he whispered.

Morgan smiled. "See? Another truth. No sting."

Tears ran from Utt's eyes, and his trembling lips were covered with white spittle.

"You know Rado's dead?"

The kid nodded. "I heard it, yeah."

"Who'd you hear it from?"

"Around."

"Not good enough. From who?"

Fear filled Utt's eyes when he yelled, "The streets, man! The streets!"

"Don't yell at me. I'm right here. Who told you?"

"I don't know, Morgan. I swear to God. People just started talking about him being dead. Then it was, like, common knowledge, you know?"

"Anyone say he was a CI?"

"What?"

"Were there rumors of him talking to the cops?"

"No one talked like that, I swear. Rado was good people. He wouldn't talk to the cops."

"He did right by me," Morgan said flatly.

Utt searched the detective's eyes, trying to determine if Morgan was indeed telling the truth. Finally, he asked, "Rado was a rat?"

He slugged Utt. Again, the junkie was unable to double over due to his shoulder being pinned to the wall. Utt's face reddened, and he coughed. When he was done, saliva hung from his chin.

"Why'd you hit me, Morgan?" he yelled. "I didn't lie!"

"Don't speak ill of the dead," the detective said. "Who would want to hurt him?"

"No one, man! I promise. I swear on my mother's life."

"Gimme someone else to talk to."

"I don't know no one else."

Morgan lifted his fist. "Roy, you better gimme someone else to sting or else you'll get stung again."

"Scrimmy!" he yelled, spittle flying from his lips. "Talk to Scrimmy."

"Scrimmy?" Liliya Scrimshaw was another junkie known to Morgan. "Why?"

"She and Rado was hooking up. They were talking about gettin' clean, gettin' jobs, startin' a family. Stupid shit like that."

While he held on to Utt, Morgan thought about Scrimshaw. Utt didn't bother to fight back or to seek escape while the detective's thoughts drifted. When he determined what Utt had said was probably true, he let go of the junkie's shoulder and stepped back.

"Was that so hard?"

"Yeah, man. It was. You hit me."

"You lied, Roy, you lied. If you hadn't done that, you wouldn't have been stung."

"I didn't—" Utt started and looked immediately to Morgan's right hand, which suddenly clenched into a fist. The junkie nodded a couple of times and said, "Hey man, I'm sorry. It won't happen again."

"That's good, Roy. I would hope that we've moved our relationship to a new level of understanding."

Utt nodded in agreement.

"We should probably talk about those drugs in your pocket, though," Morgan said.

"The drugs?"

The detective stepped to him and studied his eyes. "Did you really think I was going to forget you were holding after you made me run?"

Utt's face fell. "No. I guess not."

Morgan waited a few moments, then reached out and patted the junkie's shoulder. "Be smart, Roy. Don't use it all at one time."

Detective James Morgan turned and headed back to where he left his car.

Chapter 25

Quinn Delaney walked into the detectives' office and tossed his keys on his desk. He powered on his computer and sat in his chair. He glanced at Marci, who was reading something intently on her computer monitor.

"Good morning," he said.

She raised her hand but continued reading.

Quinn stared at her for a moment before he muttered to himself, "Good morning, Quinn. How was your night? Oh, thanks for asking, Marci. It was nice and quiet. I worked out, read a little, went to bed early. All in all, fairly relaxing. Thanks again for asking."

He turned to his computer, typed his login password, and was greeted with his desktop image.

"You done?" Marci asked.

Quinn glanced at her.

"A bit dramatic this morning, aren't you?"

"I was feeling ignored."

"I was doing police work while you were still drifting in. The hot sheet has something interesting on it."

The hot sheet was the daily report compiled by the Crime Analysis Unit. They reviewed the latest patrol reports and field interviews and would list anything they thought might be of importance. It was used to create a bigger picture of how crime was moving and impacting the city. In years past, it previously took a day or two for information to make its way to the hot sheet. Now, it was closer to real time. As soon as a report arrived in CA, the analysts could review it, decide if the information was valuable enough to share department-wide, and then post it immediately to the digital hot sheet.

Quinn remained silent, waiting for Marci to reveal what she'd learned.

"A stolen, late-model dark Lexus was recovered yesterday."

"Okay," Quinn said. "And?"

"It was found burning behind Joe Albi Stadium."

"Stolen car found burning. Alert the news. Maybe it was some hoodlums trashing a nice car."

"It's a Lexus, you dork, not a Rolls-Royce Phantom. And maybe it was the dark car seen fleeing from the double murder scene."

He thought about it for a moment, then turned to his computer. He called up the hot sheet for himself. The responding officers had contacted the registered owner to come get the car. They cleared the scene after the fire department extinguished the blaze.

Quinn picked up the phone and called the number of the registered owner. She answered after the second ring.

"Hello?"

"Is this Amy Green?"

"Yeah."

"Amy, this is Detective Delaney with the Spokane Police Department. Your stolen car was recovered last night, correct?"

"Yeah," she said. "It's ruined now, though. Burnt up."

"Did you have it towed somewhere?"

She audibly sighed. "Not yet. It was still smoking last night. Tow truck guy came out, but he said he had to wait until it cooled off. I can't catch a break with the stupid thing."

"So, the car is still behind the stadium?"

"Unless someone stole it again." She didn't laugh at her joke.

"Okay. Thank you."

"Wait. Do you know who stole it? Are you going to arrest somebody?"

"No, ma'am. We want to take another look at it. To see if it might have been used in a homicide."

"Oh, great," Amy said. "This just keeps getting better."

The line went dead.

***

Joe Albi Stadium sits on the west end of town and is where most of the city's high school football teams play their games.

Quinn and Marci drove past the VA Hospital on their way to the stadium. Once they left the main street, the aged asphalt roads to get to the parking lot were dimpled and crumbling. When they wound behind the stadium, the burnt car was hard to miss.

A slight mist had begun to fall. Marci opened her red umbrella when she exited the car.

The Lexus sat near the woods; flames had blackened its once shiny body. The windows were completely broken, either due to the heat, vandalism, or the firefighters. The tires were flat and melted. From the inside of the car, something was still smoldering. The smell of burnt rubber and plastic was heavy in the area.

Quinn removed his cell phone and took several pictures of the car from various angles. He then repeated his steps, getting video footage with the phone.

When he was done, he stood by Marci under the umbrella.

"What do you think?" he asked. "Could this have been used in the double murder?"

"If you were going to commit premeditated murder, wouldn't you steal a car then torch it when you were done?"

"That would be reasonable."

Marci eyed him. "But we have no reason to believe this is that car, right?"

"No."

"Right. No video. No witness reports beyond descriptions of a 'dark car.' That could be anything, including this burnt-out hulk."

"Exactly."

Marci studied the car.

"You're wondering," Quinn said, "if we should grab it and take it back to the evidence room for processing."

"It's been sitting out here for how long?"

"Who knows?"

"After the fire, at least twelve hours, right?"

"So?"

Marci faced him. "I'm thinking about all the ways a defense attorney will rip this apart if we find anything on it."

"That's a big *if*."

She shrugged. "Let's process it. We can do it under the stolen vehicle report. If anything pops up, we can then tie it to our case. If nothing useful is found, it won't clutter our investigation."

Quinn thought about it for a moment, pulled out his phone, and dialed Amy Green. Since it had been found and released to her, the vehicle was technically back in her possession. They couldn't just grab it. However, if he could get her permission…

She answered on the second ring.

Chapter 26

Thomas Jessup passed through the small town of Palouse on his way to Derwood Smith's estate. He waited at the front gate to be allowed entrance. It required a second press of the buzzer before a voice came over the speaker.

"Yes?"

"Sheriff Jessup to see Derwood."

"Is everything all right?"

The voice, although tinny, was feminine and not Lupita's.

Jessup leaned toward the speaker. "Just checking on him."

For some time, nothing happened, and Jessup considered driving around the wrought-iron gate and the shrubs that abutted it. It would prove rude if the voice on the speaker had only gone to confer with Derwood, but Jessup was anxious to speak with the man.

Several more seconds passed before he finally whispered, "Screw it."

He turned the steering wheel, and the truck moved toward the dirt. The fence jerked then as it began to open, and Jessup stomped on the brakes. He straightened the truck and proceeded up the driveway to the house. A newer, white Volkswagen Tiguan was parked out front.

As he walked up the steps to the house, the front door opened. An attractive woman stood in the doorway. She was almost as tall as Jessup, who was an even six feet. She was in black yoga pants, white athletic shoes, and a light white sweatshirt that read *Capitola Pizza Company*. Her blond hair was short on the sides, but left longish on the top, flopping over to the left side. He guessed she was in her early forties.

"Adeline Smith, Sheriff," she said and extended her hand, letting it dangle slightly.

Jessup carefully took her hand, as if he was not used to the act. "Tom Jessup."

When they broke their handshake, she stepped out of the way and let him into the house. After she closed the door, she said, "I appreciate you looking in on my dad."

"Yes, ma'am."

"How long have you known him?"

Jessup shrugged. "Hard to say. You know how it is in a county like this." He didn't like avoiding her question, but intuition told him that he should keep his cards close to his chest.

"We've never met," she said with a smile. "I would have remembered a man like you."

The smile was more than polite and made Jessup uncomfortable. It was forward and flirtatious.

"Is Lupita around?" Jessup asked.

Adeline blinked a couple of times before saying, "Day off."

Jessup studied her for a moment then slowly looked around the house.

"Busy day?" Adeline asked.

"Not so much."

She slowly ran her eyes up and down his frame, stopping at the gun on his belt before returning to meet his eyes. A hint of a smile started at the left side of her mouth. "We should get you to my dad," she said and slightly extended her right hand to lead him.

Jessup glanced at her hand. "It's okay. I know my way."

Adeline pushed her lips out in a pout, but her eyes didn't reflect that feeling. "I'll escort you. It's only polite."

Jessup nodded once.

They walked side by side up the stairs.

"Did you grow up in these parts?"

"Colfax," Jessup said.

"A bulldog," she said with a small smile, still flirting. "Did you play football?"

Jessup didn't respond.

When they arrived at Derwood's room, Adeline continued inside, leaving Jessup at the door. Derwood Smith was seated in his bed with a *Wall Street Journal* on his lap, and the television tuned to *CNN* with the sound off. Derwood glanced at her as she approached.

"Dad," she said, "Sheriff Jessup is here to see you."

Derwood looked past her and smiled. He waved him in and held out his left hand.

Jessup carefully shook it. "How are you, Mr. Smith?

"I'd be better if this damn stock market would figure out what it wants to do." Derwood pointed at the television.

"Now, Dad," Adeline said.

Derwood waved her off.

Jessup turned to Adeline and asked. "Would you give your father and me a few minutes?"

She appeared slightly confused before facing her father, who was now studying Jessup.

Derwood said, "It's okay, Addy. The sheriff and I have some things to discuss."

Adeline refocused her attention on Jessup. She looked like a scolded little girl. With a slight huff, she left the room. Jessup refused to watch her go, knowing full well she would have made a show of it. He listened to her footsteps proceed down the hallway.

Jessup grabbed the chair and moved it to the bedside near Derwood. The older man's eyes were still on the television. "You follow the market, Sheriff?"

"No."

"Damn thing is bi-polar. Can't make up its mind whether it's going up or down. I'll tell you one thing, buy gold."

Jessup turned to the screen.

"Don't tell my daughter this, but I've started doing just that."

The sheriff faced the older man.

"Never hurts to have a hedge, just in case the whole thing implodes. If it corrects itself, I can always put it back in."

Jessup didn't understand the stock market, and, frankly, he didn't care.

"What's on your mind, Sheriff? By the look on your face, whatever it is, it's something serious."

"I've got bad news, Mr. Smith."

"Call me, Woody. The few friends I've got left call me that, and if what you're about to tell me is what I think you're going to tell me, well, I think I'd like to hear it from a friend."

"Woody, I did what you asked. I found Leland."

The older man turned his attention back to the silent TV. "He's dead, too, isn't he?"

"Yeah."

Derwood closed his eyes and nodded several times. "How?"

"Heart attack."

"Tsk." The older man opened his eyes. "How long ago?"

"A few months."

"Been a bad run for the Smith boys, huh?"

"It has been, yes."

They sat quietly for several moments before Derwood asked, "What kind of life did he have? Did it look like he had a good one, I mean?"

"Seemed so. He was a pharmacist. Retired."

"Was he married? Did he have children?"

"Not married. No children."

Jessup thought about telling Derwood about his sexual orientation but figured it didn't matter and wouldn't make any difference at this point.

"That's too bad. A man should get married and make a family. That's where happiness lays. You have a family, Sheriff?"

"Yes, sir. A son. He lives back East now."

"No wife?"

"She passed a number of years ago."

Derwood nodded. "My wife passed as well almost twenty years ago. Aneurism. Never took up with another. Never seemed to be a reason. No one could replace her."

Jessup didn't comment.

"Not much to do now then, I guess. Regarding my brothers, I mean."

"Actually, I think there is."

"How's that?

"Tell me what happened. What happened that led the four of you to never speak to each other again?"

A further sadness descended on Derwood's face. He folded the newspaper in his lap and set it aside. He folded his hands. "It's a bit of a story. You sure you want to hear it?"

"It could be important."

Derwood Smith lifted the oxygen mask to his face, inhaled deeply, and then slowly lowered his hand.

"My grandfather moved to Colfax in 1912," Derwood said. "Didn't take him long to meet my grandmother, get married, and buy a stake of land to farm. That's all he ever wanted to do—farm. His grandparents, which would be my great-great-grandparents, had immigrated to this country and began to raise a family in Boston.

"Their children, my great-grandparents, didn't want to be in the big city and under the watchful eyes of their parents and nosy siblings. Therefore, they decided to move to the Midwest. They made it to a farming community outside Kansas City and became sharecroppers. You've heard that term before?"

Jessup nodded, remembering the term from a long-forgotten junior high school class.

"When my grandfather came of age, he fled that community and moved further west to Colfax. He didn't want to be a sharecropper like his father, and he wanted to get away from his family, be his own man. You can understand that, right?

"So my grandparents began farming. They were very conservative with their money and very astute with how to invest it. They bought land whenever they could, continuing to add to their acreage. What they couldn't farm, they leased out to someone else to tend.

"They continued that process throughout their lives until they died and left everything to my father. After he was born, my grandmother couldn't have another child. She tried, but the other children, they died in birth. I believe my grandparents stopped trying after the second death. It was a rarity for a farm family to be so small."

Derwood lifted the oxygen mask and inhaled. Jessup thought he heard footsteps in the hallway. He turned to look at the doorway, expecting someone to enter, but no one did. When Derwood continued speaking, Jessup returned his focus to him.

"They were simple folks, my grandparents, never wanting for anything more than the farm and to build a legacy. Even when they had amassed considerable wealth, they never traveled beyond the immediate area. It wasn't their way.

"Growing up an only child on a farm impacted my father greatly. In his mind, he desperately wanted a large family. Our generation of the Smith family would provide him with five boys. Myself, Leland, Clayton, Renard, and Eugene."

Eugene? Jessup thought. This was the first mention of a fifth brother.

"My mother died when I started high school. She took her own life. My father found her in the bathtub, fully clothed. She'd taken a bottle of sleeping pills while we were at school, and he was working the field. It was no secret that she hated her life, the life of a farmer's wife.

"She used to tell me her dreams of being an actress and living in a big city like New York. They were always filled with a certain amount of sadness and regret. Instead of chasing her dreams, she married her high school sweetheart and got stuck in Colfax with five boys who were essentially hooligans."

Derwood chuckled at a memory.

"The five of us were always stirring up some sort of trouble, and my father loved it. That's what he wanted from a big family. Those kinds of memories. Those kinds of problems. My mother, however, shook every time she got a call from the school, or worse, the police. My father took great delight in the fact that we tortured her. Don't get me wrong, Sheriff. He loved my mother more than heaven and earth, but he thought little boys were supposed to be mischief-makers to their mothers."

Jessup imagined five boys must have been hard on Mother Smith.

"She should have left him," Derwood continued, "and pursued her dreams, but a woman didn't do that in those days, especially not a woman from around these parts. It was frowned upon. She descended into further depression until there was only one way out for her.

"Her death shook my father to the core. It broke the man in a way I didn't know a man could be broken. It was like he died inside, but his body didn't know it yet. He was a robot. No, that's not right. He was a zombie. We lost our father when she died, except no one realized it then."

Jessup wondered about his relationship with William. Had he ruined his own relationship with his son following Mia's death? Was it his fault? Had he turned into a robot, or worse, a zombie?

"Us boys," Derwood said, "we handled our mother's death as you would imagine. Drugs and alcohol, of course. I was particularly fond of the booze. Some of the looser girls kept our minds off our motherless upbringing. Yes, even back then, there were girls like that, and we were more than happy to make their acquaintance. We did everything we could to convince ourselves our mother's absence didn't matter."

Derwood took a break to draw several breaths from the oxygen mask. Jessup strained to hear if someone was in the hallway. He couldn't make out anything over the hiss of the oxygen tank. Jessup stood and quietly walked to the hall. No one was there. When he walked back, Derwood watched him with interest.

Jessup sat and nodded.

The old man continued, "The Vietnam war loomed over our family. Five boys meant some of us were bound to go. Leland and I, being the oldest, we both decided the smart thing to do was sign up and choose where we went. I joined the Navy, and he went into the Coast Guard. Neither of us ever ended up near the war. We were lucky. It may not have been the bravest course of action, but we served our country.

"Clayton and Renard took a different—some would argue—less honorable path. They both went to college to avoid the draft. Clayton went to Berkley, Renard attended Oregon State. They stayed in all the way through, both getting their master's degrees. They protested the war, and they even protested Leland and me. Can you believe that? It was the start of the cracks in our family. When Leland returned from the Coast Guard, he protested the war, too, but in a different way. He straddled a line, though, telling Clayton and Renard that he had *earned* the right to protest and that they were too scared to make a commitment. His argument didn't make a lot of sense, but not much did during those days.

"As soon as he could, our youngest brother, Eugene, enlisted in the Army. He chose to be an infantryman, guaranteeing he would be sent to Vietnam. The others were upset with him for joining. My father was furious. He saw the evening news reports. He knew what was going on over there. I was the only one that supported his decision, seeing the man that Eugene was growing into. He told us it was for patriotism, but I knew why he made the decision. It was to escape the depression surrounding our childhood home. He'd been left alone with our father after the four of us had abandoned our little brother."

Derwood lifted the mask to his face and took a deep breath. His eyes were sad as he remained that way for a few moments. When he dropped his hand, he continued.

"Eugene arrived in country just in time for the fall of Saigon. He barely made it out. When he rotated back to the States, he was assigned to Fort McClellan, Alabama, going to help train recruits attached to the basic training unit there. Even though I supported his decision to join, I was happy he was going to be safe. What could be safer than training a bunch of fresh-faced recruits?

"A few weeks after he arrived, we were notified he was killed in a training accident. He rolled a Jeep and was crushed. God knows what he was doing, but he killed himself joyriding around in a Jeep. Nineteen years old. A damn shame."

Tears filled Derwood's eyes. He rubbed them with shaking fingers. He took another hit off the oxygen mask.

"They sent his body home, and we had a funeral. Clayton and Renard returned to Colfax for it. Leland was there. I was attending college at State by then, having gotten out of the Navy. None of us really spoke to the other, we were all in a daze about Eugene, and we didn't like each other much by then. We barely talked to my father. The funeral came and went, and everyone went back to their respective lives.

"Eugene's death ruined what was left of my father. He was the good son, and we all knew it. He was the one who had planned to come home to take over the farm. The rest of us didn't want anything to do with farming, but Eugene had always said he would take it over someday. He loved the land.

"My father turned inward after that. His wife was dead, his youngest son gone. The rest of us had moved on with our lives and gotten wrapped up in our own selfishness. I'd drive up from Pullman on the occasional weekends to visit him for an hour or two. I was only a few minutes away, but I couldn't be bothered to see the old man. I was wrapped up in my own life, going to school, partying, living a life I thought was so damn important. Each visit home, my father seemed less communicative, and he was already cold. It didn't make me want to see him. The rest of my brothers essentially abandoned him. I guess I did, too.

"Finally, one weekend I came home, and he told me he sold the farm. I didn't know how to respond. I didn't care, I mean. I didn't want the farm after all, but it seemed like it was some sort of familial heritage, like it should be sort of important. He said he decided he no longer wanted to be in Colfax and was moving to Spokane. He was going to start over, look for something else in life. Remember, it was the mid-1970s, and a lot of people talked that way, always looking for the thing that would make them happy, give their lives some sort of meaning. It was odd to hear my father talk like that."

Derwood placed the oxygen mask over his face for a moment then removed it before continuing.

"After he got to Spokane, he used the money from the farm to start buying real estate. I didn't know he was doing it then, but that's what he did. He didn't tell my brothers or me what he was up to. We didn't find out about it until years later. He never remarried. I don't think he ever met anybody. I don't know if he even tried.

"My father divested himself of all his funds. He lived modestly in a two-room rancher. As I went about my life, and my brothers went about theirs, my father's investments grew. He never talked to us about it. He became more and more cantankerous, so much so that I eventually quit calling him. He was a miserable man. I hadn't talked with him in almost ten months before he died in November of '83.

"It was then we all discovered what he did. In his will, he left his entire estate in a trust. We didn't know what was inside that trust except for real estate. As beneficiaries, we had no voting rights and no access to any funds. Distributions were initially forbidden. The trustee was not allowed to sell any of the assets, and he was not allowed to tell us what was inside the trust nor how it was performing."

"You don't know which properties your father owned?"

"I tried to find out, Sheriff. Believe me, I tried. I can't imagine how many hours early on that I spent looking for them. This was before the Internet, and we spent a considerable amount of time looking. I even hired a real estate broker to help me, but we were never able to locate what might be there. As I said, the trust was forbidden to release any information to us.

"We were told that it was directed to first pay off the debt of each property, then continue to manage them, placing the funds in whatever interest-bearing accounts they deemed appropriate."

"It's a blind trust then."

"That's exactly what it is," Derwood said and lifted the mask to his face. When he removed it, he said, "We were told when everything was paid off we would receive annual distributions."

"Do you receive those payments now?"

"We do. We started receiving them about five years ago. I've thought about it for some time, and I believe he intended to bring us together, force us into being a family again. In his own way, I believe he loved us. I don't think he did this to hurt us. His mind was just twisted after the death of Eugene. Things probably didn't make a lot of sense to him anymore.

"Unfortunately, the trust made us blame each other further. We brothers, we pointed the finger at one another. We always distrusted each other because of what happened to our mother, to Eugene, to our father, and now there was the family fortune to back up our animosity.

"What little communication remained between the brothers stopped fully. We fractured to the point where we were irrevocably broken. There was no putting us back together."

"Who handles the trust?" Jessup asked.

"An attorney in Spokane. Baumbach. Ezra Baumbach. I can get you his number."

"It's okay, I can find it," Jessup said. He stood. "Thank you for your time, Woody."

"Anytime, Sheriff."

Jessup said, "Quick question. Adeline?"

"My daughter."

"Only child?"

"No. I have a son as well. Heath. He lives near Spokane."

Jessup extended his hand, which Derwood took.

The old man said, "I hope I was helpful."

"You were, Woody, you were. Take care."

***

She was seated in the living room, reading a book. Several floor-to-ceiling bookcases lined the south wall, and a picture of a sunset hung on the east wall. Large windows on the north end provided a view of the rolling hills of the Palouse. A couch and two recliners sat facing each other in the middle of the room.

Adeline sat in the corner of the couch and lowered the book as Jessup walked in. "Have a nice talk?"

"Informative."

"That's good, I hope."

Jessup walked over to the window. "Impressive view."

Adeline stood and joined him. "It's lovely, isn't it?"

"What did your father do? For work, I mean."

"He was a professor at WSU."

Jessup glanced at Adeline then looked back out the window. "And he afforded this?" he asked with a sweeping gesture.

"Oh," she smiled. "No, not from that. He invented a gasket."

"A gasket?"

"It's a little more technical than I understand, but it was a part of a respirator—the kind a hospital uses. He invented it, patented it, then sold it to a medical company. He built this home with the proceeds from that sale. It's nice, isn't it?"

"Did you grow up here?"

"I wish. We lived in a modest home in Pullman. It was nice, but nothing like this."

"You have a brother, right?"

Adeline frowned. "Yes."

"He lives in Spokane?"

"Spokane Valley, thank God."

"Don't like your brother?"

"He's all right, but he's an acquired taste. I like his kids better. They come down occasionally and visit their grandfather. We get together when they do."

"What about you? Where do you live?"

"Me? I'm still in Pullman. I couldn't leave this part of the world. As far as I'm concerned, this is God's country. I've got a little apartment, couple blocks from campus. I used to have a house, but I downsized. I decided I needed less stuff in my life if I was going to focus more on me."

"What do you do?"

"I'm going back to school to get my teaching degree."

Jessup studied her. "What did you do prior?"

"Accounting, but it never really spoke to me. That might sound funny, but who wants to spend their lives doing something they hate? That's why I decided to start over, chase my dream. I've always wanted to be an elementary school teacher."

He thought about asking if she listened in on the conversation with her father, but he left it alone. He also wanted to ask her about the housekeeper, Lupita, but he decided it could also keep for another day.

"I'll let myself out," Jessup said and moved toward the front door.

"Sheriff," Adeline said and hurried toward his side, catching him as he arrived at the front door.

"Hmm?"

"Are you married?"

"Excuse me?"

"Would you, maybe, like to have coffee sometime?"

He forced a polite smile. "Thank you, but I can't."

Jessup opened the front door and headed toward his truck, not bothering to look back.

Chapter 27

"Someone said you and Rado were going to get clean, maybe start a family."

Liliya "Scrimmy" Scrimshaw sipped her black coffee then put the white, chipped mug down. They were at The Hoot Owl, a café in East Spokane that held a variety of Alcoholics Anonymous meetings.

"Who was sayin' that?" she asked, her eyes flat, no suspicion.

"Skinny Boy."

"Why would he say anything? Did he get hisself into some trouble or something?"

"Or something. He was trying to be helpful, Scrimmy. I'm looking to find who did Rado. You know I liked the guy."

Scrimmy picked up her cup and swirled around the remaining bit of coffee. "He thought you was okay. For a cop. I guess you always did him right."

She was a tiny woman made even smaller by her drug use. Morgan couldn't imagine what she'd put into her body over the years but was sure she'd probably sampled a bit of everything and did a lot of one thing—heroin.

Her rap sheet went as far back as sixteen years old and ran the gamut from prostitution to drug possession. She even had a conviction for Felon in Possession of a Firearm, a charge she earned by carrying a weapon for a former boyfriend. She was in her mid-thirties, which was ancient for the type of life she had lived. She was about ten years older than Cadillac Jones.

"So it was true, Scrimmy? You two were gonna get clean, start a family, drive off into the sunset?"

She held up the chipped mug. "I ain't drinkin' this for my health."

Morgan watched her as she lowered the cup, suddenly lost in her thoughts.

She let out a small, sad laugh. "Maybe I am drinkin' it for my health, right? I guess that's the point. Yeah, Morgan, we was gonna get clean, try to be legit. I loved him, and he loved me. Is that so hard to believe? I didn't want to be in the life no more. Neither did he. We just wanted to get away from here, live a different life, be different people."

"Did you have a plan?"

"On how to get clean? Me? I figure it's like what the program says. One day at a time."

"You're sticking with it?"

"Just because he's dead doesn't mean I want to go back to drugs. I started to get clean for him. He made me believe we could do it. I want to see it through, you know? This is the last thing I can give him."

"Can you get into a program, Scrimmy? A real one, away from here."

"With what health care? I ain't never had a real job, Morgan. I've got to work through this on my own. Go full Rambo on it, beat it with willpower."

"What did Junior think of you shacking up with Rado and getting clean?"

"He didn't know."

"Your pimp didn't know about you and Rado? C'mon. He knew."

She shook her head.

"Maybe he did. Maybe he was the one who killed him."

"I was careful, Morgan. Real careful. Besides, Junior wouldn'ta killed him. He'da made him pay. You don't get money from a dead man, Detective, or don't they teach you that in your cop school?"

He leaned in and studied her. "What did Rado think of you still working the stroll?"

"It's what put junk on the table. He knew the life."

Morgan leaned back and sipped from his mug. The bitter coffee did nothing but buy him time with his thoughts. "If not your pimp, then what did Rado get himself into?" the detective asked.

Scrimmy looked up from her coffee and ran her fingers through her long, unwashed hair. "He didn't get into nothing, Morgan. He was further along than me, getting clean, I mean. He was serious about it. Had a vision of what we could be, where we could go. A little house, white picket fence. He even had us a dog picked out, a Jack Russell terrier. Ever hear of that? Jack Russell. What kinda person gets a dog named after a person? He showed me a picture of the dog inna book at the library. I thought it was a funny-lookin' dog, but he said it would be perfect for us. He was gonna make it so we would have a home, a family. He was gonna name the dog Spaz 'cause I guess that kind of dog is spastic or something. Spaz."

She grabbed the cup, sipped the last of her coffee, and put the mug back on the table. "None of that is ever going to happen now, is it?" She flicked the cup handle with a finger. The resulting ding was lost in the noise of the café.

"How was he going to pay for that? The house, the move, the dog. That would require serious scratch. Where was Rado working?"

Scrimmy looked up but remained silent.

An elderly waitress walked over. She wore blue jeans and a white sweater, and her silver hair was piled on top. She began refilling Scrimmy's coffee mug.

"What about you, hon?" she asked Morgan. "Want a warm-up?"

He covered his half-empty mug with his hand, never letting his eyes drift away from Scrimmy's.

"Suit yourself," the waitress mumbled and walked off.

"What was he doing for money?"

"I dunno."

"You were his woman. You knew. You don't talk about running away with a man and not know how he was making his money."

She looked away into the distance, over his shoulder. "All I know was he told me he was going to help a guy do a job."

"What kind of job?"

She glanced around the diner before whispering. "B&E."

Breaking and entering. In Washington's criminal code, it was known as burglary, but most people called it B&E due to movies and TV.

"Did he say what he was going to break into?"

"An old couple's place."

Morgan's adrenaline spiked, and he leaned forward. "An old couple?"

She nodded and slowly turned her coffee cup in circles. "Supposably, yeah. I guess they had some cash and jewels squirreled away in their house. That's what Rado's guy told him."

"What guy?"

"Rado called him Casey. That's all I know."

"Casey."

"Yeah."

"Get a last name?"

"We don't get last names down here."

Morgan knew that truth too well. "You ever see Casey?"

"Nuh-uh, but I saw what he was driving."

"Yeah? What was he driving?"

"The first time he was in an older car. Like a Camaro or something."

"You remember the color?"

"Orange."

"An old orange Camaro?"

"It was like one of those muscle cars the jocks drove back in high school."

"Yeah?"

"A real rumbler, you know?" She mimicked a noisy engine, her lips and cheeks popping and throbbing in rhythm with the sound.

"You said that was the first time you saw him?"

"The second time he showed up, he was in a black Lexus. That's when Rado got in. I never heard from him again."

"Why didn't you call the police?"

"What was I supposed to do? Call the police to say my boyfriend was dead. Oh, by the way, before he left, he told me he was gonna rob an old couple, and then I heard on the news you suspect him of killing a couple of gray hairs. Yeah, that's exactly what I'm gonna do. I ain't stupid, Morgan."

The detective held up his hands in a defensive position.

"At first," Scrimmy said, "when he didn't come home, I figured something didn't go right with the job. Maybe he was hiding out, or maybe he got pinched. Then, when I heard he was dead, well, I guess I knew things didn't go right. That's the life, isn't it? It's gonna get you one way or another. None of us are getting out alive. Rado just got taken sooner than me or you."

"Do you know how I can get ahold of Casey?"

"No, but you know I would tell you if I did."

"Yeah, Scrimmy, I know."

Liliya studied her coffee cup then. They remained quiet for several moments.

He was staring out the window when he asked, "Did Rado tell you how he met Casey?"

She looked up, and Morgan turned to face her.

"Yeah," she said. "He did tell me that."

Chapter 28

By all accounts, Ezra Baumbach's office was on the cutting edge of fashion... for the late 1970s.

When Quinn Delaney and Marci Burkett walked into the small office at the Gateway Plaza building, it was like stepping into a time warp. Quinn smiled, the odd flashback reminding him slightly of watching old sitcoms with his grandfather.

Wood paneling lined the walls. The receptionist's desk was white metal with an oak top. An orange telephone sat on the desk.

The early 2000s computer with its large monitor seemed futuristic in the setting.

The Chi-Lites "Have You Seen Her?" played through stereo speakers behind the receptionist's desk.

The late-twenties receptionist appeared out of place. Her mousy brown hair fell past her shoulders and onto her thick green sweater. She looked up from her cell phone and raised her eyebrows to the two detectives standing in front of her desk.

"Yes?"

"I'm Detective Burkett," Marci said. "This is Detective Delaney. We set an appointment to meet with Ezra Baumbach."

She blinked several times then consulted her calendar. "You did?" she asked her finger scanning through various appointments.

"We called a bit ago. Maybe an hour."

"Oh," she said. "I wasn't here."

"I talked directly with Mr. Baumbach," Marci said.

"Which is why it's not on the schedule," the receptionist muttered, clearly irritated. "He's with a client now. I'll let him know you're here. Can I tell him what this is about?"

"He already knows," Marci said.

The receptionist set her jaw, picked up the telephone's receiver, stabbed a button, and waited. In a moment, she said, "There are two detectives here to see you." She hung up the phone and said, "He'll be out in a minute." Without delay, she turned her attention back to her cell phone.

Marci shrugged and headed toward the green fabric couch in the corner; Quinn followed her. They both sat, lost in their thoughts.

Finally, Quinn leaned over and said, "This place is amazing."

"Yeah," Marci said, no sense of awe in her voice. "Really amazing."

"You don't like it?"

"What's to like? It's old, and it smells musty."

"It's the seventies, Marci," Quinn said, his eyes scanning the décor. "It's so cool."

"Far out." She didn't bother to hide the sarcasm in her voice.

Quinn shook his head. "You don't appreciate classic Americana."

"You're right. I don't appreciate it." Marci's eyes drifted back to the receptionist. "What do you think of her?" she whispered to Quinn.

He looked at the young woman who was deeply involved with her phone. "What about her?"

"Get any vibe from her?"

"No. You?"

"Yeah."

"What kind?"

"Don't know. Maybe. Like she was shocked to see us or something."

Quinn relaxed. "Most people act that way when the police show up."

"It wasn't that."

The door to the back office opened, and two older men exited. The younger of the two, a man in his early seventies, continued to the front door of the office.

The older man who remained behind said, "Detectives?"

He appeared to be in his eighties and was dressed in tan slacks, a white shirt, and a blue argyle sweater vest. It was hard to tell how tall he was due to his permanent hunch. He hobbled toward them with his right hand forward. "Ezra Baumbach," he said.

Quinn shook his hand first. "Quinn Delaney. This is Marci Burkett."

When he shook Marci's hand, Ezra covered hers with his left and said, "You are quite lovely, my dear."

Marci smiled. "Thank you."

He waved them back to his office. "Follow me." Ezra turned to his receptionist. "Please hold my calls, Crystal."

When they were inside Ezra's office, the older man shut the door and headed slowly toward his desk.

Quinn stopped to take it all in. He smiled, enjoying the visuals. The wood paneling that had been in the receptionist area was gone and replaced with cream-colored walls. On the north wall was a yellow, orange, and brown stripe that ran its length, turned onto the east wall, then suddenly curved downward to the floor before the windows.

A framed picture of a basset hound, its ears spread wide as if in flight, hung on the west wall, near the door.

Ezra sat at a large mahogany desk near the head of the room. Behind the desk, on the south wall, was a floor-to-ceiling bookcase filled with binders and books. A small ladder stood nearby.

Quinn and Marci sat in orange-fabric chairs in front of the desk.

A stack of files was on the edge of the desk. A black push-button phone, an adding machine, and a penholder were the only other items present. Ezra didn't have a computer in his office.

He reached for a file in the stack and carefully yanked it out. He put on a pair of reading glasses and opened it. Quickly, he scanned the top page, then removed his glasses.

His smile was warm and friendly. "Now, how may I help you, Detectives? You mentioned on the phone you wanted to talk about the Smith Trust?"

Quinn leaned forward. "Mr. Baumbach, we're investigating a homicide related to the Smith children."

Baumbach's face slackened. "You are? Who?"

"Clayton."

"Oh, that's terrible."

"Two other brothers also died."

His face now whitened. "When did this happen?"

"Recently," Quinn said. "At first, the deaths looked normal, but in light of the recent homicide, there is suspicion they weren't."

"Who were the others?" Ezra asked, his eyes back on his file.

"Renard and Leland," Quinn said.

"Oh, that's terrible. Just terrible."

Ezra reached for a notepad, clicked his pen, and made some notes. He scribbled for several moments, without talking to the detectives.

Quinn's eyes shifted to Marci, who watched the lawyer patiently.

When Ezra finished writing, he looked up and said, "Then only Derwood remains."

"Yes, sir."

"Oh my," he said then made some additional notes.

"Ezra," Marci said, "can you tell us about the trust?"

Ezra looked up from his notes. When he focused on Marci, his smile was kind and gentle. "I'm sorry, Detective. I can't do that. It's confidential. I hope you understand."

"We do understand. If we get a warrant, you'll show us the trust paperwork?"

Ezra's smile faded, but his eyes remained gentle. "Of course, my dear. My duty to my client will have remained intact."

Chapter 29

Jessup drove up to South Lake Street and parked his truck out front.

His mother opened the door as he climbed the stairs. "You look tired, Tommy."

He kissed her on the side of the cheek. "It's the job."

"Want something to eat?"

"That would be great, Mom. Anything you got. Nothing special, okay? Where's Pop? I want to ask him a question."

"The living room. I'll bring a plate for you."

Jessup found his father with a baking sheet on his lap. A magazine was opened and laying on it. His head was bowed, and his glasses had slid to the edge of his nose. He was rubbing his hands as he read. His arthritis must have been acting up.

"What are you reading?" Jessup asked as he took a seat in the low-back chair in the corner of the room.

"Mmm? Whassat?" Dwight Jessup said, looking up.

Jessup pointed at the magazine.

Dwight's face brightened, and he lifted the publication to show Jessup the cover of a World War II magazine. "I'm readin' a story about the P-38 Lightning. Did you know the—"

Jessup held up his hand to interrupt him. Once his father got going on any military history subject, he would be hard-pressed to get him to stop and focus on something else. "Pop, I've got a question for you."

Dwight's forehead creased.

"You remember a Smith family ever living in town?"

Dwight rubbed his chin with his gnarled hand. "Lots of Smiths have lived in this town, buddy. That ain't that special of a name, you know? Not like Jessup." His smile was a mixture of pride and mischief.

"They lived here in the fifties and sixties, maybe the seventies. Five brothers."

"The Smith brothers!" Dwight said with a laugh and clapped his hands together once. "I remember them, for sure. Boy, did we have some fun times together." He closed the magazine and set it, along with the baking sheet, on the coffee table. "We was all about the same age, 'cept the little one, Gene. He sort of came after. The little guy always tagged along, but I guess lookin' back, he wasn't too much of harm. Anyway, why you askin' about them? Nothin' too bad, I hope."

"I've come into contact with some of the family recently and—"

"They moved back to the area?" he asked with a smile. "Which ones? I'd love to see whoever it is, even that weirdo Leland."

"None are in town, Pop."

Dwight's smile faded. "That's too bad."

"Derwood lives in Palouse, though."

Dwight made a face.

"What?"

"*Woody*," he said, his voice flat.

"What about Woody?"

"He never really liked me none."

"Why?"

"He was the oldest. I always hung out with Clay and Renny. We was the same age. Woody and Leland, they were older, so they tended to look down on the three of us. They played with us when we were smaller, but once they got to high school, they got too cool for us. Probably, the same thing we did to lil' Gene, now that I think about it. He was so skinny for a while we used to call him String Gene." Dwight chuckled. "Kids are sort of tough on each other, I guess."

"You were close with them?"

"As close as kids can be."

"You remember when their mom passed."

"That was something terrible, for sure."

"She killed herself, right?"

Dwight nodded. "Terrible shame what that did to them boys. She left them alone with Joe. That man was not especially nice."

"Joe was their father?"

"Yeah. Ol' Joe Smith."

"You said he wasn't nice? Did he hurt them?"

"Oh, no, nothing like that. Maybe nice isn't the best word. *Warm*. He wasn't especially warm. Fathers back then aren't like they are today. They weren't even like they were when you were growin' up. They had a tough time showin' emotions, and Joe was the worst. Them boys were a holy terror runnin' around town back before their mother died. Joe took great delight in that, but when she died, he sort of died, too. Do you understand what I'm sayin', Tom? He didn't take any delight in them boys anymore. I think it was the exact opposite. I think he resented them."

"He resented his sons?"

"Sure. At first, he thought it was a hoot to have a brood of boys runnin' around town like a pack of wild dogs, drivin' his wife, their mother, crazy. I remember my parents complainin' about it. I can't tell you how many times I was told not to play with them, that they was a bad influence to be around. Now, you tell an eight-year-old boy that another boy's a bad influence, and that's like handin' him an engraved invitation to play with that kid."

Jessup smiled.

"Anyway, after their mother died, Joe didn't take no pleasure from being around those boys anymore. He stopped going to their sportin' events, their school events. He stopped playin' with them. He just closed himself off. Nobody saw him around town with a smile anymore." He thought about it for a few seconds. "I suppose those boys were a reminder of what he lost. Anyway, I'm tryin' to remember when he left town, but I think it was shortly after Gene was killed in the war. After that, he sold off his land and left. Nobody ever heard from Ol' Joe after that. Actually, I don't think nobody really heard from the brothers either. It was like they all just moved on. Strange how people vanish from your life like that."

Vera walked in with a plate and handed it to Jessup. There was a pastrami sandwich, a pickle, and some potato chips. Jessup took it and smiled at his mother.

"What are you boys talking about?"

"Tommy's taking me down memory lane."

"What for?" Vera asked.

"He never said. I think I interrupted him."

Jessup had just taken a bite of the sandwich, so he finished chewing before he said, "It's part of an investigation, Pop."

"Investigation?" Dwight repeated.

"Into what?" his mother asked.

"It's ongoing. You know I can't say."

"With the Smith boys? Must be something crazy," Dwight said with a smile. "I wonder what they got themselves into?"

Chapter 30

River City Boxing was located at the corner of Helena Street and Sprague Avenue, in a part of Spokane that struggled through repeated attempts at urban renewal. It was as if the neighborhood had tried to put on a brave new face but could never entirely hide its past hurts or disappointments.

Some buildings had been updated and contained new businesses. Other structures remained dilapidated and housed industries that were throwbacks to yesteryear—antique stores, a vacuum repair shop, a shoe repair business, and the like. Regardless of the attempts to change the East Sprague neighborhood, its soul was still stained, marred by years of abuse and community apathy.

Prostitutes walked along the streets in this part of town, unafraid of City Hall's push to change the district's narrative. Drug deals occurred in the back alleys, drug houses, and parking lots of the neighborhood. The city may have wanted this area to transform, some real estate investors may have even been at the value-add trough, but the inhabitants—the ones who lived there daily— were resistant to change.

The city had recently re-branded this part of town the International District, but Detective James Morgan considered that liberal bullshit at best and corporate meddling at worst. To him, no matter how much makeup and perfume the city tried to apply to her, East Sprague was, and always would remain, Spokane's dirty whore. She was the type of woman the average citizen hurried past, refusing to make eye contact, thereby leaving her alone to deal with those who weren't afraid to stare maliciously at her and use her for whatever they damn well pleased.

Morgan parked his car, got out, and surveyed the neighborhood. This was the Spokane he grew up in, the town he knew, and had a love/hate relationship with. He quietly closed his car door, even though there was no need to do so in the middle of the day when he was not sneaking up on someone. It was habit.

Before stopping, he had circled the block, looking for an orange Camaro, hoping it would be parked on a side street or in a nearby parking lot. It was too much to hope for and had proved to be exactly that.

River City Boxing stood on the corner, its large windows showing various young men and women training inside. It was clear the establishment was doing more than training them to box. It was there to bring some light, some small ray of hope, to the neighborhood.

When he pushed the door open, his senses were hit immediately. Hanging in the air was the cloying smell of sweat and menthol, probably from the overapplication of Tiger Balm or Icy Hot. The noise level was also high. The sounds of fists hitting heavy bags and speed bags mixed with the thumping beats of a hip-hop song pounding from unseen speakers.

Morgan stood at the entryway and took it all in, enjoying the spectacle of young gladiators preparing for battle. He remained still for several seconds, letting the sights and sounds wash over him.

"Help you?" a deep voice called from across the room.

Morgan searched for it until he saw a heavyset black man in the middle of the open room. He sat on a stool near the boxing ring. The man watched Morgan with intense curiosity.

Two white men, both wearing boxing headgear of different colors, moved around the ring, flicking jabs and throwing punches at each other. They paid no attention to Morgan as they continued to work. As far as Morgan could tell, no one else in the gym turned to look at the detective, their focus remaining where it was intended—on the heavy bags, speed bags, or ring opponent, not to be broken by some temporary outside distraction.

Morgan approached the man and opened his leather jacket to reveal the badge on his belt. "Detective Morgan, SPD. Can I ask you a question?"

"As long as you ask it here. I got a gym to run." The man's eyes drifted to the fighters in the ring. "Stick and move," he yelled. "Stick and move."

"What's your name?" Morgan asked.

"Am I in trouble?"

"No. I just like to know who I'm talking with."

The man's eyes went back to the ring. "Move your feet, Kyle. You look like you're stuck in molasses." When he focused again on Morgan, he said, "Al Kimpson."

Morgan studied Kimpson for a moment, then smiled. "No kidding."

"That mean something to you?"

"K.O. Kimpson, right? Didn't you fight with Muhammad Ali?"

Kimpson chuckled and waggled a finger. "Oh, no. I never fought the man. Sparred with him, and lightly at that. Warm-ups, if you will."

"But still," Morgan said, impressed he was finally meeting the local boxing legend.

The big man smirked. "There's a big difference between fighting and sparring. Regardless, it was an honor just to stand with him in a practice ring, even if it was in the latter part of his career, and mine was just starting. I learned a lot by being around the man."

"I can imagine."

Kimpson didn't respond then. Instead, he watched his fighters bobbing and weaving around the ring.

"You got a fighter here named Casey something or other? Maybe drives an orange Camaro?"

The man's eyes moved back to Morgan.

The detective stared at him, not making a move or asking a follow-up question. A bell rang, and the two fighters moved to opposite corners of the ring.

Kimpson slowly broke his gaze, slid off the stool, and turned to the fighters. He put his hands on the edge of the ring and leaned forward. "Last round, men. I want you to work with each other on this one. Don't just clobber one another, okay? Give and take, know what I'm sayin'? You're workin' technique the next three minutes. Kyle, focus on gettin' your hip around on your cross. It'll get you deeper into that punch. Ed, focus on combos. You're leavin' too many opportunities wasted because you flick the jab while you're moving. You're not hangin' around long enough to see if the damn thing was even effective."

Both fighters nodded at Kimpson's instructions. He glanced down at the electronic timer. "Get ready."

He slid back onto the stool as the digital bell signaled the start of another round. The two fighters moved into the ring, starting their violent dance again.

"You were askin'?" Kimpson said.

"Casey. Orange Camaro."

"Why you lookin'?"

Morgan thought about being hard, acting like he would to any punk on the street, but Kimpson wasn't that. Not only was he a citizen, he was also a guy making a difference in his community. Besides, he'd once worked his way up the heavyweight ladder to fight professionally. He may never have fought for the heavyweight title, but the guy stood in a ring with some of the most famous bruisers of the fight game. He had earned Morgan's respect in a lot of different ways.

Playing hard with Al Kimpson was simply out of the equation.

"A victim of a homicide," the detective said, "met with your fighter outside your club. His girlfriend told me that's where they first met. I'm only looking to make connections."

Kimpson pursed his lips and returned to watching his fighters. Morgan left the man to his thoughts and watched the men throwing hands inside the ring.

"Gimme your card," Kimpson said quietly. Morgan almost missed it due to the song playing over the radio.

Morgan pulled his wallet from inside his coat, removed a card, and handed it to Kimpson.

"Now, make a scene leaving," Kimpson said, his voice still low.

"What?"

"Everyone's watching, so make it convincing."

Morgan didn't turn his head, but his eyes swept the room. The various fighters continued their work on the heavy bags and speed bags. It didn't look like they were paying any attention to him and Kimpson.

"How can you tell?" Morgan asked, his voice low.

"The rhythm of the bags is off. They're payin' attention to us, not to what they should be doin'."

Morgan listened to the bags but couldn't hear what Kimpson could. However, he knew he should trust the older man. He suddenly flicked his hand dismissively, then stomped toward the door. He turned and pointed at Kimpson. "You call me or else," he yelled.

The older man looked at the business card, ripped it in half, then tossed it to the floor.

Morgan spun around, opened the door, and slammed it as he left.

Chapter 31

"It's called a blind trust," Ezra Baumbach said. He leaned back in his chair with his glasses pushed up on his forehead, and his fingers interlaced over his stomach.

A couple of hours after their first meeting, Quinn and Marci had returned to his office with a signed search warrant for the information pertaining to the Smith family trust documents. When they arrived, the receptionist wasn't in, and Ezra's door was open. They walked back and found him reading some papers.

"Where's your receptionist?"

"Out for lunch." He checked his watch. "Been a little long now. She should be back soon."

Quinn handed the warrant to Ezra, and he carefully read each line. He nodded with satisfaction when it was done and put the order to the side. He handed a file to Quinn, who opened it so Marci could read it along with him.

"What's a blind trust?" Quinn asked, looking up from the file.

"It's used in various scenarios," Ezra said, "but it's often used when people, especially politicians, want to avoid conflict of interest scenarios."

"What's it do in this scenario?"

"In this scenario, it hid all of Joseph Smith's assets from his sons while providing them with a monthly stipend."

Quinn and Marci glanced at each other.

"I can see by the looks on your faces that you're confused. Perhaps I should tell you how this trust came about."

"We'd appreciate that," Marci said.

Ezra glanced up to the ceiling as he spoke. "I met Joe in the eighties some time, 1981, I'd guess. Anyway, he asked me to start helping him with the legal work surrounding his burgeoning real estate portfolio. Of course, I was happy to oblige him. As we continued to work together, I grew to know the man. He was nice, not necessarily kind, mind you, but nice, nonetheless. There was something that haunted the man. I'm not sure what it was, though, as he didn't share much about himself. It seemed he didn't enjoy much in life. He worked at building a real estate empire, and that was about it. Nothing else seemed to excite him."

Quinn glanced at Marci, who was studying Ezra intently. He closed the file and placed it on the attorney's desk.

Ezra continued, "When he was diagnosed with lung cancer, he contacted me and said he wanted to create a trust. Leave something for the family legacy. He was very specific about how he wanted it created, though. All proceeds from the real estate were to pay off the mortgages associated with the properties. Only when they were debt-free, and reserves had been created would a stipend begin to be paid to the four sons."

Quinn lifted his hand to interrupt. "When Joseph died, the sons didn't get an immediate inheritance from their father? Even though everything was already in the blind trust?"

"Exactly. He left them nothing following his death. From what he told me, there wasn't much of a relationship left between him and his boys. I'm still not quite sure why he built what he did or why he even left it to them. Maybe it was a sense of duty. I don't know. It was the damndest thing I'd heard of, but we built it to accommodate his wishes."

"Do you know how the sons reacted to the news?" Quinn asked.

"Curiosity at first. It was only natural. I think we'd all have that reaction. They wanted to know what was inside the trust. I couldn't tell them, of course. That's the core purpose of the blind trust. To keep assets hidden."

"How did they know," Marci interjected, "that you were doing what you were supposed to be doing with the properties? I mean, you could have taken the money for yourself."

Ezra's smile was kind. "I wouldn't do that, Ms. Burkett. I'm a professional."

"But how would they know that?"

"I provided them with quarterly updates to show loan balances, reserves, and bank balances."

"But you wouldn't show them which properties were included in the trust?"

"No."

"You just showed them numbers?"

"Yes."

Quinn said, "You would have figured one of them would have tried to sue to find out."

"Clayton did."

"He did?" Quinn asked.

"And he lost," Ezra said flatly. "The brothers weren't communicating with each other, and this was something that drove the wedge even further. The trust had to defend itself, which caused it to spend money. Derwood didn't want the action taken and contacted me, asking me not to use his portion of the money for the lawsuit. I told him that's not how it worked. The trust was a singular entity. If it was sued, it had to defend itself wholly."

"When did this occur?"

"Shortly after Joe's death. Late 1983."

Both Quinn and Marci made some entries into their notebooks.

"You mentioned the stipend," Marci said. "When did that start being paid?"

"About five years ago."

"How much?"

"The payment record is in there," Ezra said, pointing at the file he'd handed Quinn, "but each of them receives about twenty thousand a month."

Quinn whistled. "Twenty thousand? That's a quarter of a million a year."

"Cash flow," Ezra nodded. "That's what Joe wanted to leave them. A fully paid-off portfolio. It took a while, but we did it, and now it's theirs forever. Well…" Ezra's voice trailed off.

"What occurs when one of the brothers dies? Does that stipend go to his family?"

"No," Ezra said flatly.

Quinn's eyes snapped to Marci, then back to Ezra. "What?"

"Joe didn't want that to occur. If one of the sons died, his portion of the stipend was to be divided up between the remaining brothers."

"So the twenty thousand a month," Quinn said, "would be split three ways and the three remaining brothers would get—"

"—a little over twenty-six thousand a month, yes."

"Do you know what that is?" Quinn asked.

"It's a form of joint tenancy. Wherein, the brothers share an equal interest in the property, and the last surviving brother gets total control of the property. But in this case, it's a trust, and the last surviving brother will be endowed with the family's assets."

"No," Quinn said. "What you've just given us is motive. We've been searching for a possible connection between the deaths, and you just handed us one."

Ezra glanced between the two detectives. "I guess I have, haven't I?"

"When did the brothers discover this?" Quinn said. "The survivor's benefit and how it would be divided."

"As far as I know, they never have," Ezra said. "It was part of the trust's internal workings, and the brothers were not privy to that information. Joe made sure of it. Since I just learned of the brothers' deaths, we have never modified a payment to them."

Marci shook her head as she spoke. "Surely, you had to imagine something bad like this would occur at the end of the trust?"

"Murder?" Ezra said. "How would I foresee that? Of course, I told Joe the concept was a bad idea, but I counseled him strictly from the vantage that his sons were already involved in a toxic relationship with each other. It was vitriolic. That's some of the reasoning why he didn't want to leave them anything immediately upon his death. He thought they were emotionally immature and selfish. I don't know if any of that was true. I just know how the man felt. He was disappointed in his boys and how they behaved."

"So, the last remaining brother..." Quinn said, at a loss for the name.

"Derwood," Marci said.

"Derwood," he repeated. "How does it work for Derwood now?"

"First," Ezra said, "I will have to verify what you have told me. I must get proof of death for the other brothers. Once that occurs, we will notify Derwood of the change in his monthly stipend."

"I thought you said he would be endowed with the assets of the trust."

"He would be," Ezra said.

"Meaning?"

"Since he is the last surviving son, the trust will be opened to him. Also, the assets become transferrable now."

"Transferrable?"

"He can sell them if he chooses. He can pass them down to his heirs."

Quinn glanced at Marci.

"I would be happy to keep managing the trust for him. It's one of my oldest accounts. I don't have any desire to stop working. I believe if a man stops working, he'll die, and I have no interest in dying."

"How could they have found out?" Quinn asked. "Could someone hack your system?"

"I'm very secure, Detective. None of my files are on the computer. They are all paper copies," he said, tapping a file on his desk.

"Who has access to your files?"

"Just me and my secretary." Ezra glanced at his watch. "Who is taking an awfully long lunch today."

"Is that like her?" Marci asked.

Ezra looked up. "Sometimes, but she always makes up for it by staying late. She's a very responsible young woman."

"She been with you a while?"

"About a year. My previous assistant had a terrible accident. God rest her soul."

Quinn and Marci slowly looked at each other. Together, they both said, "What was the name of your previous assistant?"

"Carol Harden."

Marci jotted in her notebook.

"And the name of your current assistant?" Quinn asked.

Ezra studied the detective for a moment before saying, "Crystal Braemar. I hope you don't think she's involved. She's a lovely young lady."

Marci added the receptionist's name to her notebook. "We do backgrounds on everyone," she said.

They sat quietly for a few moments until Quinn stood and pointed at the folder for the Smith Trust. "Thank you for your time, Mr. Baumbach. We appreciate it. Will you copy that for us?"

"Of course," the elderly man said as he walked around his desk to shake Quinn's hand. "I'm glad to help in any way I can."

When Ezra turned to Marci, he smiled and reached out for her hand, which he again shook with both of his. "You, my dear, are so lovely."

"You are a flirt, Ezra."

"But I'm very harmless."

"Oh, Mr. Baumbach, I doubt you were ever harmless."

He patted her hand and chuckled.

Chapter 32

The small town of Garfield was a little more than twenty minutes northeast of Colfax. Sheriff Tom Jessup covered most of that distance in silence.

She had called him that morning, and he had answered on the second ring.

"Jessup."

"Sheriff?" she asked, her accent heavy.

"Yes, this is Sheriff Jessup."

"This is Lupita DeLeon."

"Lupita?"

"Can you come and see me? I hope to talk with you about Mr. Smith and his daughter."

He skipped breakfast and headed to Garfield.

The little yellow house was on Union Street. Its clapboard siding had been recently painted and was vibrant but did little to hide the imperfections that were immediately apparent on the surface. An older red Toyota Camry was parked in front of the house. It was the same car he had seen previously parked at Derwood's.

As he approached, Lupita opened the front door. "Good morning, Sheriff."

Jessup glanced up and down the quiet street before entering the house. Lupita closed the door behind him. It was warm inside and smelled of coffee and cinnamon.

"Would you like coffee? I just made a pot."

"That would be nice. Just black."

She moved off to the kitchen, allowing Jessup's eyes to sweep over the living room. A cross hung near the door, along with a picture of Jesus Christ wearing a crown of thorns. Several family photos were clustered together. They appeared to be large family gatherings.

Jessup located Lupita in each of them, and she was always smiling brightly.

The couch was blue fabric with little flowers and had grown threadbare in spots. A reddish-orange recliner sat nearby. An oak coffee table covered with magazines was in front of the couch and recliner. A large flat-screen TV and DVD player were on an entertainment center placed against the opposite wall. Several DVDs were stacked near the corner of the TV. Jessup craned his head to look at the titles. They were written in Spanish, so he shrugged and looked away.

When Lupita returned, she handed him a cup and kept one for herself. She sat on the couch and offered him the recliner.

"What can I do for you, Lupita?"

She stared into her coffee.

"Lupita?"

She looked up.

"You called me for a reason."

She nodded, then said, "I worry about Mr. Smith."

"About his health?"

"Yes, of course, but his daughter, she is no good."

"What do you mean by 'no good'?"

"She is not there to take care of him."

"Why do you say that?"

"She watches me very closely when I am there. She does not like how I care for him."

Jessup shook his head, trying to understand what she was saying. "I don't understand. That doesn't mean she doesn't want him to be okay."

"I do my job, Sheriff. I take very good care of Mr. Smith. He likes what I do. He tells me so."

"Okay."

For a moment, Jessup worried he'd gotten himself into a domestic squabble. Something he should have foreseen and been smart enough to avoid.

"I think she wants him to die," Lupita said.

"Excuse me?" Jessup said, leaning forward.

She nodded emphatically. "Yes, yes. She tells me to go away, that she will take care of him. When I come back, he has not been fed, and he has not been cleaned or taken care of. She is only there to get his money. I know this." Her gaze was intense.

"She doesn't take care of him when you're gone?"

"It's my job to take care of him. Make him meals. When she sends me away, she wants to hurt him. She wants him to die."

"Have you seen her hurt him?"

"No, Sheriff, she does not hurt him like that. She hurts him by not caring for him. Do you understand?"

Jessup leaned back, considering what Lupita had to say.

"I cannot confront her, Sheriff."

He sipped his coffee, thinking.

"If I do, she will have me fired."

"You work for Mr. Smith, right? How can she send you away?"

Lupita nodded. "She asks him to. She says she wants to spend time with him. He is very soft in the heart for her."

"I don't know if there is anything I can do, Lupita."

"Sheriff, I am afraid something is going to happen to him."

He could see the fear in her eyes. "You're that worried about him?"

"Yes."

Jessup thought about it for a moment. "I will talk with her."

***

When Jessup left Lupita's house, he called Autumn at the station. She answered after the third ring.

"Hey, kiddo, do me a favor?"

"Sheriff?"

"Run Adeline Smith. Get me everything you can on her."

"Who is she?"

"The daughter of Derwood Smith, probably forty or so. I'm not sure what's going on with this family, but let's do a little homework."

Chapter 33

The office of the Criminal Task Force was on the third floor of the Monroe Court Building, which stood next door to the Public Safety Building. When the police department outgrew its space in the PSB, it started expanding into neighboring facilities. Morgan liked the digs in the MCB but would have preferred to be far away from the watchful eyes of the brass.

The CTF was in a large bullpen, and even the sergeant of the task force didn't rate an office of his own.

Sergeant Ken Bynum was propped back in his chair, feet up on his desk, with a phone cradled between his ear and shoulder. When Morgan walked into the office, Bynum pointed his finger and thumb at him. Morgan raised his hands in mock surrender and walked toward his desk. Bynum continued to talk into the phone while dropping his thumb. Morgan moaned, "Uh!" then clutched his heart and did a pirouette before staggering into a nearby desk.

"A bit dramatic," Nyala Senai said.

Morgan smiled at her as he lay across the empty desk. She was the newest member of the team, having rotated over from Property Crimes. Her dark skin and angular features highlighted her Ethiopian heritage. Her mother had migrated to the area when she was a little girl. They had left her home country after her father was killed in a terrorist attack. Senai was a perfect fit for the team: attractive, tenacious, and hungry to prove herself.

"You're not even going to come save me? Maybe gimme a little mouth-to-mouth?"

"I'd give a rabid dog mouth-to-mouth before I gave it to you. There'd be less chance of catching something."

Bynum hung up his phone. "Damn, Senai. Go easy on the old guy."

"Old guy?" Morgan said, still laying across the desk.

Even though Bynum was ten years younger than Morgan, he was the assigned Sergeant and officially led the team. Morgan had refused to ever take the sergeant's test. He was one of the most senior detectives in the department, which gave him his choice of assignments. He chose CTF and fought every year to remain on the team.

"Give Morgan an inch," Senai said, "and he'll take a mile."

Morgan stood from the desk and gave her a practiced leer. "Nyala, baby, I'll give you more than an inch."

"That's what I'm afraid of," she said. "Keep your angry inch to yourself."

Both men laughed.

Morgan walked over to his desk and dropped into his chair. A red light blinked on his phone, indicating a new message. He picked up the receiver, pressed the Voice Mail button, and listened.

"Detective, this is Al Kimpson. Please call when you have a chance." Kimpson then recited his phone number.

Morgan quickly hung up, then dialed Kimpson's number. He answered after several rings.

"Hello?" the old man said.

"Al, this is Detective Morgan."

"You in your office?

"Yeah." He gave Kimpson the address.

"Gimme fifteen," he said and hung up.

***

Roughly fifteen minutes later, Al Kimpson walked into the Criminal Task Force office. He stopped just inside the front door. His eyes swept past Senai and Bynum before settling on Morgan. He walked over to his desk and eased himself onto the folding chair in front of it. He tossed the two pieces of Morgan's ripped-apart business card onto the desk.

"I'm glad you found the place," Morgan said.

"I appreciate your bit of drama back at mine. Got the boys back to work."

"I understand."

Kimpson reached into his pocket and pulled out a folded piece of paper. He also tossed this onto Morgan's desk.

The detective opened it and saw *Casey Braemar* handwritten on it. There was also an address.

"Thank you," Morgan said.

"He's not one of my boys," Kimpson said. "He started a few months ago. Comes in and works out mostly by himself, uses the heavy bags, never the speed bags. He's a martial arts type. Really intense. Likes to mix it up with a couple of my guys who will spend the time with him."

"If he's not training for a fight, why let him in?"

"I ain't doin' what I do for charity, Detective. Besides, I get a lot of rich white folks who like to come down and pretend they could have been fighters. Rocky wannabes. When they work out near the fighters, it gets their blood up, if you know what I mean."

Morgan nodded.

"The only ones I gotta watch out for are the upper-class broads." Kimpson's eyes flicked over to Senai. "Sorry, miss, I mean the ladies. I ain't used to being in polite company. Those ladies, they like being around the warrior lifestyle, the blood and sweat, but they're just treating it like a singles bar while their husbands are away. I gotta politely shoo them on. Sometimes, not so politely, if they don't heed my advice."

"How often does Braemar work out?"

"Hit and miss. Doesn't keep to a set schedule as far as I can tell. What should I do if he shows up? Call you?"

"I'd appreciate that."

"You really think he was involved in a homicide?"

Morgan shrugged. "I don't know if he was involved, but he's connected somehow. How that is, I don't know."

"I don't want someone suspected of something like that in my school."

"You can ask him to leave, but call me if you see him, okay?"

Kimpson stood slowly and limped toward the door.

Morgan immediately turned to his computer and typed in Casey Braemar's name. When he ran him through the system, the only thing he came back with were driving and parking infractions. The address on file with the Department of Licensing was different from the one that Kimpson had given him.

When Kimpson was gone, Sergeant Bynum asked Morgan, "What are you working on, Hoss?"

He leaned back in his chair and turned his attention to the sergeant. "I'm looking for the guy who killed Rado."

"Rado Jones?" Bynum glanced to Senai, then back to Morgan. "I thought that was Delaney and Burkett's case."

"It is."

"You going to notify them that you're poking around?"

"The Glory Hounds?" Morgan said, snapping his chair upright. "Why would I do that?"

"Didn't your mother teach you about playing nice in the sandbox?"

Morgan squinted at Bynum.

"Why did I ask?" the sergeant grumbled. "Get someone to watch your back then. I don't need you to go out, kick a hornet's nest, and have it blowback on me."

Morgan stood and snatched his jacket from the back of his chair. "Grab your coat, Nyala."

She pushed her chair back as she stood. "Are we not making friends today, Morgan?"

"We're CTF. We're all the friends we need."

***

The little blue house stood at the dead-end of West Fourteenth Avenue and backed up against Polly Judd Park. They stopped a block away and walked over.

Morgan never considered calling dispatch to let them know where he and Senai were. The omission violated policy, and it violated officer safety norms, but he didn't care. It was the attitude of CTF—take care of business. If they needed help, they'd call for it. Until then, policy was a concept designed to keep them under the department's thumb, and none of the CTF team members liked the idea of that. Even though Senai was new to the team, she was catching on quickly and didn't point out that he should have notified radio.

"No cars in the driveway," Senai said as they approached.

"You see a garage?" Morgan asked.

"No."

They continued walking, both scanning the neighboring houses. The mid-spring sun was directly overhead as they approached. The neighborhood was quiet, most of its inhabitants, hopefully at work due to the time of day. A small dog barked from inside a house nearby.

"Take the front," Morgan said as he hurried to the back, drawing his gun as he went. The yard was yellow and mushy, a victim of the wet spring. As he approached the backdoor, he heard Senai banging at the front.

He listened for movement but didn't hear any. When Senai's knocking stopped, he continued listening. There was still no movement.

The detective glanced toward the neighboring houses to ensure no one could see him. He looked over his shoulder and could see the park from the rear of the house, but no one was there now.

He turned back to the door and tried the knob. It wouldn't turn. It was an older Kwikset lock.

Lucky, he thought.

Morgan holstered his gun, then pulled out a small leather bag from inside his jacket. He dropped to a knee and unzipped it. After removing a metal ball rake and a tension strip, he set the bag down. He inserted the strip and applied some pressure before inserting the ball rake into the lock to manipulate the pins inside carefully.

Morgan had learned how to pick locks from an actual burglar after he busted the thief for possession of stolen automatic weapons. The burglar wasn't the intended target of the investigation, only a peripheral player who was coerced into a crime of which he didn't know the full extent. Morgan realized this and offered to toss him back into the wild in exchange for lessons. The burglar jumped at the opportunity, not realizing he was giving the detective a type of skill most cops would never have nor dream of using.

When the lock eventually released, Morgan quietly turned the knob and pushed the door open. He put the tools back in his pocket.

"Morgan," Senai whispered as she approached from the side of the house.

He stood and drew his weapon. He looked around the corner and caught her eye. "The back door was open," he said.

"Does it look forced?"

"No," Morgan said. "It was just open."

Senai glanced around. "Is our guy still around?"

"He didn't answer your knocks."

"Should we do a health and welfare check?"

"Yes," he said and entered the house without waiting for Senai. "Spokane Police," he yelled.

It was a two-bedroom house with a single bathroom. There were no decorations on the walls in the living room. Along one wall, a flat-screen television sat precariously on the edge of the box it came in. An antenna hung on the wall by a nail and was connected to the back of the TV. A single folding chair sat in front of it.

The first bedroom had a neatly made bed and not much else. Again, no pictures were on the walls. A basket of folded clothes sat near the foot of the bed. Another basket with presumably dirty clothes was in the far corner.

As he moved about, Morgan continued to say, "Spokane Police."

In the next room, several cardboard boxes had their tops folded closed. Nothing else was in the room.

When the house was clear, Morgan said, "Secure the back door."

"Why?" Senai said.

"Let's take a minute to see who we're dealing with."

Senai watched him with suspicious eyes.

"I'll take a quick look around, and then we'll go."

She disapprovingly shook her head and slowly moved toward the back of the house.

Morgan returned to the front bedroom, where the cardboard boxes were. He opened the top one. Inside were paperback novels, mostly science fiction titles from authors like Bradbury, Asimov, Dick, and Clark. Morgan refolded the top and set it aside.

He opened the next box and discovered it was full of papers. He quickly thumbed through them, stopping when he found some that read *U.S. Air Force.*

"Huh," he muttered.

"You say something?" Senai called from the other room.

"Keep watch," Morgan said.

He pulled several documents from the box and photographed them with his phone. Then he placed them back in the stack as they were and reclosed the top. Then he put the box of paperbacks back on top.

He hurried to the rear of the house.

"Let's go," he said to Senai.

As he left the house, he reset the lock before pulling the door closed.

***

"He's trained," Morgan said.

"I heard that old man say something about that. Martial arts or boxing, right?"

Morgan signaled a turn and spun the steering wheel almost simultaneously. A car behind him honked.

"He was trained by the Air Force."

"He's a pilot?" Senai asked. "What kind of training do they get? The same cake-eater stuff they do for jarheads?"

Morgan grimaced. "You're playing with fire."

Senai laughed.

He knew she was aware of his experience in the Corps. It was the only thing he loved more than being a cop. Her grin showed the glee she took in tweaking the older detective.

Morgan pulled out his phone and looked at its screen while he drove. He could have easily told her, but he wanted her to see what he saw. When he found the picture, he handed her his phone.

"Check that out."

"What am I looking at?" she asked as she took the phone.

"That's his graduation certificate from Pararescue."

"Pararescue?" Senai repeated.

"Those are the guys specifically trained to jump into hostile territory and get downed pilots and airmen out. You know FBI's Hostage Rescue? That's these guys, but they do it in from the air."

"This isn't SEALs, right? He's not a trained killer."

"In the military, everyone is trained to kill, Nyala," Morgan said, "but no, they're not like commandos, if that's what you're asking."

"What does this mean for us?"

"I don't know." Morgan pointed at the phone. "Scroll to the next picture."

She did so and squinted as she read. "A graduation certificate from SERE school. That's here in Spokane, right? At Fairchild?"

Just west of Spokane, Fairchild Air Force Base was the home for the Survival, Evasion, Resistance, and Escape school.

Morgan turned left on Monroe Street and pressed the accelerator. "Yeah."

"Isn't that where they teach them to survive torture?"

"Exactly," Morgan said.

"And if you can survive it…"

"Then you can dish it out," Morgan finished.

"You think this guy did Rado?"

"I have no idea, but he just got a helluva lot more interesting."

Chapter 34

The first thing Quinn Delaney and Marci Burkett had done that morning was a search for Crystal Braemar, Ezra Baumbach's assistant.

Searches through the National Crime Information Center (NCIC) and Washington State Department of Licensing (DOL) resulted in virtually nothing. Crystal Braemar was twenty-nine years old, had a lengthy history of unpaid parking tickets, and disputed speeding tickets, but no criminal arrests. She may have had a poor history of sharing the road, but she wasn't a menace to society.

A Google search of her name also came up with nothing. They were also unable to locate any social media accounts tied to her. It was the lack of social media accounts that was surprising. A person in her twenties was likely to have at least one account. Therefore, it was likely she had purposely deleted her digital footprint.

Department of Licensing listed her last known address as an apartment complex in the Spokane Valley, a neighboring city to Spokane.

When the detectives drove into the complex, they passed the sign announcing its name—The Whimsical Pig.

"I've never understood that name," Marci said.

"You would think their marketing department could have come up with something, anything, better than that. Even the Whimsical Bullfrog sounds better."

"Barely," Marci said, "but yeah."

Quinn banged on the door for Apartment H-131. Footsteps hurried to the door. A young woman who looked nothing like the receptionist in Ezra Baumbach's office answered. She was stocky with short, dark hair.

She wore a Batman T-shirt and pink pajama bottoms that were frayed near her black Adidas tennis shoes.

"What?" she said.

"Is Crystal here?" Quinn asked.

"Who?"

"Crystal Braemar. Does she live here?"

"You got the wrong guy, Jack," the woman said and started to close the door.

Quinn put his hand on the door to stop it from closing.

"Hey!" the woman exclaimed.

"How long have you lived here?"

"Why?"

Both Quinn and Marci opened their jackets to reveal their badges and guns.

"Oh!" the woman exclaimed, her hand jumping from the door handle like it was hot. "Why didn't you say so?"

"How long have you lived here?" Marci asked.

"About three months."

"And you don't know Crystal Braemar?"

The woman shrugged. "Never heard of the bitch."

Before leaving the complex, the detectives stopped at the management office. They introduced themselves to Shirley Haidt, a silver-haired woman suffering from a cold. A sore-throat lozenge clicked against her teeth as she moved it around her mouth.

"Shirley, did Crystal Braemar leave a forwarding address?" Quinn asked.

"Mmm, don't think so," she said and clicked the lozenge against her teeth again. She bent into a cabinet to pull out a manila file. She laid it on her desk, flipped it open, and ran her finger down the paper. The lozenge continued to click inside her mouth while she worked. Her head bobbed in rhythm to the clacking. "Like I thought, no forwarding address."

Marci glanced at her partner and shrugged.

"Is she in trouble or something?"

"We don't know yet," Quinn said. "We'd just like to talk with her."

Shirley flipped the file closed. "She always seemed like a nice girl." The lozenge continued to click in her mouth as the detectives left the office.

***

"Talk with Derwood Smith again," Quinn said.

He was seated in the department's conference room with Marci. Both were leaned in toward the speakerphone in the middle of the large table.

"Why?" Tom Jessup's voice came through the phone. "What's going on?"

"We spoke with Ezra Baumbach," Quinn said.

"And?"

"We now have a motive for murder," Marci added.

"I'm listening."

Quinn laid it out then, explaining what they learned about Joseph Smith, the establishment of the blind trust with Ezra, and the process for the transfer of ownership interest upon the death of one of the Smith brothers.

"If I understand this right," Jessup said, "everything in the trust now belongs to Derwood. Is that right?"

"That's correct," Quinn said.

"Do you think Derwood could have masterminded the murder of his brothers?" Marci asked.

"I don't know, maybe," Jessup said, "but why would he call me after reading about his brother's death in the paper? He didn't have to do that."

"Maybe he did it to establish an alibi," Marci suggested. "Or divert suspicion."

"Yeah, okay," Jessup said, "but we were unaware of the connections until he called. If he hadn't told me, I wouldn't have gone up to Spokane, and maybe we would never have linked them together."

"And they would have gotten away with it," Quinn said, looking at Marci.

"Who is they?" Jessup asked.

"There has to be a they, right?" Quinn returned his attention to the phone. "You said he was bedridden, so he couldn't pull this off on his own."

"I don't know if he's fully bedridden. I've just seen him in bed, attached to some oxygen. I'm assuming he's bedridden."

"Well, regardless, whether he was healthy or not, he would need accomplices, right? Who would help him?"

"I would start by looking at family," Jessup said.

"Us too," Quinn said.

Marci nodded in agreement, then as almost an afterthought, leaned toward the phone and said, "Yeah, uh-huh."

"Have you interviewed the son yet?" Jessup asked.

"Not yet. We're going there next. What about you? You met the daughter. Did she seem capable of doing something like this?"

"Not really, but I wasn't looking at her like that. I was planning to talk with her again, but this just made it more important."

Quinn asked, "So you'll talk with Derwood, too?"

"Yeah. I'll touch base with the daughter first. Then I'll circle back to dad. I'll call you with an update."

"Sounds good. We'll talk with the son, then wait to hear from you."

Quinn pressed the red button on the phone, ending the call.

***

"Heath Smith?" Quinn said.

"Yeah?"

His eyes were half-closed, like he had just woken from a nap. He wore a Cannondale logoed T-shirt, ripped blue jeans, and rubber Croc sandals. Underneath a Yeti baseball hat, thick salt-and-pepper hair feathered out. He stood about six feet tall and was lean. He appeared to be a once physically fit man who'd recently lost weight, most of it muscle.

"I'm Detective Delaney with the Spokane Police Department. This is my partner, Detective Burkett."

Heath's eyes slowly shifted between the two detectives.

"Can we come in and talk for a few minutes?"

For several seconds, he just stood there, blinking and breathing.

"Mr. Smith?" Quinn said.

"Yeah?"

"Did we wake you?"

"No."

"Can we come in and talk?"

He opened the front door wide, then stepped out of the way, allowing the detectives to enter. Once inside, Heath closed the door and led them deeper into the house. On the back of his left arm was a thick scar. Heath's walk was unsure, and he ran his hand along the wall to steady himself.

The house was well kept. Everything appeared to be in its place. On the walls were framed mountain bike posters and rock concert flyers. It presented a child-like atmosphere yet in a tidy world.

Even though it was late afternoon, it was dark inside. The living room curtains were drawn, and several ferns hung in the corners.

"Personal Jesus" by Depeche Mode softly played through the large speakers near the over-sized television.

"May we sit?" Quinn asked.

Heath motioned toward the furniture as he continued an unsteady shuffle around the coffee table.

Marci sat on the chair nearest the entrance to the room. Quinn took the recliner. Heath shuffled slowly over to the couch and sat, moving a controller for a video game system out of the way. He settled into position, his head on the back of the sofa.

"Mr. Smith, do you know why we're here?" Quinn asked.

"Yeah."

"And why is that?"

Heath rolled his head so he could look between the two detectives. Then he stopped and stared at Quinn.

Several seconds passed before Quinn asked again, "Why are we here, Mr. Smith?"

Finally, Heath shrugged.

Quinn's brow furrowed. "Are you high, Mr. Smith?"

"No," he said, his face reddening.

Quinn looked at Marci, who shrugged.

He asked, "When's the last time you talked with your father, Mr. Smith?"

"Been a while. We don't talk so much."

"I'm sorry," Quinn said.

Heath struggled to sit upright and began looking around as if he was searching for something. His eyes scanned the coffee table. Then he moved several throw pillows to look behind them.

Quinn leaned forward, on alert, paying attention to what Heath was doing. "What's wrong, Mr. Smith?"

"If you're going to give me bad news, I should take a pill."

"A pill?"

Heath looked up. "I get anxieties."

Quinn relaxed then. "We're not here to make you anxious, Mr. Smith. We only need to ask a few questions about you and your father."

Heath stopped and stared at Quinn. "My father?"

"Your father's health isn't very good right now."

"Oh," Heath said and dropped back into the couch, the look of worry slowly dissipating from his face.

"You look relieved."

"He's been that way a while. He's not going to die."

Quinn said, "You don't get along with your father?"

"Not really."

"Why not?"

"He thinks I wasted my life."

Marci leaned forward and asked, "You got worried we were going to tell you something bad. What did you think that was?"

"Something about my family."

Quinn looked around. "Are you married?"

Heath shook his head. "Never been."

Marci added, "But you're worried about your family?"

"I had a girlfriend. We were together a long time. She left." Heath's eyes drifted down as he drowned in sadness. When he looked up, he realized he was being watched. "It's okay. I don't blame her."

"What family were you were worried about then?" Marci asked.

"My kids."

"Kids?" Marci said. "You were never married, but you have kids?"

Heath nodded. "Uh-huh. Yeah."

"Do they live with you?"

"They're grown. They have their own lives. They don't talk to me much."

"Why is that?" Marci asked.

"That's the way family is. My family, at least."

"You don't talk with your father?" Marci asked.

"How it goes."

"That's kind of sad," Marci said.

Heath's shrug was halfhearted.

"Where do you work?" Quinn asked.

"I don't," Heath said.

Quinn looked at him inquisitively.

"I'm disabled," he said.

"Oh," the detective said.

"I've got—" he tapped the side of his head "—an injury."

"A brain injury? How did it happen?"

"I don't think you're supposed to ask. It's private. You're supposed to respect that."

"That's not how that works," Marci said, softly.

Heath's eyes slanted, and he studied the female detective for a second. Then he relaxed and said, "Since my accident, I have to be careful. People can bully me. That's what my counselor says. Don't let people bully you, Heath. People aren't nice."

"We're not bullying you, Mr. Smith," Quinn said. "We only want to ask some questions."

"What kind of accident did you have?" Marci asked.

"A bicycle accident."

Marci turned to look at the mountain bike pictures on the wall. "On a bike like that?"

Heath's face brightened when he looked at the bicycles. "That's how this happened, too," Heath said, pointing to the scar on the back of his arm. "I also broke some bones."

"I bet it hurt."

"Yeah," Heath said. "It hurt a lot."

"Were you wearing a helmet?"

"I was supposed to." The look of remorse returned to Heath's face. "My girlfriend, she got mad at me for not wearing my helmet. She stayed mad for a long time."

"Is that why she left?" Marci asked.

"She said it wasn't, but I know it was." He closed his eyes and scrunched his face. When he opened his eyes, he said, "My brain doesn't work as good as it did before, but I'm not stupid."

Marci scooted to the edge of her seat and leaned forward. "Since your accident, do you still ride?"

"I wish. I'm not very stable. My walk, I mean. I'd be liable to get in another wreck." He clucked his tongue as he slowly mimed knocking on the side of his head.

"Do you run instead?" Marci asked.

"Nuh-uh. Same problem. I go to physical therapy a couple of times a week."

"How long ago did this accident happen?"

Heath blinked several times as he thought. Finally, he said, "Six years."

"Six years," Marci repeated. "Wow."

Quinn jumped back into the conversation. "How often are you in contact with your uncles?"

Heath looked at him and blinked. "Uncles?" he finally said. "Never."

"You've never been in contact with your uncles?"

"Why would I be? They weren't around when I grew up."

"Your whole life," Quinn said, "you've never met your uncles?"

"I don't think so. Maybe when I was a baby," he said, struggling to recall memories. "I don't remember them, though. They never came around, and we never visited them."

"Never even a birthday card or Christmas card from any of them?" Quinn asked.

Heath shook his head.

"How do you afford all this?"

Heath tapped the side of his head. "Disability payments. I had a job before. A good one. I had saved my money and had some insurance."

"Does your father help?" Quinn asked.

"What do you mean?"

"Does he send you money?"

"Why would he do that?"

Quinn smiled. "Because he's your father. He loves you."

Heath frowned. "He doesn't love me. We're not that kind of family."

"Were you abused?"

"No," Heath said, his face beginning to redden.

"I'm sorry," Quinn said. "I didn't mean to offend you."

"We don't show affection. We don't help each other."

Marci's eyes had surveyed the house while Quinn and Heath spoke. When she reentered the conversation, she asked, "Do you clean your house, Mr. Smith?"

He turned his gaze to Marci. "My daughter does it for me. I do a pretty good job, but she does it better. She comes once a week. It's a big help."

"That's sweet of her. What's her name?"

"Crystal."

"Crystal?" Marci repeated, glancing at Quinn, who met her eyes. "Really?"

"Yeah." Heath's face scrunched in suspicion. "Why?"

"We met a Crystal the other day. It's not a very common name, so it sticks out, you know? Does she have the same last name as you?"

"She has her mother's."

Marci leaned in as she asked, "And what's that?"

Heath's suspicion remained, but he said, "Braemar."

"Braemar," Marci repeated. "Crystal Braemar. What does she do?"

"She's a bookkeeper. Why?"

"A bookkeeper, huh? Not a receptionist? The Crystal I met was a receptionist."

"No," Heath said. "I'm sure she said, bookkeeper."

"Do you know where?"

Heath's eyes moved from Marci to Quinn then back to the female detective. "I'm sure she told me, but I don't remember. Why do you want to know?"

"Do you have Crystal's phone number and address?"

"Why?" he asked. His face pinched as he struggled with his thoughts. "Why do you want to talk with Crystal?" he finally asked.

Quinn jumped in, pulling Heath's attention away from Marci. "We like you. We just want to make sure Crystal is doing her best to take care of you."

His face continued to contort as he thought. "No. Uh-uh. That doesn't sound right. Crystal is a good person. She takes care of me."

"I'm sure she does," Quinn said. "We'd just like to talk with her."

"This feels like bullying." Heath's cheeks and ears were entirely red now.

"We're not bullying you," Marci said, her voice soft and gentle.

"You are. I know you are." He unsteadily stood. "You should leave."

"We'd like to ask you a few more questions," Quinn said.

"Please leave, or I will call the cops."

Quinn stood. "We are the cops."

Heath put his hands on the sides of his head.

"Please, Heath," Marci said, "we didn't mean to upset you."

As Heath shuffled away, Quinn and Marci followed him.

"Where are you going, Heath?" Marci asked.

"What are you doing, Mr. Smith?"

Heath walked into the kitchen, his hand dragging along the wall, helping to support him. Several times, he bumped into pictures, knocking them askew. Finally, he found what he was looking for on the kitchen table. He picked up his cell phone.

"Who are you calling?" Marci asked.

"The police."

"We are the police," she reminded him.

"Yes," Heath said, slowly into this cell phone, "This is Heath Smith. There are two detectives in my house that won't leave. I've asked them to leave, but they won't go. My address?" Heath then provided the location of his house along with the personal information the dispatcher was requesting.

Quinn and Marci glanced at each other. They had checked out with radio prior to walking into the house. Even though they wanted to continue the conversation with Heath, they had no reason to detain him further, even if it was inside his own home. If they were to continue the interview, it could be viewed as hostile or even tainted if they later needed to rely on statements garnered from this moment.

The best course of action was to disengage and come back another time.

"Mr. Smith," Quinn said, "we're sorry for the inconvenience. We'll go."

As they headed for the front door, they could hear Heath tell the dispatcher, "They're leaving now."

****

Outside the residence, Quinn called dispatch to inform them they had cleared the house and that if a supervisor needed to call them, they were available. Otherwise, they would file a report on the contact when they returned to the department.

Quinn dropped into the driver's seat as Marci slammed the passenger side door.

"What did we miss?" Quinn asked.

"As far as I'm concerned, a lot. Things suddenly got interesting, but it went sideways in a hurry."

"So we confirm his daughter is, in fact, Ezra Baumbach's assistant. If so, that's not a coincidence."

"Dude. Her name is Crystal *Braemar*. How many Crystal Braemars do you think are in Spokane?"

Quinn dropped the car into gear and pulled away from the curb.

"You think he could be involved in the murder?"

"Heath? Not a chance," Marci said. "He could barely walk, let alone run. His brain doesn't function at a high rate. He's basically at three-quarters capacity right now."

"So now we talk with Crystal and figure out her involvement with this."

"Exactly."

They rode in silence for several minutes until Marci said, "He said kids, right?"

"What?"

"I'm pretty sure he said kids, like plural, but he only identified Crystal. We never followed up on that question. You think he might have another kid?"

Quinn's face purpled as he continued to drive. Finally, he hit the steering wheel with the palm of his hand.

Chapter 35

Sheriff Jessup saw her walking across campus and lifted his hand to get her attention. She noticed the movement and nodded, changing course toward where he had parked near the lower soccer field. He shoved his hands into the pockets of his jacket and leaned against the back of his truck.

Jessup had called Adeline Smith, requesting to meet. She said she had an English class but could meet him for an hour before. They agreed to meet on the campus of Washington State University.

She wore faded blue jeans, a cream sweater, and green ankle-high hiking boots. Her walk was full of confidence and joy. She nodded at other, younger students as she passed them. They nodded or waved back.

Adeline smiled as she approached. When she was close enough for him to hear her, she said, "It must be important if you'd drive all this way to see me."

"It is."

She stood directly in front of him, unafraid and unintimidated. "Is this sheriff business or personal business?"

The insinuation in her voice was undeniable, but Jessup ignored it.

"Because I was hoping you called to see me. By the look on your face, I can tell that's not the case."

"What's the deal between you and Lupita?"

"The help? You're here to ask questions about her?"

"Yes."

"Why?"

"She said you sent her away, that you don't want her taking care of your father."

The joy in her eyes was replaced by disbelief. "I didn't realize the sheriff of Whitman County did community outreach."

"I'm investigating a homicide, and this popped up. I don't know if it's related or not, so I'm asking questions."

"My concerns with my father's help are definitely not related to your investigation."

"So convince me."

Adeline removed the backpack from her shoulder and dropped it to the ground. She leaned a hip against the side of the truck and stared at Jessup. "I don't trust the woman."

"She doesn't do a good job?"

"She does fine, I guess, but I still don't trust her. She's cozying up to my father a little too much if you ask me."

"In a romantic way?"

"Something like that."

"And that bothers you?"

"You're damn right, it bothers me, Sheriff. I've been looking out for him for years, especially since his health started declining, now he hires this woman to cook and clean for him, and she thinks she can weasel her way into his will?"

"You think that's what she's doing?"

"I think so, yeah."

"Why do you believe that?"

"Because he mentioned it. He's considering putting her in because she's done a good job for him. I know I'll already have to split the inheritance with that damaged brother of mine, and he never checks in on my father. Why should I split anything with her?"

"What's wrong with your brother?"

"He had a bicycle accident. It left him with some brain damage. I don't mean to sound calloused, but he didn't care much for my father before the accident. Now, because of it, he hasn't helped one bit. He wouldn't have helped, even if he was functioning normally. I may end up having to take care of him as well."

"What about the trust?" Jessup asked.

"What trust?" Adeline said.

They stared at each other for a moment until Adeline repeated, "What trust? Has my father set one up?"

"I don't know." Jessup lied when he realized he might have relayed some private information Derwood Smith had kept secret. "I figured there must have been. Don't most rich people have them?"

Adeline shook her head. "My father isn't like that. I mean, maybe he set one up, but I would highly doubt it. He's got it in his head that my brother and I are to make our own ways in life. He's not one for handouts and help during a crisis. He's always wanted us to work our way out of our problems. I know there's a will that my brother and I are supposed to share fifty/fifty. That's why I'm worried about Lupita injecting herself into a discussion of an inheritance. He may not have helped me much when he was living, but I damn well expect to get something when he dies."

Jessup stared at her, letting her words sink in.

She rolled her eyes. "Okay, yeah, I know that sounded bad, but you understand what I mean. At least, I hope you do."

"Lupita said you're not taking care of him the way he should be taken care of. That he's not regularly being fed while you're gone and that the house isn't being cleaned."

"Are you kidding? I'm here, at school, part of the day. I rush over there before and after class. He's still getting taken care of. It's not like she's there twenty-four/seven either. No one can be. People need a life. Even you, Sheriff."

"I understand."

They studied each other for a moment as students continued to walk past them. Neither of them bothered to make eye contact with anyone else.

Finally, Jessup said, "I'll stop by and check in on your father."

"How is this even part of your concern? This seems like a whole bunch of family drama that you shouldn't be involved in."

"There are bigger things at play, and I'm making sure all my bases are covered."

Adeline picked up her backpack and slung it over her shoulder. "Well, while you're covering your bases, Sheriff, don't forget to enjoy your life."

She turned and headed back toward campus.

***

Jessup drove the twenty minutes to Palouse to meet with Derwood Smith. He proceeded up the driveway to the gate and buzzed for entrance. When there was no answer, he buzzed again and waited. After no response, Jessup backed his truck up and drove around the gate and shrubs before returning to the asphalted driveway.

When he arrived at the house, he saw Derwood Smith shuffling outside. He wore a long winter coat, a wool beanie cap, and gloves. He pulled along an insulated oxygen tank behind him. A rubber tube ran up to his nose.

Jessup parked his truck and climbed out. Derwood gave a small wave and shuffled toward him. "What brings you out, Sheriff?"

"Some follow-up questions, Woody."

"About?"

"Your father and his trust."

"Whatever you need," the older man said. "Ask away."

"Would you like to go inside where it's warm?"

Derwood waved a gloved hand. "No, sir, I would not. It's nice to be outside, even in this chill. Lupita and Addy both want me inside, but I don't want to spend my remaining hours cooped up on that bed."

"Speaking of Lupita and your daughter…"

The older man's eyes shifted to the sheriff. "What about them?"

"There seems to be a power struggle."

Derwood nodded. "I've noticed. You know, Lupita does a fantastic job, regardless of what my daughter says. Addy can't take the time to help me every day. She's busy going to school. It's sweet of her to think so, but she just can't. Unfortunately, she won't get it out of her head that Lupita is going to take me for some money. Resentment has built up that I have to be watchful about."

"So, you're not worried about Lupita?"

"Not at all. She's a wonderful gal. She cooks and cleans. She even drives my car to errands when I need to go somewhere."

Jessup looked back up the driveway. "Where is your car?"

"It's in the garage. I no longer drive. Lupita loves using it. It's much nicer than hers. If something happens to me, I plan on leaving it to her along with a little something to help her along in life. But everything else will go to Addy and her brother. I think it bothers my daughter that Lupita will get something, no matter how small."

"It does bother her."

"That's too bad. My daughter doesn't realize that sometimes we must ask for help in this life. It's nice to reward those willing to lend a hand. Addy is still young enough to think she can do it all, that nothing will ever strike her down. That's the folly of youth, believing we can go on forever, but life comes for us all sooner or later. I would have thought she would have grown out of that belief by now."

"Can you tell me more about the trust your father set up?"

"We already talked about this, Tom. Didn't we?"

"We did, but I'm trying to understand why your father would set it up the way he did."

"Let's walk so I can warm up a titch." Derwood shuffled down the driveway with Jessup by his side. "My father," he said, "was a complicated man, cut off from us, maybe even cut off from himself. I don't know, and it's too late to figure out why he became the way he did. Sometimes you just have to accept a man for who he is."

A brief thought of his son entered Jessup's mind. He quickly pushed it away.

"I'm not sure of the real reason why my father set it up. He could have easily gifted each of us with an inheritance, but instead, he put it into that damn trust. The fact that we had to wait for the money was also troubling. We were young men just starting. We could have all used an immediate leg up."

Jessup thought about Adeline's words concerning Derwood before saying them to the older man. "Maybe he wanted you to make your own way, not rely on the family's wealth to determine who you would be in life."

Derwood continued to walk but briefly looked at Jessup. "Perhaps, and I had thought about that before. I treat my children the same way. A man needs to teach his children how to fly on their own, to not live forever in the family nest."

Jessup nodded, even though Derwood wasn't paying attention to him now.

"You know, the upsetting part was he made it so we couldn't see what was in the trust or how it was being run. Why would he do that? That's disconcerting, don't you think?"

"Could he have set it up that way so you and your brothers wouldn't fight over the money?"

"I considered that, and maybe that truly is why he did it. But why not come out and say it then? He could have told us, 'I don't want squabbling between my boys, so I created a trust to handle the Smith legacy.' Instead, everything was handed down to us in sort of secrecy. It sullied it."

"How so?"

"He didn't love us enough to trust us with the truth. Or he did it to for some weird control beyond the grave."

"But he built something to leave you. Many families never get anything like that."

"I guess," the old man said.

"Have you ever learned what was inside the trust?"

Derwood stopped and looked at Jessup with a kindly smile. "I tried, Tom, I really did. Shortly after we found out there was property in there, I hired an investment attorney to advise me on the subject. He called up Ezra Baumbach. Have you talked with him yet? No? Well, he's a very smart man, and my attorney said to save my money, that I was bound to lose. I heeded his advice. What did my idiot brother Clay do after I shared that information? He still sued Baumbach and the trust. I told him I didn't want any part of it. I wasn't willing to throw any money away on something like that. Leland didn't have any money at the time, so he couldn't jump in, but Clayton promised him he would spot him if he joined the fight. So one more idiot brother joined in the folly.

Renard was doing his own thing like he always did and didn't want to go against our father's wishes. Even though he was dead, Renard was still afraid of the old man.

"The four of us weren't talking, and life had grown us apart. Maybe it was the way we were raised. Who knows? Anyway, Clay and Leland started communicating, but it was strictly mercenary. The trust had to spend money to defend itself, which made me furious since they were technically spending part of my inheritance. Renard, the wimp, didn't want to take sides, and I told the lot of them that I didn't want anything to do with them ever again. As far as I was concerned, they were all dead to me.

"Our father might have tried to protect us with the trust, but it was the final nail in the coffin for me. I no longer needed my brothers."

Derwood stopped walking and struggled for air. When his breathing returned to normal, he said, "This is probably far enough, Tom. I should head back now."

The older man turned around and shuffled toward the house, Jessup quietly by his side.

"So the lawsuit?" the sheriff prompted.

"They lost, of course. They didn't learn anything and wasted time and money. Clay eventually demanded reimbursement from Leland for his portion of the lawsuit."

"I thought you said he would cover Leland's end."

Derwood chuckled. "He did when he thought they would win. When they didn't, Clay wanted his money back. That tore what bit of relationship those two had left. And that was it. That's the true family legacy laid bare."

"Were you surprised when the stipends began showing up?"

The older man nodded. "Pleasantly, yes. We knew the plan was to get something someday. We were told that much. The trust was to pay off the associated mortgages, build a reserve, and then start sending monthly stipends. It was rather exciting when the payments arrived."

"You didn't hear from your brothers then?"

"No," he said. "It had been so many years that I had no inclination to call them. Maybe the others spoke to one another, but I didn't have the desire to communicate with them. Since they're gone, I probably should have thought differently, but that's how I looked at the situation then."

"Do you know what happens now?"

Derwood glanced at Jessup. "What do you mean?"

"Now that your brothers have passed, do you know what happens to their portion of the stipend?"

The older man shrugged as he continued walking. "I would imagine it would go to their family or wherever their wills dictate." He stopped. "Did some of them have family? It's embarrassing to ask that, to not know my own brothers' lives. You told me about Renard's son, which is a damn shame."

"I don't know about Clayton and Leland. I'm sorry."

A sadness washed over Derwood's face, and he became unsteady. Jessup reached out and grabbed him by the arm. It took a moment for the older man to steady himself. When he did, he straightened and looked directly at the sheriff.

"Wasted years," Derwood softly said. "I should have been there for Renard. His wife left him after his boy's death, isn't that correct?"

"From what I understand."

"Sad," Derwood said. He shook his head and began walking again toward the house. "I should have been there for them all."

They walked in silence for a bit, until Jessup said, "The trust doesn't work that way."

"What do you mean?"

"The way it was written, when a son dies, his portion of the stipend was to be shared among the remaining brothers."

Derwood continued for a few more steps, then stopped. "Excuse me?"

"When a son dies—"

He waved a hand to stop Jessup. "I heard that, but that's a horrible concept. Why do that?"

Jessup studied Derwood.

"That's a terrible thing," the older man said. "If his family had grown accustomed to that money, then to have it stopped immediately upon the death of their husband, their father... That makes no sense. Why would my father have written it that way?"

"Maybe he didn't want it to go to a second generation," Jessup said. "Maybe he wanted the remaining brothers to figure out they needed to come together to take care of the missing son's family."

Derwood's face was twisted with grief. "No. It was vindictive."

"How so?"

"He made us wait for it. Fine. I lived my life, built a fortune without his help. When it finally came, it was a bonus. I don't know about my brothers, but I didn't need it. Maybe they did. Maybe the money would have changed their lives. But my father put that provision in there so their families would lose it upon their deaths, and it would go to the remaining brothers. That's mean. It's wrong. There was no love in his decision."

"I don't know if you realize this, Woody, but you're the last Smith brother."

Derwood stared at Jessup.

"The trust is now yours. You've inherited it all."

His face reddened, and his lips twisted in anger. No, they were curled in disgust. "Well, I don't want it."

He turned and shuffled off, pulling the oxygen tank behind him.

Chapter 36

Morgan was parked in his Dodge Charger on Ash Street at the corner of Fourteenth Avenue, waiting and watching. Casey Braemar's house was at the dead-end of Fourteenth. There was only one way in, and Morgan had made it his mission to be there when Braemar returned home.

Why would an expert on escape and evasion choose to live in a house on a dead-end street?

To Morgan, it seemed like an easy trap. Or was he missing something? Was there a way for Braemar to escape if he was boxed in? There was a park to the north he could run through; then, there was a cliff to the east that dropped down to the rail lines.

Someone could traverse that drop, but it would be tricky. Maybe it wouldn't be difficult for a SERE-trained pararescue operator. On the other side of the rail lines were South Inland Empire Way and a poorer part of town known as Vinegar Flats. Perhaps Braemar had a second car hidden down there.

That would make sense, Morgan thought.

If Braemar fled the house, he could run down the hill, which would be tough for someone unfamiliar with the terrain to follow, then he could cross the tracks, head to his previously hidden car, and escape.

Yeah, Morgan thought, *I bet that's exactly what he's done.*

The patrol radio chirped with activity. Morgan had been listening to the continuous traffic between dispatch and officers. A stolen vehicle had been pursued and stopped on the northside of Spokane. Three suspects had run from the car, but they had been subsequently caught. It sounded like most of the department had joined that pursuit. Now that it was over, Morgan knew what would happen. Most of the involved officers would stand around, congratulating themselves on a job well done, reliving the moment with their buddies, even though they had all been part of the same experience. Morgan smiled at familiar memories; he had done the same thing many times himself. It was a way to let off steam and build camaraderie.

The brass hated guys standing around after a call but screw them. They'd forgotten what it was like to be a line-level officer. He hadn't.

Morgan let his mind drift back to the problem at hand: the murder of Cadillac Eldorado Jones. Somehow Braemar was tied to him. Why would a trained pararescue operator work with a junkie like Rado Jones?

Drugs? It was possible Braemar began using and ran across Rado somewhere in the underworld. More than likely, though, Braemar targeted Rado solely for a fall guy. As an operator, he would be trained to watch and evade. He would be experienced at observing, and Rado wouldn't be hard to follow. Hell, Morgan had watched Rado several times himself without the snitch knowing it. It wasn't particularly difficult.

Braemar would have done something he wasn't trained for and approached a subject to get Rado to go along with him. Perhaps he could have grabbed Rado, taken him forcibly by overpowering him. Rado was thin, drug thin, made weak by years of repeated usage. It wouldn't take much to subdue him. That would make sense if he just needed someone to take the fall, but Scrimmy made it sound like Rado and Braemar had some conversations before the job took place. So maybe he wasn't grabbed. Perhaps he was coerced.

Morgan had trouble rationalizing exactly what Braemar would do. Had he been trained like Morgan, a

Marine, he imagined Braemar would attack the problem more like a hammer, swift and brutal. But Braemar was trained as a rescuer. How would someone like that deal with a problem?

Morgan closed his eyes and drummed his fingers on the steering wheel while he thought. When he opened his eyes, they drifted to the rearview mirror. An orange Chevrolet Camaro was coming up from the rear. As the Chevy approached, it slowed considerably as it passed him. When it was even with the detective's car, a white male glanced over. He wore sunglasses and a baseball hat.

"Shit," Morgan said.

The Camaro lurched forward, its engine roaring, then raced southbound on Ash Street.

Morgan dropped his car into gear and stomped on the accelerator. His vehicle jumped ahead as if it relished the opportunity to chase prey. He activated the lights hidden in the front of the car's grill, and the emergency siren wailed.

He grabbed his microphone and called, "Ida seventy-seven."

"Seventy-seven, go ahead," responded the dispatch operator.

"Seventy-seven, I'm in pursuit of a late sixties Chevy Camaro," he said and then read off the license plate. "We're southbound on Ash Street approaching Nineteenth."

"Copy, seventy-seven. Channel is restricted."

"Speeds are forty miles per hour," Morgan advised. "Streets are clear and dry."

"Copy. Seventy-seven, the plate number you gave is coming back stolen and registered to a late-model Honda Civic."

"This is an orange Chevy, sixty-eight, sixty-nine," Morgan said. "Now eastbound on Sixteenth. Speeds are fifty miles per hour."

The Camaro raced through uncontrolled intersections, barely missing a head-on collision with a minivan. Morgan sped by the surprised female driver, whose eyes were wide with shock.

"Supervisor is monitoring the call," the dispatcher announced.

Great, Morgan thought.

Per policy, a lieutenant or captain was required to step in and monitor any pursuit call. If none were available, the duty fell to a sergeant. The supervisor could easily deem the situation too dangerous for public safety and terminate the chase. Then Morgan would have a decision to make—end the pursuit or continue the pursuit off radio and put himself out on a limb legally.

"Ida seventy-seven," the dispatcher called. "Supervisor is requesting the reason for initiating the stop."

The cars raced past a young woman walking two Golden Labradors. She jumped as the Camaro passed. The dogs furiously barked as Morgan sped by.

"Driver is wanted for questioning concerning a homicide."

"Which homicide?" the dispatcher asked.

What a stupid question, Morgan thought. *Why does it matter? And what pinprick of a supervisor would think it matters?*

The Camaro's brake lights lit up for a brief second before it disappeared by making a hard right turn.

"Southbound on Cedar," Morgan announced into the microphone.

"Copy," the dispatcher said. "Advise speed and traffic."

Morgan's eyes flicked to his speedometer. "Sixty and no traffic. Roads are dry."

"Suspect in which homicide, Ida seventy-seven?"

The cars raced along Cedar Street, which had now turned into South High Drive. They were at the farthest edge of the South Hill. Off to the right was a cliff that led down to Hangman Creek, and neighborhoods were to the east.

Morgan's thumb hovered over the microphone's call button. If he identified the driver now, he knew what would happen.

"Ida seventy-seven, please advise, who is the driver?"

He pressed the button and said, "Driver is Casey Braemar."

It took less than two seconds for the dispatcher to respond, "Terminate pursuit, seventy-seven. I say again, terminate the pursuit."

Morgan immediately let up on the accelerator. As he decelerated, he pressed the call button and said, "Pursuit terminated." A couple of seconds passed, and Morgan muttered, "Pencil neck supervisors," then released the call button.

"Ida seventy-seven," the dispatcher said flatly, "you're still on the radio."

Morgan smiled. He pressed the call button and ignored all formality by saying, "My bad."

He hung up the microphone back into position.

Several clicks came over the radio then, the non-verbal approval of various patrol officers. That had to piss off the administration.

"Seventy-seven," dispatch called.

Morgan reached for the microphone, knowing what was coming now. He pressed the call button and as cheerfully as he could muster, "Seventy-seven?"

"Ida seventy-seven, Captain Ackerman requests you report to his office. Immediately."

Morgan clicked his microphone, not bothering to verbally agree to the upcoming ass-chewing.

Now it makes sense, Morgan thought. *Ackerman was the pinprick of a supervisor who thought it mattered.*

For a few minutes, Morgan continued to drive around the neighborhoods where he lost Braemar's Camaro. He knew it was a futile effort, but he still hoped to find the car abandoned and that Braemar had taken to foot.

A couple of patrol cars slowly rolled through the area, probably looking for the same thing. They didn't know what Morgan was driving now, as he often changed his rig, so neither of the officers bothered to glance in his direction. That was fine with Morgan. He didn't need to get into a bitch-about-the-brass session with some uniforms right now. He was already on the clock with the captain.

Morgan drifted slowly back toward Braemar's house, even though he knew it was a longshot that the suspect would return home. Only a complete idiot would do that, especially since that's where Morgan first spotted him. He wondered if Braemar would ever return home now.

When he passed the house on Fourteenth Avenue, there wasn't a car out front.

Morgan took a deep breath and slowly exhaled.

He knew what had to be done now, even if it was something he disliked.

It was time to play nice. Well, as nice as he could.

***

"What the hell was that about?" Captain Ackerman asked, his teeth clenched.

"I don't understand," Morgan said, even though he did. It was just that he took great pleasure in riling up Ackerman. It went back to his days on patrol when Ackerman was a newly minted sergeant. The two men never saw the world the same way once Ackerman put his foot on the ladder of leadership.

The captain closed his eyes, flexed his jaw, and smoothed his tie. His expensive suit was in sharp contrast to Morgan's jeans and leather jacket.

They were seated in Ackerman's office within the Public Safety Building. Morgan had quietly shut the door when he stepped in, right before Ackerman had told him to, "Sit the fuck down."

It was the first time Morgan had ever heard the captain swear. Oh, he'd heard Gary Ackerman the patrolman swear plenty of times, even Ackerman, the detective. Still, once he began to ascend the pecking order, Ackerman, the leader, considerably cleaned up his act.

It made Morgan happy to know he could still get to Ackerman after all these years.

When the captain opened his eyes, he inhaled deeply and said, "I want to know, *Detective*, why you didn't respond to dispatch when requested?"

"I was in pursuit."

"Not good enough."

"Seriously?"

"Seriously what, Detective?"

"When's the last time you've been in a pursuit, Gary?"

"It's Captain."

"I was in a pursuit, through a neighborhood, making sure I was keeping it as safe as possible, thereby protecting uninvolved citizens."

"Yet you heard the call to terminate."

"Yes."

"But you didn't hear the request for the reason for the pursuit?"

"I answered it as soon as I heard it."

"We called more than once."

"I missed it. What do you want? An apology?"

"Well, now you can't ignore it. Why were you pursuing," Ackerman looked down to his notes, "Casey Braemar?"

Morgan scratched his head as he thought. He was delaying, and it was a ham-handed tactic to look exactly like he was stalling.

Ackerman's face reddened.

Just as the captain opened his mouth to speak, Morgan said, "He's connected to the double murder that Delaney and Burkett are investigating."

Ackerman's mouth slowly closed. "What?"

"At least I think he is," Morgan said.

"Explain."

"You know the couple I'm talking about? Their suspected killer, Rado Jones—"

"Rado? I thought the suspect was named Cadillac."

"Rado is his nickname. And Rado isn't a killer."

"Anyone can be a killer if pushed far enough."

Morgan fought back a smirk. "Not Rado," he said, remaining stone-faced. "He's a junkie turd, but underneath he's sort of a sweet kid. Messed up for sure, but kind of sweet. You remember the type?"

"No."

"Right. Anyway, I don't see it. I feel it in here," Morgan said, tapping his chest. "The kid didn't do it. That's when I did some asking around."

"It's not your case."

"So?"

The two stared at each other for several seconds until Morgan began speaking again. "One of the things I learned was Rado was planning a heist of an elderly couple.”

Ackerman leaned forward. “How did you learn this?”

“His girlfriend told me.”

“Have you told Delaney and Burkett?”

“Not yet.”

“Why not?”

“It’s fresh info. I’m bird-dogging it now. It may be bad intel.”

“You should have told them, gotten them in the loop. They could help you.”

“I’ll bring them in as soon as I leave here.”

The captain studied Morgan. “Your intel proves Jones was at the murder scene?”

“No, that’s not what it proves. It proves someone had approached him about a heist. That’s all I know.”

“The person who approached him, was it this—” Ackerman again looked to his notes. “Casey Braemar?”

“That’s correct.”

“How’d you come across him?”

“Rado’s girlfriend described his car and where Rado was picked up. I backtracked the info to a source and got the name there.”

“And that source is reliable?”

“Seems so.”

Ackerman’s eyes flicked down to the paper on his desk. He put his finger on something, then asked, “Were you sitting off Braemar’s house, waiting for him to come home?”

“Yeah.”

“He spotted you.”

“Seems so.”

The captain tapped the desk once, then crossed his arms in self-satisfaction. “Had you brought this to Delaney and Burkett earlier, brought everyone into the loop, we could have put a couple of uniforms in the area, maybe had a net set up for this guy."

"Listen, Gary—"

"Captain."

"I didn't know if the info I got was good or bad. I deal with scumbags all day long."

"We all do," Ackerman interjected.

Morgan smiled. He knew he shouldn't loft the softball, but he did it anyway. "Captains deal with scumbags?"

Two seconds passed. Morgan knew due to the audible ticks on the clock. That's how long it took for the captain to swing at it.

"I'm dealing with one now," Ackerman said.

Morgan's smile broadened as he stood. "And here I thought you were getting civilized."

Ackerman said, "We're not finished, Jim."

He thumbed in the general direction of the detectives' office. "I need to bring Delaney and Burkett up to speed. We should get a uniform on Braemar's house. Every minute we wag our dicks at each other is another minute he's on the loose. You really need another minute to tell me something I already know?"

Ackerman stared at Morgan for a moment until he waved his hand dismissively. The detective turned and left, quietly closing the door.

***

He walked past Dallas Nash on the way to the detectives' office.

The quiet detective looked up at the last moment, distracted. When he made eye contact with Morgan, he smiled and nodded.

Morgan didn't bother matching either the smile or the nod. Instead, Morgan thought, *Screw Nash*. He was one of the good boys of the department, always getting a pat on the head for something. The guy did decent work, but he was a sellout, just like Delaney and Burkett.

Just like most of the department.

They wanted the easy way—to play nice with the administration and city hall.

That isn't the easy way, Morgan thought. *That's the road to hell.*

To the administration, line-level officers and detectives were a renewable resource. No matter how much they pretended to care, and how much whining they did about the cost of training a new officer, they always knew another batch of wide-eyed rookies was just waiting around the corner. If the brass cared, they'd stand shoulder-to-shoulder with the union against city hall, against the evil that lurked about masquerading itself as city leadership.

Morgan remembered one of his training officers, a grizzled veteran who was in his final year before retirement, telling him the majority of stress an officer would experience would come from inside the department rather than outside. That man was a damn fortune teller.

He arrived at the desks of Burkett and Delaney to find them empty.

Morgan grabbed a yellow sticky note from Burkett's desk and wrote, *Call me. Important. - Morgan*

He stuck the note on her telephone and headed back to his office. He'd done what he needed to do and now had plausible deniability if the Glory Hounds said he had tried to keep them out of the loop.

Chapter 37

The office of Ezra Baumbach was quiet.

There was no one at the front desk when they entered. No bell chimed on the door to announce an entering presence. It wasn't needed when a receptionist would usually handle greeting visitors.

"Hello?" Marci called. "Anyone here?"

Quinn walked past the reception desk and stopped at the doorway to the back office. "Damn," he said.

"What?" Marci asked as she approached his side. When she saw what he was looking at, she muttered, "Oh."

In his desk chair, Ezra Baumbach was leaned back with one hand on his chest. The other hung loosely to the side. His mouth was wide open, but his eyes were closed. His glasses lay on the floor near the hand that had fallen from the chair.

"Ezra?" Quinn said. When the older man didn't stir, Quinn moved toward him. With two fingers, he looked to find Ezra's pulse in his neck. The moment his fingers touched the older man's skin, Ezra's eyes popped open.

"Huh?"

Quinn jumped back, bumping into his partner.

Marci laughed and pushed him away from her.

"Huh?" Ezra said again, reaching up to turn his hearing aids on. "What?"

Quinn glowered at Marci with a shut-up look. She continued snickering and shaking her head.

"What's going on?" Ezra asked, blinking. He reached down, picked up his glasses from the floor, and set them on his face.

"We're here to do some follow up," Quinn said.

Ezra nodded, then rubbed his eyes underneath his glasse, with his fingertips.

"Sorry, we woke you," Marci said. "We probably should have called first, but we needed to stop by unannounced."

"Why's that?" Ezra asked, blinking the sleep from his eyes.

"We wanted to talk with your assistant."

Ezra stopped everything and focused on Marci. "Crystal? Why?"

"Did you know she's connected to the Smith family? The trust you oversee?"

Ezra looked to Quinn, then back to Marci. "That can't be right."

"She's the daughter of Heath Smith, Derwood Smith's son," Quinn said.

"But her name is Crystal *Braemar*," Ezra said, emphasizing the last name. "I specifically asked if she was related to any of my clients. She said no. I explained if she ever determined that she was related to one, she was to tell me immediately."

"She didn't, though," Quinn stated.

Ezra stared at him.

"We think she may be involved with the recent deaths of the Smith brothers," Quinn said.

"Crystal? No. She's so sweet."

The two detectives watched him as he struggled with the realization. He finally asked, "You think she had something to do with this?"

They both nodded.

Ezra shook his head and whispered, "Good Lord."

"Do you have any employment paperwork for her?" Marci asked.

The old man blinked several times, then said, "Yes, certainly."

He stood and shuffled to a tall, three-drawer cabinet. Ezra pulled out the top drawer and thumbed through several file folders. He shook his head and repeated the search process. With a heavy sigh, he pushed the drawer closed and said, "It's missing."

"Her file?" Quinn asked.

"Maybe it's at her desk," Ezra muttered. He shuffled to her desk and looked. He shook his head again and muttered, "Huh."

"She has access to her own employee file?" Marci asked.

The old man continued to look at her desk but said, "We're a two-person office. She has access to everything."

"Everything?" Marci asked.

Ezra straightened and turned to her. "Yes, she would have access to those files."

"Can you ensure the trust paperwork is still here?"

The attorney shuffled to a different cabinet, opened a drawer, and in a moment, removed a folder. He opened it and nodded. "Yes, it's all here."

"Did she make a copy for us?"

"I saw her doing it," Ezra said. He slid the folder back into the drawer and closed it. He wandered about the office, looking for a copy of the file. "At least, I thought she was copying it."

He returned to his chair and dropped into it slowly.

"Didn't you hire Crystal after your previous assistant had an accident?" Quinn asked.

"It was a tragedy."

Quinn tilted his head and asked, "She died, right?"

"Yes. Very unfortunate."

"What was her name again?"

"Carol Harden."

"And what happened to Carol?" Quinn asked.

"She and her husband fell while hiking. No one was there to help them. Just sad."

"Wait," Quinn said. "Both she and her husband died?"

"Oh, yes. They were hiking Tubbs Hill. Do you know where that's at? In Coeur d'Alene. It's not supposed to be a very hard hike. They did it quite frequently. It was kind of sweet. But he had a bad hip, so a longer, tougher hike they weren't going to do. Anyway, I guess they slipped."

"That's definitely not a treacherous hike," Marci said.

"That's what I thought," Ezra said. "We've all probably done it at some time in our lives. I used to do it when I was younger. My wife doesn't particularly like to go on those kinds of walks now. The detectives came around, asking if Carol and her husband were having marital difficulties. I told them not that I knew of. Carol always seemed happy. They'd been married a lot of years."

Quinn and Marci glanced at each other.

"So, it was ruled an accident?" Quinn asked.

"As far as I know. One day she was here, and next, she was gone." A sadness settled on Ezra's face.

Quinn said, "Carol must have meant a lot to you."

"She did. She was a great help. It's interesting how you rely on certain people. She was a rock. We'd just had a burglary that really shook me up, but Carol handled it very stoically."

"A burglary?" Quinn asked.

"Somebody, probably kids, broke in, looked around. Didn't find anything of value to steal. They made a mess, then left. I'm not embarrassed to say it shook me up something fierce, but Carol cleaned up the mess and got us back to work in a jiffy. She was a wonderful woman."

"Did you notify the police?" Quinn asked.

"Definitely. I don't think it did any good, though. We never heard from them again." Ezra shrugged and raised his eyebrows at the same time.

"How did you come by Crystal?" Marci asked.

The attorney turned his attention to her. "Carol had been with me a long time, almost thirty years if you can believe that. Which meant I hadn't put out an advertisement for a receptionist in a long time. The last one I put out was the one that got her. I guess I did well with that one, but it's not like I've had a lot of practice. So I just called the newspaper and talked with one of their people. They helped me craft an advertisement. It ran on Sunday. Crystal was the first person to show up on Monday morning. Actually, I think she was the only person to show up. She had a professional resume. References.

"When I told her I would think about it, she said, 'There's nothing to think about. You need me, and I need you. Let's get started.' She sort of reminded me of how Carol did business, so I just accepted, and we got to work."

"How did Carol do business?" Marci asked.

Ezra smiled. "Sort of bossy. She was good that way. Always kept me organized and on task. That's how I hoped Crystal would be."

"Has she been a good worker?"

"No one could replace Carol, but yes, she's been fine, I guess."

"How long ago did all of this happen?" Marci asked.

"About a year ago, I guess."

"Twelve months?" Quinn said.

"Give or take. Yeah, that sounds about right. Do you think she could be involved in what happened to Carol?"

Both Quinn and Marci shrugged.

The older man lowered his head. "What have I done?"

"Ezra," Quinn said, leaning forward in his chair, "if it's proven that one of the brothers was involved in the murder of another brother, would that impact the transfer of the trust shares?"

When he looked up, he said, "I don't believe so. There's nothing written into the trust agreement preventing transfer based upon criminal action. Besides, from what we've discussed and what I remember, I don't believe there are any descendants to bring some sort of lawful action to challenge it. It's highly unlikely there would be grounds to break into the language of the trust, but without someone to bring suit, it's not going to happen. Therefore, it stands, and the remaining assets would continue to flow down to the surviving brothers."

"Or brother, in this case," Quinn said.

"Yes," Ezra said. "As you said, it all lands to Derwood Smith now."

"What's the process?" Marci asked. "How will you handle this?"

"Well, the trust is a vehicle unto itself. I won't have to go through the probate process surrounding the death of an unwilled individual. Instead, I will have to verify the death of the individual and follow the process laid out in the original trust documentation. It will take a little time, but the path has been set. The other brothers have expired, regardless of how or why, and Derwood is now the sole beneficiary of the Joseph Smith estate."

"What happens if Derwood dies?" Quinn asked.

"Well," Ezra said, "the trust's assets belong to Derwood, and his will would dictate the disbursement of such if such a document existed."

Quinn and Marci looked at each other. "Derwood's heirs would now stand to gain from his death."

"Isn't that how it is with most children?" Ezra said.

Chapter 38

The little town of Hooper, Washington, sits on the western edge of Whitman County. Tom Jessup drove out there at the request of one of its residents, Edward Ferman. They met in the parking lot of the post office, near the corner of Haxton and McGregor Roads. The Palouse River flowed lazily nearby.

"Thanks for drivin' out to meet, Tom. Means a lot for the sheriff to come through town. Gives folks a sense a well-bein' an' security."

Jessup nodded.

Ferman's age was hard to gauge, perhaps as young as the early seventies and maybe even as old as the late eighties. He'd grown up in Hooper and inherited the family farm. He had spoken with Jessup a few times over the years, even when he was a deputy. He was always pleasant and eager to share a story.

"So how you been, Tom?"

Jessup's eyes slanted.

"I ain't meanin' to pry, nothin' like that. It's jus' been some time since we talked, and I was wonderin' about ya."

Jessup studied the older man but held his tongue.

"You see, Rodney was out here."

Jessup sighed. "Rodney?"

"Deputy Howard."

"Yes, I know Deputy Howard."

"Well, he said, maybe… well, that maybe you should meet my daughter."

Jessup dropped his head.

"She's really something, Tom. Prettiest girl you've ever seen and smart as a computer."

Jessup lifted his eyes to Ferman. "Listen, Eddie."

"Don't go sayin' no, Tom. Rodney told me you been lonely. So has Connie. She's a great girl, works in the post office here, and she deserves someone nice, a good person. I figured I was gonna hafta get involved and help her find a good man. She keeps telling me to stay out of it, probably the same way you are now, but what do I care? I'm an old coot, and I don't listen to what people say. Rodney seemed to think it was a good idea."

Jessup smiled. "I appreciate it—"

His cell phone rang. It was a 509 area code, and the number looked vaguely familiar.

Had this been another meeting, he might have thought about letting it go to message. Instead, he said, "Hold on a second, Eddie," and answered the call.

"Jessup," he announced into the phone.

"Sheriff, it's Lupita." She was whispering and out of breath.

"Are you okay?"

"People are in the house."

"Your house?"

"Mr. Smith's house. They do not belong. I think they are here to do bad things."

"Can you get Derwood out?"

"No. He is in his room. I am outside. I just arrived, and the door is open. I hear them inside, talking loudly."

"Leave, Lupita. Leave now."

Jessup hung up and reached into his truck, grabbing the radio microphone. He pressed the call button. "Sheriff to dispatch."

"Go ahead, Sheriff."

"Autumn, get someone out to Derwood Smith's place now."

"The one in Palouse?"

"That's correct. Something's going down. Men are inside there now. Might be a burglary or worse. I'm on my way from Hooper. Going to take me some time."

He placed the microphone back into its slot, turned to Eddie and said, "Sorry, my friend. Another time."

Eddie called after him, "I'll invite you to dinner some night!"

Jessup pretended he didn't hear.

***

At normal speed, he was a little more than an hour away from the town of Palouse, which was on the far eastern edge of the county. Jessup activated his lights and siren and drove as fast as the roads would allow.

What the hell is going on at Smith's house? he wondered. Who could be there, and why? Was this tied into the recent murders?

It had to be, Jessup thought. Everything had to be. It was too much to all be a coincidence.

He called Lupita's phone, but she didn't answer. He wanted to get a further description of what she might have observed—perhaps a car out front or something she had overheard. For a moment, he second-guessed himself on hanging up with her so quickly, but she needed to get away from potential harm. He could get the answers to these questions when she was safe.

A side effect of law enforcement is how quickly abnormal things become normal—like driving one hundred miles per hour on winding roads. How hitting the brakes, transferring the weight of the vehicle, reaccelerating, then repeating the process becomes rote. A person's mind becomes accustomed to it, and it develops a sense of normalcy. NASCAR drivers experience this, Army parachutists experience this, and so do cops. Jessup fell quickly into a routine racing along Highway 26, which soon allowed his mind to drift to other subjects.

When his mind wandered, he silently cursed those around him and their fascination with his love life, or lack thereof. Why couldn't they stay out of it? Why did so many people insist on believing he had to be with someone to be happy?

As he passed through Colfax, switching to Highway 272, Jessup refocused and pushed the personal thoughts away. He needed to stay alert and focused on what might be occurring at Derwood Smith's place. Deputy Howard had already checked out and reported no vehicles were on site; however, he was entering the premises to check on Smith.

Jessup reduced his speed slightly while still clocking ninety-two miles per hour. He kept trying to force the personal matters out of his mind, but the intrusions by well-meaning friends and family bugged him more than he liked to admit. His life was his own, and whether he chose to spend it alone or with someone was his choice. Folks should just keep their noses out of his business.

As he entered the town of Palouse, he realized he'd made the sixty-mile drive in a little more than forty minutes.

He proceeded through the town at a reduced speed until he made it to the driveway of the Smith estate. He accelerated up the driveway, ignored the ornamental gate, and drove around it, bouncing wildly until he returned to the pavement. He then floored the gas pedal, earning a loud protest from the engine even as the truck lurched forward.

He skidded to a stop in front of Derwood Smith's house. The only car in front was Deputy Howard's.

As he ran toward the front door, Howard was stepping out. His expression was sour, not the usual jovialness that his friend displayed.

Jessup slowed up. "You clear the house?"

Howard nodded.

"And?"

"Deceased white male, lying in his bed."

Jessup's shoulders slumped. He stood there for a second, then patted Howard on the arm. "Call medics. We'll need them to pronounce his death officially."

***

The sheriff stepped inside the house and stopped, not moving. His eyes scanned everything. He'd been here before, so now he was trying to determine if anything was out of place. Everything looked as it had before.

He slowly walked the stairs. He was consciously aware he might bring in contaminated elements. His boots weren't covered, and he could be traipsing in dirt or mud from other parts of the county. He looked back over the steps he'd just walked on. They appeared clean, but at the microscopic level, it could be a different story.

Still, he had to get to Derwood Smith and see what had occurred.

The older man was in his room, the same place he had met Smith for the first time. The television on the wall was tuned to *FOX News*, the volume muted as previously done. His bed was positioned to allow him to read. In Smith's lap was a copy of the *Wall Street Journal*. A pillow lay on his knees.

Only a single pillow was underneath his head.

He heard footsteps then and turned to see Deputy Howard approaching.

"Medics are on the way."

Jessup thumbed toward the body. "Is this how you found him?"

"Exactly."

"You didn't touch anything?"

"I checked for a pulse. That's all."

"You didn't try to revive him?"

"He was already cold."

Jessup blinked several times, then reached over and touched Smith's skin. There was no warmth. He had been dead for some time.

"Damn," Jessup said and brushed past his deputy.

"What?" Howard said.

"Stay with the body until medics arrive," Jessup said and moved to the room next door. He tugged a pair of latex gloves from his pocket, pulled them on, then opened the door. It appeared to be an office. Drawers had been yanked out and dumped over. Books were swiped off their shelves and dumped on the floor.

Jessup moved to the next room. He opened the door to find another bedroom. The closet was open, and its contents appeared to be jostled about. A small secretarial desk had its drawer removed and tipped over onto the floor.

He found the same scene in the other rooms on the second floor. Whoever had gone through the rooms had made an enormous mess.

When he was done, he proceeded to the top of the staircase and was about to start down when he stopped. He looked back toward the various rooms. A thought nagged at him.

The doors were shut. Why?

Jessup proceeded down the stairs and checked the kitchen. It was still immaculate. Nothing was out of place.

He moved on to the great room. The scene was like the bedrooms upstairs. It was in shambles. Couch cushions were tossed about. The recliners were tipped over. Books were removed from their shelves and thrown on the floor.

A painted picture of a sunset was leaned against a wall.

On the wall, behind where the picture had hung earlier, was a safe. Its door was wide open. Jessup stared inside at its emptiness.

A home-invasion robbery? Jessup thought. He stepped back and crossed his arms over his chest. His eyes surveyed the scene again. The room *looked* like a disaster.

The two recliners were tipped over. Why was that even necessary?

The couch cushions were tossed about. Perhaps the intruders looked for something underneath them, but tossing them, along with the couch pillows, across the room seemed excessive.

The books from the various shelves were, presumably, grabbed by handfuls and scattered about. Why was the scattering necessary? If they were searching for something behind the books, wouldn't a simple swipe of all the books to the floor be just as effective?

He then turned back to the open safe. The picture that had covered it was laid against the nearby bookcase. The safe was empty. He thought about what might have been in it. Papers perhaps. Maybe information related to the trust. Would Derwood have kept cash in it? That's when Jessup remembered the conversation with Woody about the stock market and how the older man had been buying gold lately. If he were to keep it anywhere in the house, it would have been in the safe.

Jessup knelt to study the picture. Something about it bothered him. After a minute of not satisfying his curiosity, he stood and examined the safe. When he was done, he strode out of the house.

Deputy Howard stood near his car.

"What do you think?" Howard asked.

"Got your camera?" Jessup asked.

"Yeah."

"Then we're going to investigate this as a homicide."

Howard's eyebrows shot up. "Didn't he die in his sleep?"

"I doubt it," Jessup said. "I think it's supposed to look that way."

"Should I call State Forensics and get them started?"

"Yes, but I need to make a call. Then gear up and wait for me."

Jessup walked over to his truck and sat behind the wheel. The phone rang twice before it answered.

"Delaney."

"Hey, Quinn, it's Jessup."

"What's up, Sheriff?"

"Derwood Smith is dead. Murdered."

"Huh."

"That's all you got? Huh?"

"What do you mean?" Quinn asked.

"The last of the Smith brothers is murdered, and you respond with 'huh.' I figured you would have had a different take on it."

"It throws a monkey wrench into our theory."

"That maybe Smith was involved with his brothers' deaths?"

"Yeah."

"I told you he wasn't." Through his windshield, Jessup watched Deputy Howard pull a camera case from the trunk of his car. "Who gains now that he's dead?"

"The trust's assets go to Derwood, and then the kids will inherit them from him," Quinn said.

"Adeline and Heath Smith."

"Right. If there's a will in place."

"And if not, they still will, right? It goes through probate, and the state would likely award it to them." Jessup rubbed his chin, considering. "Which makes them suspects."

"The problem with that theory," Quinn said, "is we interviewed the son. He's messed up."

"Bike accident, right?"

"Yeah, right. It did a real number on him. I don't see him being involved in this, Tom. What about the daughter? Could she have pulled this off?"

Jessup thought about his interactions with Adeline. "She might be capable."

"Heath has a daughter we're looking into."

"A daughter?"

"Yeah. Crystal Braemar."

"Braemar?"

"Mother's name."

"How's she fit into this?"

"She was working for Ezra Baumbach," Quinn said.

"The trust attorney?"

"Yeah, uh-huh."

"That doesn't smell right," Jessup said.

"Not at all."

Jessup watched Deputy Howard move to the front of the house and wait for him.

"We're actively searching for Crystal," Quinn said. "If we get anything on her, we'll call you. Will you contact Adeline?"

"Will do."

"If you're going to interview her," Quinn said, "would you mind if one of us sat in? All the cases are intertwined now."

Jessup thought about it. Quinn and Marci were Major Crimes Detectives. They had honed their skills in this area. He could use the help, and his ego should not be a factor. "Definitely. I'd appreciate it."

"We'll talk soon," Quinn said and ended the call.

Jessup was about to get out of the truck when he paused for a second. He activated his phone, searched for her number, and pressed Send. The phone went immediately to voicemail. He heard Lupita's voice announce she could not come to the phone right now and to leave a message. He hung up without leaving a message.

Chapter 39

When they returned to the station, the first thing Quinn Delaney did was drop into his chair and fire up the computer to look for a burglary report tied to Ezra Baumbach's address. He hadn't even typed in the address when he heard Marci say, "The hell?"

He looked at her. She was holding an orange sticky note.

"This was stuck to my phone," she said.

"What's it say?" Quinn asked.

She held it up.

"I can't read that from here."

She extended her hand toward Quinn.

Call me. Important - Morgan.

"We've both got cell phones," Marci said. "He could have called one of us. Or texted."

Quinn shook his head and turned his attention back to his computer. He didn't like Morgan. No, it went deeper than that. He didn't trust him. He'd heard all the rumors and innuendo about how he did his job. Quinn wasn't one to trust departmental speculation, but this talk was different. The rumblings were about cutting corners, brutality, and lying. Things no cop should be accused of by another, yet Morgan had that aura around him. Unfortunately, there were some in the department who treated him almost like a hero.

Marci banged around in her desk. "I bet that bastard searched my desk."

While his partner continued to check her work area, Quinn found the report he wanted. Almost twelve months prior, there had been a burglary at Ezra Baumbach's office. The office had been tossed, but nothing appeared to have been stolen. A responding corporal took fingerprints, but none came back as useful.

"The report," Quinn said.

Marci stopped searching her desk and looked at him. "What report?"

"The burglary at Ezra's office."

"And?"

"It's like he said. A year ago. Nothing was taken. No evidence left behind."

"What do you think it means?"

Quinn shrugged. "Probably nothing. Or maybe someone wanted to look at something they couldn't get at legally."

"You think someone broke in to look at the trust document?"

"Might have been the only way they could have seen it," Quinn said.

Marci picked up the orange sticky note and looked at it again.

"You going to call him?" Quinn asked.

Marci slapped the sticky note onto her desk and picked up the telephone receiver.

***

"Took you long enough," Morgan said, leaning back with a grin, his hands resting on the arms of the chair.

Quinn and Marci had walked over to the Monroe Court building where the Criminal Task Force was located. At that moment, Morgan was the only member of the team in the office.

"You could have called us," Marci said, holding up her cell phone as emphasis. "Saved us some time. Maybe got to us a little quicker."

"I figured you two were busy. Besides, it's a nice day for a walk."

"It's raining," Marci said.

"Like I said," Morgan said, his grin growing wider.

"What's so important?" Quinn asked.

"Rado Jones. I found how he's connected to your double murder."

"We already had the connection," Marci said. "His driver's license was at the crime scene."

Morgan leaned forward. "That was circumstantial. You never found his prints at the scene, right?"

Marci stared at him. Morgan's eyes flicked to Quinn, who didn't bother answering.

"If we aren't going to share info, then maybe I'll just keep my intel to myself."

Marci's lip started to curl, but she tried to stop it. It was too late, though. Quinn saw it. So did Morgan, and he smiled.

She took a deep breath through her nose and let it slowly out through her mouth.

"Centering yourself, Sensei?" Morgan asked.

"No fingerprints belonging to Jones were found at the scene," Quinn said.

"That's because he wasn't there. We can all agree on that, right?"

Marci's eyes moved to Quinn, who shrugged. They both looked at Morgan. "Okay," they said in unison.

"So, who was in the house? I think I know. Do you?"

Marci's face reddened.

"Who?" Quinn said. "Who was in the house?"

"Casey Braemar."

"Who?" Marci and Quinn said in unison.

"Casey—"

"Braemar," all three of them said together.

"That's right," Morgan said. "Braemar. Does that name mean something?"

"Definitely," Quinn said. "It definitely does mean something."

Marci held up her hand. "Step back. Who is Casey Braemar? How did you come across him? And how does he fit into this?"

Morgan pointed at Marci and looked at Quinn. "I like it when she acts like a detective."

"Quit screwing around, Morgan, or I'm going to encourage her to kick your ass."

"You kidding me? This one?" Morgan's eyes ran up and down Marci, who had suddenly gone very calm. His smile faded. "You know, Burkett. I seriously like you."

Marci's eyes flattened.

"You belong here in CTF."

"Braemar," she said.

Morgan shrugged. "Rado Jones was my CI, and I liked the kid. He did right by me. I tracked down some of his known associates and chatted with them. One of them pointed me to his girl, Scrimmy."

"Scrimmy?" Marci asked.

"Liliya Scrimshaw. She said Rado was recently hanging out with Braemar. That they were talking about pulling a job, some rip from a wealthy old couple."

Quinn and Marci glanced at each other. Quinn noticed Morgan's grin had returned. He was enjoying slowly doling out his story.

"Rado left the night of the murder to do the job with Braemar, and he never returned home. Scrimmy never saw him again."

"You should have called us on this," Quinn said.

"You were busy. I didn't want to disturb you."

Marci stood still. Quinn felt the anger emanating from her.

"I take it you've run Braemar," Quinn asked.

Morgan shrugged.

"And?"

"Clean."

"Anything else?" Marci said.

Morgan thought about it for a moment before he said, "He fled from me when I attempted contact."

"Are you serious?" Quinn said, his voice rising in frustration. "Why didn't you tell us this before? We could have helped."

"I do things my way."

"This is *our* case," Marci said.

"And Rado was *my* CI."

The three of them remained quiet for a moment. Each was lost in their own thoughts. Finally, Morgan said, "So you heard the name Braemar before I told you…"

"Yeah," Quinn said.

"And?"

"And nothing."

"Listen, I shared. Now, it's your turn."

"Are you kidding?" Quinn said. "You set our investigation back by not coming clean when you found this information. Screw you, pal. We don't have to share anything with you."

Quinn turned and headed to the door. Marci was close by his side.

"Hey," Morgan called. "You might want to hear about what he's driving, where he's living, and the training he's received. I've still got a little more to share."

Quinn stopped, his hand on the doorknob.

"I promise to play nice," Morgan said.

At that moment, Quinn recalled the story of the frog and the scorpion. How the scorpion wanted to cross the pond and asked the frog for help. The frog didn't trust the scorpion, sure he'd sting him. But the scorpion convinced him he wouldn't, so the frog relented, and the scorpion hopped onto its back. Halfway across the pond, as the frog paddled, the scorpion suddenly stung him. The frog asked him why he did that, because now they would both drown.

"It's my nature," said the scorpion.

Quinn took a final look back at Morgan and said, "We'll take our chances."

***

Outside as they walked back to the Public Safety Building, Marci glanced at Quinn, a sense of bewilderment on her face.

"What?" Quinn asked.

"Really?"

"What?" Quinn repeated.

"You gave up easy."

"I'm thinking Morgan did as well."

Marci stopped and looked back at the Monroe Street Building. "You thinking he's still going after Braemar?"

"You mean Casey? I'd bet on it. For him, it's a sport now. He wants to bring him in."

"What do you want to do about it?" Marci asked.

"We could go to the captain."

"The brass? Yeah, that's something I want to do. Besides, do you think that would change anything?"

"It won't change Morgan."

"Then why waste time standing in front of Ackerman?" Marci asked. "Let's find Braemar ourselves."

"What do we know about him?"

"Nothing, but we know about the sister."

"Then, let's get after her."

Chapter 40

After the State's Forensic team processed the crime scene, Sheriff Jessup tasked Deputy Howard with putting several items into evidence back in Colfax. The coroner had arrived and coordinated the removal of Derwood Smith's body.

Jessup repeatedly called Lupita while at the house. He left multiple messages for her to call him. When he cleared the scene, he immediately drove north to her home in Garfield. She wasn't there. He stood in her front yard for a few minutes until he decided on his next course of action.

Jessup then headed south to Pullman. While he drove, he called the department and put out Attempt to Locate orders on both Lupita DeLeon and Adeline Smith.

When he arrived at Adeline's apartment, he parked his truck, trotted along the sidewalk, climbed the three flights of stairs, and knocked on the door.

For several minutes, there was no answer.

He stood on the balcony and overlooked the parking lot, thinking. He watched several cars coming in and out of the lot. He searched for a white Volkswagen Tiguan but didn't see one.

Jessup walked down the stairs, his eyes scanning for some directional signage. Finding some, he headed toward the community's office.

When he stepped inside, he immediately noticed the sole occupant, a young woman, was engaged in a phone conversation. The nameplate on her desk read *Miranda Dobson.* She turned to look at the sheriff, her eyes widening when she saw his uniform.

"Uh-huh, yeah, that's correct. Two bedrooms," the woman said into the phone, still staring at Jessup.

His eyes scanned the office. Its paint and carpet were a series of grays broken up by yellow flowers and paintings with brighter bursts of yellow.

"Right," the young woman said, "we're one hundred percent full now. Uh-huh, yeah. You have to get here before the next school year starts, or you're going to have a tough time renting. Yes, that's any place. Right. Have a nice day."

When she hung up the phone, she watched the sheriff expectantly.

"I'm Sheriff Jessup, Whitman County."

"Um, okay," the woman said, elongating the second word.

"Adeline Smith?"

"Sir?"

"Where does she park her car?"

"Excuse me?"

"Her car? Does she have a designated parking stall?"

"Oh, yes." She spun back to her desk and grabbed a printout. Her finger ran down the page until she said, "B-11."

"Perfect," Jessup said and left without further conversation.

He walked through the lot, his eyes scanning the yellow paint on the asphalt. Designated parking was underneath a series of carports. Once he discovered the numbering scheme, Jessup hurried to B-11. Adeline's Volkswagen wasn't there.

Again, the young woman looked up from her desk when Jessup returned to the office. "Yes?"

He held out his business card. "When you see Adeline or her car, please call me or my department."

She stood and took the card. "Is she in trouble?"

"I'd like to talk with her."

Concern filled the woman's eyes. "Are we in danger?"

"No. If you see her, please call."

The young woman nodded as the sheriff reached for the door.

He stepped outside and looked up into the gray sky. The gray apartments, gray walls, gray carpets, and the gray sky suddenly seemed too much. A heaviness pushed on his shoulders.

Jessup pulled out his cell phone and dialed his son, William.

It rang several times before going to his voice mail. He listened to his son's message, enjoying the sound of his voice. He hung up before the beep would signal the start of recording.

He then searched for Lupita's number and dialed.

Again, it went straight to voicemail.

***

Driving on Highway 27, the town of Garfield is about thirty minutes north of Pullman. Jessup notified Autumn where he was headed while he drove. It was a little after 5 p.m. now and dark. His thoughts meandered back to the crime scene.

Someone had murdered Derwood Smith and stolen something from his safe. The house was burglarized, but there was something wrong with the way it had been conducted. He tried to put his finger on it.

He'd seen three types of professional burglars.

The first was the most common. The mad-dash type who quickly got in and out, grabbing what they could. They were often inexperienced or chemically dependent. This could be a high school kid just getting his first taste of the criminal life, or it could be a junkie looking for a way to continue to pay for his addiction. Regardless, their work was sloppy, as it was a crime of opportunity. They hadn't planned anything ahead of time. Their only plan was to snatch something and then run away.

The other types of burglars were rarer, but they were the ones that Jessup found most interesting.

The second type ransacked a house methodically. They would enter a home and strip every room of potential hiding spots. Pictures of any size would be removed from the wall, to verify no safes existed or that nothing had potentially been secreted behind them. Drawers would be pulled out from their chests, bottom first, making their way to the top. This would allow them to discard the contents of the drawer, then open the next drawer without closing the previous drawer. It only saved a sliver of time, but that type of thinking—that seconds mattered—was the difference with this burglar. They were methodical.

The final type of burglar was similar but different in that they didn't want to leave a trace. They may search every drawer and look behind every picture, but they would put everything back in its place. Their goal was never to be noticed. They wanted to get in and out without anyone ever suspecting they were there. Because of this, they usually operated in a way that afforded them the luxury of time, hitting homes when people were on vacation, or at least at work.

Above all, burglars tended not to be violent criminals, regardless of their style. It was extremely rare for them to carry a weapon. They wanted to work in private without confrontation. Theirs was a secret world. If they were spotted, they ran.

Even though most cops disliked the slapdash burglar, Jessup learned to respect the professional burglars because of a former sergeant. He was the one who explained the thought and care they took to go through their process. They usually weren't junkies out for a score or kids out for an adrenaline rush. These burglars were working on mastering a profession and needed to be respected as such.

And that's what bothered Jessup about Derwood Smith's death. If these were really burglars at the house, wouldn't their first instinct have been to run when they encountered Derwood?

More than that, they would not, could not have possibly seen that older man as a threat from his position in bed. So why kill him?

Therefore, a significant question in Jessup's mind was timing. Derwood's murder either occurred first, and then the burglary took place, or the burglars came to the house in the small town of Palouse because of him.

Upon further thought, Jessup suspected Derwood's death was the motivating factor, not the burglary. The double homicide in Spokane had been made to look like a burglary as well. It fit the pattern of at least one other of the killings.

Therefore, Jessup's theory was someone entered Derwood's house and smothered the older man with his pillow. The death reminded him of Renard Smith's death, the brother in St. John, who looked as if he had died in his sleep. But his house hadn't been ransacked.

The burglary angle still plagued the sheriff. Perhaps they thought the older man would call for help, and that's why they killed him. Again, it seemed unlikely; it went against the burglary types that Jessup had known. The happenstance killing of Derwood Smith by a burglar seemed wrong.

Jessup had to be careful to make up his mind this early before getting all the evidence in, but he felt in his gut that Derwood was murdered, and the burglary was staged to make it look like his death was an unfortunate result.

However, the staging was poor, and the evidence pointed to that.

The neighboring rooms had been ransacked, but nothing appeared to be broken. They could quickly be put back together.

Nothing in the kitchen had been disturbed, but what was the likelihood a burglar would check a kitchen? Not likely. Jessup tried to remember how many kitchens had been burglarized in his career. A few, but they were mostly for food, not for cookware or utensils.

The great room had been cluttered with books and couch cushions strewn about, but it could easily have been placed back in order. Even the painting that had been removed was set carefully against the wall. The ransacking made no sense.

That's when he thought about the chairs. They had been tipped over.

Why? Jessup asked himself.

To make the room look more disturbed, he reasoned.

The safe behind the picture had been opened, and its contents, assuming there were any, had been taken. Had the intruder forced Derwood to give them the safe's code? That would be a reason to attack the older man and threaten to kill him, Jessup realized.

If the thief got the code and opened the safe, why bother to trash the place? Just to add to the illusion that the crime was the reason for his death?

Another thought occurred to Jessup.

Who would already know the code to the safe?

The answer was immediate. Adeline surely would know it.

If the goal was to kill Derwood and make his death look a part of something else, there could have been other crimes to cover it up with. Vandalism came first to Jessup's mind. The intruder could have trashed every room and made the death look like a crime of opportunity.

How about arson? Jessup thought.

That would probably have been best. Start a fire right in Derwood's room. If they were lucky, the whole house would burn down, especially if his oxygen tank exploded. There would be no way to determine if he had been smothered at that point. A fire would consume all evidence of a crime.

Although Jessup mused, arson might be tough to commit to the body of a loved one who had just been murdered.

He saw the fallacy in that argument, and his thoughts tumbled in on one another.

What continued to bother Jessup was the open safe. What if what was inside was the primary reason for the crime? If that was the case, Jessup wondered, then why not open the safe, take what was there and leave? The older man was up in his bed and would never know. Or at least, he wouldn't know for some time.

He thought of three immediate possibilities, although there may have been more. He'd have to let his mind work the problem later.

The first possibility, and he admitted this seemed a strong option, was the person who entered the safe was not a professional. That they wanted what was inside the safe, extracted the combination from Derwood by force, realized what they had done, and then created a scene to mask their crime.

The second likelihood and this one seemed far-fetched, was someone staged the scene to blame it on someone else. Derwood was murdered, and the stage was set to get Jessup and his department to look for someone other than the murderer. If that was the case, who was he supposed to be looking at when he should be looking elsewhere?

The third possibility, he surmised, was the murderer wanted to misdirect the reason for the murder altogether, thereby covering their tracks. Maybe the burglary wasn't the reason for the killing at all. In light of recent events, this possibility struck a chord with Jessup.

Jessup arrived in Garfield and drove to Lupita's house. Her car still wasn't there.

Even so, he headed to the front of the house and knocked on the door. There was no answer. He waited a few moments and knocked again.

He had a thought and walked around the house. There was no fence to stop him, so he was in the backyard. Although there was an alley behind her house, there was no car there.

Jessup returned to the front of the house and stuck his business card between the jamb and the door.

Chapter 41

By refusing to play ball with James Morgan, Detectives Quinn Delaney and Marci Burkett might have created more work for themselves. Some would have considered that shortsighted, but they both felt it was better to avoid lying down with dogs and getting fleas.

For Quinn, it took barely any time or effort to find what they needed. He knew Morgan's call sign, and he knew he'd been in a pursuit. After a couple of taps on the keyboard, he had what he needed.

Morgan pursued a stolen vehicle in the area of Fourteenth Avenue and Ash Street. The suspect vehicle was a late 1960s orange Camaro with stolen plates. Captain Ackerman had terminated the pursuit.

"Quinn."

The detective turned to see Captain Ackerman standing behind him.

"Sir?"

"How are things with the Smith murders?"

"We're making progress."

"Anything I can relay to the chief? I'm on my way to meet with him now."

"We've got a lead we're working."

"Braemar? The guy Morgan was chasing?"

"Right," Quinn said. "We're going to notify patrol to be on the watch for an orange Camaro."

Ackerman nodded. "Oh, they'll love that."

"I hope so."

The captain patted his shoulder. "All right, big hitter. Get it done. I'll let the chief know."

***

As for Marci, she had returned to Ezra Baumbach's office to search for anything that might lead them to Crystal Braemar.

"I'm sorry, my dear," Ezra said. "I've searched every file. There's nothing here."

"Mind if I search her desk?"

Ezra held out his hand. "Be my guest."

She dropped into the receptionist's chair, pulled the drawers from the desk, and rifled through the various items kept there.

In the bottom drawer, she found an envelope labeled to Crystal Braemar. Its address was in Spokane Valley on Conklin Road. She opened the envelope and pulled out a letter. Her eyes skipped over the contents.

It was from Crystal's doctor.

***

While the apartment community was beautiful and new, the fact that it was built around Shelley Lake was a bit of a misnomer.

At its deepest, the lake was fifteen feet. It was sixteen hundred feet in length and thirteen hundred feet at its maximum width. It was pretty to look at it, but it was more of a glorified pond than a lake. However, *pond* doesn't sell houses or rent apartments.

Quinn pulled into a parking stall next to an orange Camaro. His eyes shifted to the car next to him. "See that?"

Marci leaned forward and studied the car. Her eyebrows raised, and a smile formed. "Maybe we get a two for one?"

Quinn backed his car from the stall and parked it perpendicular to the Camaro, blocking it in with the sidewalk. They got out and examined the lettering on the sides of the various buildings.

"Which one is she in?" Quinn asked.

"Says A-317," Marci said and pointed at the building in front of them. "Building A. Third floor, right?"

They searched along the length of Building A until they found apartment 317, then they climbed the stairs to the third floor. Marci rang the doorbell.

There was no answer.

Quinn banged the flat of his fist against the door.

There still was no answer and no movement inside the apartment.

"This has to be it, right?" Quinn asked. "How many orange Camaros are there?"

"Not many."

He banged his fist again.

"Hey, what are you doing?" a woman yelled somewhere in the distance. "I'm gonna call the cops."

Quinn glanced at Marci, who shrugged in return. He banged harder on the door. "Spokane Police! Open up!"

A door below them opened. A woman wearing red WSU sweatpants and a purple University of Washington sweatshirt hurried onto the stairs and looked up at the detectives. "He's getting away!"

"What?" Marci said.

"The guy you're looking for. He just climbed down to my balcony, and he's jumping down to the first floor."

"Damn it!" Quinn yelled, running down the stairs.

He hopped down the last stairs and ran toward the sidewalk. He saw a white male climb into the orange Camaro.

The Chevy roared to life and lurched forward, jumping the curb. It drove onto the wet grass, wildly throwing mud and particles. As Quinn sprinted toward his car, he looked back over his shoulder, not seeing Marci anywhere near him.

He opened his car door, slid in, and started the engine. He dropped the car into Reverse, immediately flooring the accelerator. The engine whined, and the tires squealed as the vehicle raced backward. Quinn slammed his brakes as he almost collided with a mother and her young son carrying groceries from across the parking lot. The woman screamed profanities at him.

Quinn put the car into Drive and accelerated away, his eyes searching for the Camaro. He turned a corner and slammed the brakes again, this time avoiding a collision with a large F150 pickup. The driver stared at him with fascination. He activated the emergency lights and drove carefully around the truck, his head swiveling, searching for the Camaro.

Around the back of the apartment community, he found tire tracks where the Camaro had left the grass and entered the pavement. Two muddy lines continued for a short while before they faded into nothing.

"Damn," Quinn muttered.

He spun the wheel and drove slowly back to the apartment. Marci stood at the edge of the sidewalk, waving him down with a large smile on her face.

As he pulled up alongside her, he rolled down his window. "What happened to you?"

"I quit running," she said.

"Why?"

"Because I'm the brains of this outfit."

"What?"

"Say it."

"Huh?"

"This wasn't his apartment, right?"

Marci stepped out of Quinn's line of sight, and that's when he saw her. Seated at the bottom of the stairs, with her hands behind her back, was Crystal Braemar.

"It was a diversion," Marci said. "Her brother ran so we would chase him, and she could slip away. I realized that when I saw only him. I turned back around and waited underneath the steps. She came running down a couple seconds later." She gave Quinn a self-satisfied grin. "So say it. I'm the brains of this outfit."

Quinn smiled back. "I'm not saying it."

"You'll say it sooner or later."

Chapter 42

James Morgan was pissed.

He didn't like getting shown up, especially by a couple of do-gooders like Delaney and Burkett. After his confrontation with them in his office, he stewed. Their holier-than-thou bullshit ate at him. He was a good cop and a damn good detective. He didn't need to be preached at, especially not by them.

They played the game their way, and sometimes criminals walked. He played the game his way, and no one walked on his cases, ever. Even when the system failed to do its job, Morgan made certain justice got its due.

And that's why the death of Rado Jones ate at him. Rado had ratted for him. Yeah, the kid was a junkie punk, but he was Morgan's junkie punk, and that meant something in his world. That meant Morgan protected him and owed him a debt. He owed it to Rado to bring his killer to justice. And right now, Morgan was pretty damn sure Casey Braemar was the killer.

When members of the CTF team started to filter back into the office, Morgan found an excuse to leave. Everyone knew he was a moody son of a bitch, so he didn't bother hiding his irritation. That was one of the benefits of being the way he was. It kept the bar low. Expectations weren't high, so if he behaved as anticipated, everyone accepted it. If he exceeded their expectations, well, those folks were pleasantly surprised. Either way, Morgan didn't care.

Spring was still in early bloom. Dampness filled the air, and night fell early, which meant people were tucked into their homes by seven. Morgan parked his car a couple of blocks away and walked to the little house on

Fourteenth Avenue. He repeated the same process he had earlier by picking the Kwikset lock on the back door. It relented quickly, and he was soon inside the house alone with his frustration.

Morgan's anger turned inward.

He was mad—not for breaking into the house, but for doing it unprepared. Oh, he was equipped correctly with his duty weapon, an extendable baton, a knife, and a backup gun, but what he really wanted was something to eat and drink.

He didn't dare open the refrigerator door, though. To do so would cause the light to turn on, thereby signaling anyone watching the house that someone was inside. If Casey Braemar wanted to return home, he wouldn't come be-bopping up to the door and just walk in. No, he would take his time, watch the house for a while as well as the neighborhood. Any movement inside would tip Braemar that a trap was set for him. Which meant Morgan needed to stay down and remain hungry. And for that, he was mad. It was a stupid mistake. He hadn't thought a step ahead.

It wasn't that Braemar had gotten into his head. He was just prey. Like a number of other criminal turds he'd chased over the years. He might be better trained, but Braemar was still a turd.

No, it was the other detectives that got to him.

Major Crimes.

The golden ticket.

He would never get invited to play in that league, not with his reputation. He played it off that he didn't want to be in Major Crimes, but that was bravado. Of course, he wanted to be in the big leagues. Everyone did. It bothered him that they had recently promoted a couple of real meatballs to the section. Either the department was hurting for quality, or they had something on the ball that

Morgan couldn't see. He decided it was the former and let his anger drift back to Delaney and Burkett.

Burkett, Morgan thought, *she would be attractive if she wasn't such a—*

There was a noise at the back door.

Morgan tensed, controlled his breathing, and listened. A key was inserted into a lock. The back door opened, and the moon backlit a male figure. When the door quickly closed again, darkness and silence returned.

His heart raced. Was Braemar quietly moving through the house? Did he know Morgan was already inside?

Morgan's hand slowly reached toward his gun, his fingers resting on the safety snap that held it snuggly in the holster. To release it now would surely alert Braemar. The noise, a sharp pop, would be out of place, a signal to the other man exactly where Morgan was hiding.

Perhaps Braemar had waited at the door to make sure no one had followed him.

There was movement now. A drawer in the kitchen slid open, then closed. A cabinet door opened and closed.

Braemar wasn't disguising his movements now. He banged around in the kitchen. Another cabinet door opened and closed, then the faucet turned on briefly. Glass of water, Morgan figured.

Morgan stood from his position in the corner of the living room. Braemar didn't, or couldn't, see him. The man was now eating a sandwich. A jar of something was on the counter.

Braemar left the kitchen and walked toward the living room. He was an over six-foot shadow, his weight tough to gauge, but his shoulders were broad and his waist trim.

He suddenly stopped his sandwich at midbite. In the darkness of the house, Braemar somehow knew the detective was there. Either he saw him as his eyes adjusted to the dark, or he sensed him. Whatever it was, the game was up, and Morgan was forced to make his move.

"Police," Morgan said softly.

Braemar threw the sandwich at him and ran toward the back door.

Morgan burst from his hiding place, only a step behind him.

Braemar grabbed the doorknob and began to pull the door. That split second was all Morgan needed. He shoved Braemar into the door, the resulting slam echoing through the house.

The man spun quickly, immediately dropping to the floor and wrapped himself around Morgan's leg. The detective felt the pressure applied to his leg, the knee locked, and he went down, slapping the floor as his back hit.

Braemar mounted him quickly as Morgan punched up at him. A brief pulse of fear shot through the detective.

The fight had quickly changed to life or death. Morgan didn't dare pull his gun out now; Braemar might take it away and shoot him. He had to get Braemar swiftly off, or the man could incapacitate him and still take his weapon away.

Morgan's fist bounced off Braemar's forehead, and another blow clipped him harmlessly on the chin.

Braemar, though, landed one devastating punch after another. He rained them down with such ferocity and pace that Morgan had no answer but to cover his face with his hands and forearms. It was a ploy known as turtling, and it was a strictly defensive move. It was apparent Braemar had seen it before because he quickly set to punching Morgan in the ribs.

The detective couldn't drop his hands from his face, though, and expose his head to more beating. He struggled to control his breathing and push down the panic that had risen inside him.

When Braemar tired, he suddenly dropped his weight on top of Morgan, his arms snaking under and along his neck, looking to apply a chokehold. The detective knew he would be quickly rendered unconscious if he didn't do something fast. Morgan wasn't a trained martial artist and didn't know a quick way to escape.

Therefore, he did the only thing he knew *would* work. He applied a higher level of pain.

His right arm was pinned under Braemar's weight, so he reached over with his left hand, grabbed Braemar's right ear, and yanked it from his head. Even though he knew it was coming, the tearing sound surprised Morgan, and it paused Braemar.

Then the man jerked, screamed, and immediately let go of Morgan.

He rolled off the detective and held his head in his hand while he continued to scream.

Morgan sucked for air as he stood, thankful for the opportunity to breathe easily. He took a quick look at the ear in his hand and dropped it to the floor. He then pulled out his gun and pointed it at Braemar. "Stay down."

"You tore off my ear!"

With his free hand, Morgan pulled his cell phone from his jacket and dialed dispatch. His chest heaved as he struggled to control his breathing.

"You tore off my ear!" Braemar screamed again.

"Yeah, yeah, I hear you," Morgan said, then took a deep breath. "I'm trying to get you some help."

Chapter 43

Jessup's cell phone rang as he put the frozen burrito into the microwave. He answered it on the third ring.

"Jessup," he said.

"Sheriff, this is Miranda Dobson."

"Uh-huh." His finger tapped in one minute on the microwave's keypad.

"From the Prairie View Apartments."

The image of the young woman behind the desk suddenly flashed in Jessup's mind. "Yes," he said. Jessup pulled his hand away from the microwave and leaned against the counter. "Ms. Dobson, what can I do for you?"

"She's here."

"Adeline Smith?"

"That's right. She just returned home."

"I appreciate the call."

"Should I do anything else?"

"This is enough. Thank you," Jessup said and ended the call.

He opened his phone contact list, found the phone number for Pullman's Police Department dispatch, and called it.

The female voice on the other line was bright and alert. "Dispatch."

"Hi, this is Sheriff Tom Jessup from Whitman County."

"Yes, Sheriff, what can I help you with?"

"Got a unit available?"

"Yes, sir. We've got a couple. What do you need?"

"I'm heading your direction to interview a possible homicide suspect. I need a unit to make sure she doesn't leave her apartment before I get there."

"We can do that, but why didn't you call this in over the radio?"

"I'm not sure if she or someone she knows might be listening. Would you mind doing this quietly? Just in case. Don't dispatch it over the air."

"Sure, Sheriff, no prob. What's the address, and who are we watching for?"

Jessup quickly provided the address, then Adeline's name and description.

He hurried over to the microwave and pressed the Start button. The appliance whirred to life.

Since he'd called it a day, he was in jeans and a black T-shirt. He put his boots back on, clipped a plainclothes holster to his belt, and shoved his gun in place.

The microwave dinged, signaling his dinner was ready.

Jessup affixed a clip-on badge to his belt, near the gun. He ran his fingers through his hair before putting a black WSU baseball hat on.

He removed the burrito and its paper plate to let it start to cool.

Jessup then grabbed a black Marmot jacket, slipped it on, and headed out to his truck. He stopped, ran back into the house, and grabbed his dinner. He didn't know how long the night would be, and the first rule of police work was never begin on an empty stomach.

***

When he arrived in Pullman, he drove straight to Adeline Smith's apartment. He spotted a patrol cruiser sitting in the parking lot near Adeline's car. The patrolman hadn't bothered staying out of sight.

A small smile crossed his lips. Sometimes the most blatant approach was the best. There was no way she could leave without the officer seeing her.

Jessup parked and walked toward the patrol car. The officer saw him approaching and quickly got out of his car.

"Sir?" the officer said, his tone and demeanor full of caution.

Jessup brushed his open jacket aside to reveal his badge. "Sheriff Jessup."

The officer relaxed. "Scott Yeoman," he said, extending his hand.

Jessup took his hand and thumbed toward the buildings. "I'm going to make contact."

"Want me to go with?" the officer asked.

"No. But hang here until I'm done, will you?"

"Yes, sir."

Jessup headed up the three flights of stairs and knocked. Adeline answered the door with a glass of red wine in her hand. She was in light blue yoga pants and a loose white shirt. Her face was free of makeup, and she looked freshly showered. Her wet hair hung down near her shoulders. A pair of reading glasses covered her eyes, which were red as if she'd been crying.

She blinked a couple of times until recognition set in. Jessup realized she hadn't seen him in plainclothes before.

"Sheriff?"

"May I come in?"

"Of course." Her voice was flat.

Jessup studied her for a moment, then stepped in.

"Is this social?" The smile she forced looked almost painful.

He immediately knew something was wrong.

She turned and walked into the living room. Soft jazz music played in the background. Several candles burned. On the coffee table in front of the couch, a textbook was open, and a pad of paper sat next to it. Nothing was written on it.

"You caught me in the middle of studying, Sheriff." She placed her wineglass on the coffee table and dropped onto the couch, tucking her legs underneath her.

"Where were you today? This morning, actually."

Her eyes slowly lifted to him. "Why?"

"Today," he repeated. "Where were you?"

"Where was I?"

"Answer the question, Adeline."

She stared at him, her mouth silently opening and closing a couple of times before she said, "On campus. Probably at the library."

"Probably?"

"At the library." Her voice took on a defiant tone.

"You didn't have class?"

"No."

"Were you with anyone?"

"No," she said, her voice sterner than necessary.

"Anybody see you there?"

"What's this about?"

"Adeline, can you confirm your whereabouts this morning?"

Adeline lowered her head, and her eyes darted back and forth. Her mouth dropped as she thought. When she finally looked up, she asked, "Are you trying to pin something on me, Sheriff?"

"Pin something on you?" Jessup said.

"You know what I mean."

"I'm asking where you were today."

"I told you. The library."

"Did you check anything out?"

"Does it matter?"

"There are cameras on campus. Are you aware of that?"

Adeline remained still, not revealing anything.

"I'm going to make sure you were there today. If you weren't, then you're lying, and we have a problem."

"You suspect me of something, don't you? What is it?" Her face reddened and tears welled in her eyes. She glanced off into the distance as she thought. Suddenly, her focus snapped back to Jessup. "Lupita. She said I did something, didn't she? What is she accusing me of? Whatever it is, it's bull. You can't trust her. You can't believe her."

"Your father—" Jessup began.

"My father? *He* accused me of something?" Tears streaked down her face. "No, not possible. Unless she got to him." Her expression contorted in anger. "That's what happened, isn't it? Of course, that's what happened. She's around him all the time now. So what is it? What did he accuse me of?" She leaned forward to grab her glass of wine and held it close to her chest. "C'mon, Sheriff, hit me with your best shot. Today just keeps getting better."

"He's dead."

"What?" The word came out in a strained whisper.

Jessup watched her struggle with the news. He softened his voice when he continued, "Your father is dead. I have reason to believe he was murdered."

Adeline leaned forward to put the glass back on the table, hesitated, and pulled it back. She gulped down the remaining wine before setting the empty glass down. She covered her face with her hands and wept. After a minute, she looked up and yelled, "And you think I did that? To my own father?"

Jessup calmly said. "I asked where you were this morning."

She sucked her trembling lips in and closed her eyes, tears flowing down her face.

"You were at the library," Jessup continued. "That's the story you've told."

She nodded a couple of times before shaking her head.

"You weren't at the library?"

"No," Adeline whispered and burst out crying.

"Where were you, Adeline?"

***

Jessup walked over to the window, opened the window shades, and signaled to Officer Yeoman with a wave. The patrol car's door opened, and the officer exited. He headed toward the building. The sheriff moved to the front door and heard him trotting up the stairs. Jessup opened the door and remained where he could keep an eye on Adeline.

When Yeoman arrived, he said, "Sheriff?"

"I need you to sit with her," Jessup whispered.

"Why?"

"So I can follow up on her alibi."

The officer leaned over to look at Adeline. "What's going on?"

"She said she was with someone this morning."

Yeoman's eyes slanted.

"Sounds like they had an encounter that got out of control, and she may have been attacked."

"Rape?" the officer whispered and leaned over to look at Adeline again.

"Maybe. I don't know. She was evasive when I asked her direct questions. It's hard to make out what happened because she's so emotional right now. Listen," Jessup said, with a glance back to Adeline, "this is important. I came to talk with her about her father's murder, and I stumbled into this. I don't know yet if this is real or a smokescreen. Understand?"

"Got it," Yeoman said, nodding.

"Don't let her call anyone. Don't interview her. Just watch her. I don't know what this is, but for an alibi, it's the strangest thing I've ever heard."

"Yeah," the officer said, his eyes still focused on Adeline.

***

Erick Gunderson lived off-campus on D Street in a Craftsman-style house. Jessup stopped his truck a couple of houses away and walked up. It sounded like there was a party going on. Loud rock music was coming from inside.

Jessup stood at the edge of the property and tried to count moving bodies through the window. He saw at least six. For a moment, he considered calling for a backup officer, but he passed on it. Most of the work he'd done through his career was alone, so he wasn't intimidated to handle six college kids by himself. It was the nature of what he might be investigating that warranted the additional officer consideration.

His phone rang then. He pulled it out and looked at the caller ID screen. It was Marci Burkett. He wanted to answer, but this took priority. He'd call her back when he was done.

He continued up the path to the house, climbed the stairs to the porch, and knocked on the front door.

The music grew louder when the door opened. A young woman greeted him, a beer in her hand. Her eyes were glassy, and her smile lopsided.

"Erick Gunderson?" Jessup said. "He home?"

She turned without another word and walked off. "Erick!" she yelled. "Your dad is here!"

A moment later, a head peered around a corner. His eyes were initially full of curiosity. They soon filled with suspicion. The man stepped into view and walked confidently toward Jessup.

He was a big kid with broad shoulders and thick arms. It was apparent he spent time in the gym, and the red T-shirt he wore appeared almost skintight. His face was pleasant, with carefully manicured eyebrows and an expensive haircut. When he smiled, his teeth were straight and bright.

"Yeah?"

"Erick Gunderson?"

"Depends."

"I'm Sheriff Jessup."

"Sheriff?" Gunderson's watery eyes darted away from Jessup for a moment, then quickly returned to him. "What are you here for? Noise?" Gunderson leaned out of the doorway and looked up and down the street. "We'll turn it down. Sorry to bother you, boss."

Someone in the other room lowered the music.

"See? Already done," Gunderson said, closing the door.

"I'm not here for that," Jessup said, putting his hand on the door, preventing it from shutting. He pushed it back open.

Gunderson looked at Jessup's hand, then asked, "Then why?"

"Adeline Smith."

Jessup watched for a response, or as poker players call it, a tell. Gunderson didn't flinch, though. He pulled his hand back, shoved both into his pockets, and asked, "She okay?"

"Why would you ask that?"

"You're here. That's not normal. I figure something happened to her."

"What do you think could have happened to her?"

"How would I know?" Gunderson said with a smirk. "The woman's a hot mess. Anything could happen to her."

"How do you know her?"

"We share a class."

"That's it?"

Gunderson pursed his lips and nodded. Jessup thought he might be trying to suppress a grin.

"And you determined she was a 'hot mess' from a class together?"

"Well, we've talked before and after class, but yeah, I mean, if you've met the woman, you'll know immediately what I'm talking about."

Jessup studied Gunderson.

"What? I'm not a dick. I like her. She's nice, but something's off. Maybe it's a menopausal thing. When my mom went through it—"

Jessup cut him off by asking, "Were you with her earlier today?"

Gunderson glanced back over his shoulder, then stepped out onto the porch, pulling the door closed behind him. As protection from the evening chill, he crossed his arms over his chest. "We hung out together. So?"

"What time was this?"

Gunderson shrugged. "I dunno. Coupla hours. Maybe around ten."

"You hung out here?"

"Yeah."

"Did you have intercourse?"

Gunderson again glanced back over his shoulder through the door's window before turning back to Jessup. "What's this about, Sheriff? She okay or what?"

"Is that your girlfriend in there?"

"No. I mean, I'm trying, but no, not yet."

"That's why you closed the door? You don't want her to hear you had sex with another woman today?"

Gunderson's eyes widened. "I didn't!"

Several people were laughing inside the house.

"Who else is in there?"

"Just a couple other friends," Gunderson said, dismissively. "Listen, Sheriff. I didn't have sex with her."

"Your friends—they don't know what you did earlier?"

"What I *did*? I didn't *do* anything," Gunderson said, his expression now one of horror.

Jessup crossed his arms.

"Chrissakes, man. I mean, she's good looking for ancient and all, but she's old, almost as old as my mom. I don't need that getting attached to my name."

"It was consensual?"

"I told you. We didn't have sex. She tried; I'll give you that."

"She *tried*? What's that mean?"

"I mean, why else would a woman her age come back to college?"

"An education."

"Right," Gunderson said with a chuckle. He moved from side to side, the evening's chill getting to him. "She's having a mid-life crisis. I think she came back to college to go after a bunch of young dudes. Today was just my day. Unlucky me."

"Unlucky you?"

"Well, yeah, you're here."

"Tell me what happened."

Gunderson glanced around for a moment before deciding to answer. "We were flirting at school, and then we came back here. She pushed on me, like almost immediately, but I turned her down."

"The way she made it sound, it wasn't consensual."

"Then, she lies."

"She never said 'no'?"

"Never," Gunderson said, spreading his hands back and forth like he was waving out a fire. "She never said that."

"Why would you bring her back here if you weren't going to have sex with her?"

Gunderson rolled his eyes. "Okay, maybe that was the original plan. Like I said, she's good-looking and all, but when we got back here, things took off way too fast."

"You're saying it was going too fast? You wouldn't like that, her being forceful and all?"

"You've gotta believe me, man. She was pushy. I mean really pushy. It creeped me out. It was super unattractive."

Jessup studied the younger man's face. It seemed the guy was embarrassed by that admission. "I'm not convinced."

Gunderson clucked his tongue. "Damn, man, you ever have an older woman throw herself at you? I mean, it was sad. Like she was desperate or something. Ever been with someone desperate? It's not sexy—exactly the opposite. Something is wrong with her. I told her no, which just riled her up more. The more I said no, the angrier she got. Then she started crying. Man, it was weird. That's the only way I can describe it. Just plain weird."

"You're telling me nothing happened?"

The young man stared at Jessup for a moment, then rolled his eyes. "Well…"

"You wear protection?"

Gunderson held his hands up defensively. "Whoa, we didn't need protection. We didn't have sex."

"Then what did you do?"

He glanced back over his shoulder and looked through the window in the door. When he turned back to Jessup, he said, "I let her use her hand."

"That's sex."

Gunderson smirked. "It is most definitely not sex."

"It most definitely is."

The younger man whispered. "I just wanted to be done with her, so I gave in to that. I mean, she's a MILF, know what I mean?"

Jessup stared at him. The kid had just confirmed Adeline's alibi.

"You don't believe me," Gunderson said.

"I'm trying to determine who to believe."

"I'll tell you this. It was the weirdest handjob I've ever gotten. As soon as she was done, she started crying again and ran off. It's hard to feel like you got something good at that point."

***

Jessup returned to the Prairie View Apartments and, from where he parked, he could see the door to Adeline Smith's apartment was partially opened. Officer Yeoman stood near the door.

The sheriff nodded to the officer as he approached.

"She say anything?" Jessup asked.

"She just sat there staring at nothing. She started crying a couple of times, though."

"Gimme a minute," Jessup said and stepped into the apartment. Yeoman pulled the door partially closed again.

He walked over to Adeline, who looked up at him, her eyes red from crying.

"You found him?"

"Yeah."

She looked down.

He remained quiet as she thought. Finally, without looking up, she said, "I'm sorry."

"Why didn't you just tell me?"

"I was embarrassed."

"Embarrassed?"

She looked up at him, tears reforming in her eyes.

"I don't get it," Jessup said.

She reached for the empty wineglass and stopped. When she leaned back, she said, "The last time I was in college, I was special. Now, I'm not invited to parties. I'm not invited to hang out with anyone. I'm alone on campus. I threw myself at someone today, and he turned me down. Do you know what that feels like? It was humiliating."

Jessup watched her silently.

"I begged him to let me… He probably told you. Did he tell you?"

She looked up at the sheriff, and he continued to study her.

"Great, just great. I didn't think it could get more humiliating."

"You hinted that he forced you."

She shrugged. "I'm sorry."

"That's not good enough, Adeline."

"You just want to keep piling it on."

"I need to know why."

Tears streamed down her face.

"When you showed up here, unannounced, in regular clothes, I thought for a moment that maybe you were here to see me. I was sitting around, feeling sorry for myself, and you showed up. But right away, it was obvious you were all business, so my night went from bad to worse. Then you said my father was dead, and you were asking me where I was because you thought I might be involved. It kept getting worse. I didn't want to admit what I had done. When I started talking, it seemed better to suggest something else happened than to admit what really occurred. I didn't want to seem so… pathetic."

"You're a grown woman. You can do what you like."

She shook her head. "You don't get it."

"Just to be clear, it was consensual."

"Oh, God, Sheriff, would you stop?"

Jessup sat on the recliner near her.

Her eyes shifted to him. "My father?"

"Yeah."

"How?"

"If I had to guess, I'd say suffocation. Nothing is confirmed yet."

She lowered her head and began crying again. "Why would someone do something like that?"

Jessup leaned forward and asked, "When is the last time you spoke with your niece?"

"Crystal? It's been a while. Why?"

"Is she close to your father? Her grandfather?"

Adeline shrugged. "Not really, no. They visited him a couple of times last year. Before then, not so much."

"They?"

"Crystal and Casey. They're young. Not many young people are close with their grandparents, are they?"

"Who is Casey?"

"Crystal's brother. My nephew."

Burglars, Jessup thought. *Plural. Brother and sister. There were burglars in Derwood Smith's house.*

"Why do you ask about Crystal?"

"Because we believe she is involved in killing your uncles. Maybe Casey, too."

Adeline wiped away her tears. "What?"

"Remember, I asked about a trust?"

She nodded.

"Your father was part of a trust with his brothers. It was set up by your grandfather."

She blinked several times.

"Your grandfather left it to him and his brothers."

"My father… he never told us."

"Your niece, Crystal, is working for the trust attorney."

"I don't understand."

"Neither do we. Not entirely. We'd like to talk with her, but we haven't found her yet."

Adeline shook her head. "She's a good person. She wouldn't be involved with this."

Jessup watched her, studying her reaction.

"What about Casey?" he asked.

"I can't imagine either of them doing this."

"Got addresses for them?"

Adeline nodded and opened her phone. She pulled her notebook to her and wrote down the addresses for her niece and nephew. When she was done, she tore the sheet off and handed it to Jessup. "Do you really think they're involved?"

"I don't know. It's a strange coincidence she was working for the trust attorney, the only one who knew how the trust worked. Crystal had access to that file. Then your uncles started dying."

"So you do think she's involved." A look of disgust passed over Adeline's face. "What does killing them, killing my father, her grandfather, get her?"

"The trust was structured so the last surviving brother got everything."

Adeline gazed at Jessup.

"Everything in the trust went to your father."

"How much?"

"We don't know for sure. Millions. Tens of millions, maybe."

Her face pinched. "Why would someone set up a trust like that?"

Jessup shrugged. "Who knows? And that's a discussion for another day. What we need now is to find where Crystal and Casey are."

"You think they'll go to my brother's house? Should we warn him?"

"I don't think they'll hurt him. Not now, at least. I think they would come after you first."

She lifted a hand to her chest. *"Why?"*

"You said your father had a will, and you're splitting it fifty/fifty."

"Right."

"Knowing that, you would be the next logical target."

"Why would they want to hurt me?"

"You don't have any children, correct?"

She shook her head.

"To put it bluntly, if you're out of the picture, then everything should go to your brother, which would then flow to his children."

"No. I won't accept that. I've been good to them. They wouldn't do something like that."

Jessup's cell phone rang. After checking the caller ID screen, he said, "Excuse me," and stepped away to answer the call.

"Jessup," he said. "Sorry, I meant to call you back."

"No problem," Marci said, "but this is important, and I didn't want to let it sit until tomorrow."

"Okay."

"Long story, but we've found Crystal Braemar."

"Great," Jessup said. "Did you know she has a brother?"

"Damn. We didn't tell you about him, did we?"

Jessup lowered his head. "No, you didn't. I just learned about him."

"How?"

"Adeline Smith. She told me."

"You're talking with her?"

"Uh-huh."

"She's with you now?"

"That's right."

"Last time we talked, you couldn't rule her out. What's your gut say now?"

Jessup watched Adeline as she stared off into the distance, lost in her thoughts.

"Clear," he said.

"You think she's in the clear on this?"

"That's right," Jessup said, being careful not to reveal too much.

"Well, we've caught Crystal today. Her brother is still missing. I'm almost positive they're involved, Tom. We wanted to let you know. Dude, I'm really sorry we forgot to tell you about Casey. We just learned about him, too."

"No worries. I get it. Information comes quick, and we're sixty miles apart. You going to make a run at her tonight?"

"We're just getting started. We'll be at it for a while if you want to come on up."

Jessup thought about it for a second, then said, "I'll be up in the morning. We'll touch base then." He hung up and looked at Adeline. "They've arrested Crystal."

"You really think she's a part of this?

"The Spokane Police Department does. I tend to believe them."

She looked down for a moment, then back up. "Can I see my father?"

"I can arrange that, but not right now. Later, okay?" He turned toward the door.

"Sheriff?"

He looked back.

"I'm sorry for lying. I was just… embarrassed."

Jessup nodded, stepped outside, and shut the door.

Chapter 44

Detective Marci Burkett waited as Crystal Braemar sipped her coffee, her eyes peering over the rim of the cup as she drank. Marci had just read the Miranda Warning to Crystal and asked if she understood the rights as they were read to her.

Crystal was seated, unhandcuffed, in the interview room of the detectives' office. For officer safety, most suspects would be handcuffed to a rail along the wall, but Marci and Quinn had decided beforehand to let her feel more comfortable in her interview. She had displayed a certain level of attitude on the way into the station, and they wanted her to remain confident.

When Crystal lowered her Styrofoam coffee cup, she said, "I understand my rights."

"Will you waive those rights and speak to me?"

Again, the younger woman lifted her coffee cup to her face. Marci watched for movement in her throat. Not seeing any, she inwardly smiled. She was stalling.

Marci's eyes drifted to Quinn, who leaned against the far wall, his arms crossed over his chest, feigning a look of disinterest.

Crystal put her cup on the table and said, "I'll talk."

Marci pointed to the red light on the far wall. "We're being recorded, both audio and visual. Understand?"

"Yeah, sure," Crystal said.

"Your father is Heath Smith, correct?"

The younger woman stared at Marci.

"I can answer that for you. Yes. Yes, your father is Heath Smith. See how easy that was?"

"If you can answer these questions, why am I here?"

"Because there are some that I'll need your help with. Here's another I can answer. Is Casey Braemar your brother?"

Crystal's face remained impassive.

"Yes," Marci said, "Casey Braemar is your brother. See? Two questions in and we already have two affirmative, truthful answers. This is going well."

Crystal reached for her coffee.

"When was the last time you spoke with your Aunt Adeline?"

Her brow furrowed. "What?"

"Or does she go by Addy?"

"Why does that matter?"

"Maybe it doesn't. I don't know yet. That's why I'm asking."

"It's been a while, I guess. Months maybe."

"What about your great uncles?"

"What?" Crystal said, then slowly sucked her lips into her mouth.

"Your great uncles," Marci said, looking down to consult her notes, "Leland, Clayton, and Renard."

Crystal pushed her lips out and asked, "You building my family tree or something?"

"When was the last time you've been in contact with them?"

"I haven't."

"Never?"

"No."

"Why not?"

"That's not how we were raised."

"Did you know where they lived?"

"Why would I?"

"Do you remember when we met at Ezra Baumbach's office?"

"I remember."

"We were there to talk about a trust that your great-grandfather left to his sons."

Crystal lifted the coffee cup to her mouth. "A trust?"

"You don't know what a trust is?"

The female Braemar held the cup before her lips for a moment without taking a sip, then placed it back on the table. "I know what a trust is, sure."

"The paperwork for this particular trust was at Ezra's office, but you knew that because you already saw it, which means you knew where your great uncles lived."

Crystal crossed her arms. "I didn't look through every file. I have no idea that the file you're talking about even exists."

Quinn coughed slightly to enter the conversation. They both looked his way.

"What did you do before you worked at Ezra's office?" Quinn asked.

Marci turned back to Crystal. "Good question. What *did* you do?"

"I was an office manager."

Marci's pen hovered over her notepad. "Where at?"

"What?"

"Where? We'd like to call and confirm."

"Is this now a job interview?"

"We'd like to know what qualified you to get a job with Ezra Baumbach."

"I was qualified. Besides, why does that matter?"

"We get to decide what matters," Marci said.

"It's irrelevant," Crystal said. "Ezra could hire who he wanted."

The two women stared at each other for several seconds until Crystal said, "Lilac City Coffee."

Marci started writing, paused, then finished. She set her pen down and looked up. "You were an office manager for Lilac City Coffee?"

"Yes."

"And that qualified you to assist Mr. Baumbach?"

"I did more at LCC than I do for Ezra."

"I don't doubt it," Marci said. "How much did you make at the coffee company?"

"What?"

"It's a simple question. Did you make more money or less as an office manager? I see their coffee stands around town, plus I know they do their own roasting, right? They're selling beans to other stands, so I would imagine there's distribution to worry about. It seems they would pay you more than a one-man attorney's office could."

Crystal put her hand around the coffee cup. "I was burned out. I needed a break."

"So, you went to an attorney's office?"

"Yes."

"The one attorney in the entire county handling the trust for your grandfather?"

"It was a coincidence."

"What a big one," Marci said. "When did you first learn about the trust?"

"I don't know what you're talking about," Crystal said, and half shrugged. "I just learned about it from you."

"I don't believe you."

"That's your problem."

"Actually," Marci said, "it's *your* problem."

"What do you mean?"

"It's motive for murder."

"Murder?" Crystal said flatly.

"Your great uncles were murdered."

The younger woman questioningly lifted her eyebrows.

"I can see you're broken up about it."

"I didn't know them," Crystal said. "Why should I get broken up about it? That's like reading an obituary in the newspaper and getting upset. That would be stupid."

Quinn's phone buzzed, and he checked the caller ID screen. He then stepped out of the interview room.

"So the trust is motive for the murders," Marci said, "and we've narrowed it down to four people: you, your brother, your aunt, and your father."

"I think you need to widen your search," Crystal said.

"We believe we're right on target. We also believe we can clear your father."

"That's good," Crystal said. "He wouldn't be involved in something like you're suggesting."

"Yeah, he's kind of messed up."

"He was in an accident!"

Marci held up her hands. "Relax. I'm sorry. I was just saying these murders took some planning, some coordination. Your father doesn't seem to be the type who could pull that off."

Crystal eyed Marci with disdain.

"And your aunt, well, we haven't met her, but there's a local sheriff who's vouching for her."

Crystal's eyes slanted further.

"So that leaves you and your brother."

Quinn stepped back into the room, closed the door, and smiled.

"Something to share?" Marci asked.

"We caught her brother."

"*What?*" Crystal said.

"He's at the hospital now."

"Is he okay?" Crystal asked, worry now on her face.

"He'll live, but he's dinged up. He fought with a detective, and it sounds like it didn't go well."

Crystal's demeanor changed at that moment. She suddenly looked cornered.

"This plan. Was it his or yours?" Marci asked.

"I don't know what you're talking about," Crystal said.

"Sure, you do. One of you found out about the trust fund. Maybe while visiting your grandfather. You did that, right? That's the only point where we can figure you would have seen any information on it. Then one of you broke into Ezra's office to find the paperwork. Once you realized how the trust was structured, you decided to take action. Kill all your uncles until only your grandfather was left, which guaranteed the inheritance would come down your family line. To both of you." Marci pointed at her. "And sooner rather than later, I'm thinking."

Crystal remained silent as Marci spoke.

"Your employment at Mr. Baumbach's office is a red flag. Any prosecutor will build a case around that. Even if it's considered circumstantial, they'll describe the break-in at Mr. Baumbach's office and the death of his assistant prior to your arrival. Your insistence on being hired after leaving a higher-paying job will also look bad. See how this puts you in a suspicious light?"

Crystal stared into her coffee cup.

"If you don't give us something to work with, we'll paint the picture as an equal partnership. Brother and sister working together to steal the family legacy."

"What he did wasn't right," she whispered.

"Who? Casey?"

"My great-grandfather," Crystal said, her voice still soft. "Why would he do that? Why would he set a trust up like that? It wasn't fair."

Marci's voice softened when she said, "No, it wasn't fair. It's really cruel, isn't it?"

"Yeah. That's what it was. Cruel. Those brothers were lucky they didn't know how the trust was built. If they did, don't you think they would root for each other's deaths?"

"Maybe that's why it was kept secret?" Marci asked, her voice low.

"Maybe," Crystal said, thinking. "Probably. Yeah."

"How did you find out about the trust? At your grandfather's?"

Crystal nodded. "I saw a check from it. He refused to talk about it when I brought it up. It said *Smith Family Trust*. I wanted to know what it was, but he wouldn't tell me."

"So you saw where the check was from, and that's why you broke into Baumbach's office."

Crystal lifted the coffee cup and swallowed the last of the remaining liquid. She slid the cup away from her. She didn't look up.

"Ezra's?" Marci prompted. "You broke into his office to find out about that check?"

She nodded. "With Casey, yeah. He knows how to do that stuff. We found the file on the trust and photocopied it while we were there. We made a mess afterward, you know? To make it look like someone broke in looking for something else."

"That's when you realized how the trust worked. That if your grandfather died before his brothers, your family—your father—would get nothing."

She nodded.

"Is that when you decided to kill Baumbach's assistant?"

Crystal remained silent.

"Is that when—"

"I don't know what you're talking about."

Marci breezed past her denial. "After his assistant's death, you waited and watched Ezra's office, knowing he would need a new one. Then you showed up with your resume in hand, refusing to leave."

She stared at Marci.

"Why kill the assistant? To get a job at the attorney's office? It doesn't make sense."

Crystal shrugged.

Quinn coughed slightly again before entering the conversation. "The deaths were months apart. You needed a way to control the information flow to and from the attorney as well as the remaining brothers. They weren't communicating, and you wanted to stop them from having a reason to start doing so now."

Marci nodded and turned to the younger woman. "That's why. You did it so if any notice came into the office, you could intercept it before it made it to Ezra. You wanted to keep him in the dark as long as possible."

Crystal tried to maintain eye contact with Marci, but her eyes eventually dropped down to the table.

"The question I've been waiting to ask, the one I'm having the most trouble with," Marci said, "is why kill your grandfather?"

"What?" Crystal asked, her face scrunching.

"I mean, you would have to kill him at some point. Or if you're lucky, he dies in his sleep. But doing it now means everything is going to be split between your aunt and father now. It's stupid after all the killings you just did. The family fortune is cut in half. Unless that's what you wanted all along. Are you close to your aunt?"

Crystal blinked several times.

"If you killed her first, then the entire trust would have gone to your father and later down to you. That seems like the smartest play."

"My grandfather is… dead?"

Marci nodded. "Yeah. He was murdered. It looks like suffocation. Similar to how we suspect you killed Renard."

Crystal's face reddened. "You're lying."

"I wouldn't lie about that," Marci said. "This is serious."

The female Braemar looked to Quinn, who nodded in agreement.

"Why would he... I don't..." Crystal said, "I... I'm done."

"What?"

"I'm done talking. Book me or let me go."

"Just a couple more questions," Marci said.

"I want to talk with an attorney," Crystal said. Tears welled in her eyes. "I don't want to answer any more questions."

Chapter 45

The mid-morning sun felt good on James Morgan's face as he strode toward Deaconess Hospital. Inside, he stopped at the security checkpoint and flashed his badge. The on-duty guard nodded once and motioned for him to pass.

Morgan stepped around the metal detector and headed into the emergency room, where he approached the nurses' desk. A dark-haired woman with tired eyes ignored him for a few moments as she finished writing something on a chart. When she was done, she looked up.

"Casey Braemar," Morgan said. "Brought in last night with a missing ear."

Her fingers swept over her keyboard. "Seventh floor," she said and returned to her previous task.

When the elevator doors opened, Morgan spotted an officer sitting at the far end of the hall. His head was bent over a paperback novel.

The officer, Lee Sheets, heard the detective approach and closed his book.

Morgan extended his hand, and Sheets shook it. "How's the battle?"

"Getting paid to read isn't bad."

Morgan looked through the small window in the heavy door. Inside the room was Casey Braemar. He lay on the bed with his head bandaged in gauze, his wrist shackled to the bed frame.

Before leaving for the night, Morgan was advised Braemar would likely be in surgery for hours. When the detective woke up this morning, he phoned the hospital for an update and, as advised, Braemar had been under the knife for more than four hours and would be required to stay in the hospital for up to a week. He then talked with Quinn Delaney, who said he and Burkett were headed in later to conduct a preliminary interview.

"How's he doing?"

"Okay, I guess," Sheets said, standing to look through the little window with Morgan. "The nurses have been in and out all morning. You really did a number on him."

Morgan eyed his fellow officer in disbelief. Last night, he had taken considerable heat from the on-duty lieutenant for the use of force. Now he was taking crap from a patrol lifer? "He was choking me out. The hell was I supposed to do?"

"Relax, Morgan, I'm not beefing you. I don't think I would have thought of it at that moment. I guess we'll discuss this at a training day now."

The detective slowly nodded, not fully believing the backpedaling explanation. "Yeah, well, that's what I need to be—another teachable moment for the department. Can I wake him?"

"Ask her."

Morgan turned to see an older woman in pink scrubs approaching him from behind. She brushed by, pushed the door into an open position, and hurried into the room. Braemar opened his eyes, and they exchanged some words. He noticed the detective standing outside the room before returning his attention to the nurse.

"Have the Glory Hounds shown up yet?" Morgan asked.

"Who?" Dan asked.

"Delaney and Burkett."

"I didn't know they were supposed to."

Morgan continued to watch the interaction between Braemar and the nurse.

"You don't like them?" Sheets asked.

"Who?"

"Delaney and Burkett."

Morgan smirked and looked at the officer. "Who does?"

Sheets thought about it for a moment, then said, "I guess I do."

"You guess a lot."

"What?"

As the nurse left the room, Morgan stopped her. "Any medical reason I can't ask him some questions?"

The woman eyed Morgan with disdain before walking away.

"I'll take that non-answer as permission."

"What did you do to her?" Sheets asked.

"Who knows? She's probably some libtard who feels this turd shouldn't have been treated rough while he tried to kill me."

Morgan stepped into the room, closed the door behind him, and approached the bed. Braemar's eyes were closed.

"Let's talk," Morgan said.

Braemar didn't open his eyes.

"I know you're awake. I saw you talking with the nurse."

No reaction.

"C'mon, man, are you hard of hearing?" Morgan asked with a chuckle. "Jeez, those jokes will never get old."

Braemar's eyes slowly opened. "You're the guy."

"Yeah," Morgan said, tapping his chest. "I'm the guy."

"When I get out of here, I'm going to kill you."

"You don't even know who I am."

"I'll find out."

"How about I tell you? It'll give you a head start."

Braemar stared at him.

"I'm Detective James Frederick Morgan with the Spokane Police Department. I'm not going to give you my home address, because that would make it too easy for you, but if you're enterprising enough, which I think you are, you can find it on your own and come get me."

"James Frederick Morgan," Braemar repeated softly.

"That's right. You can call me Morgan. All my friends do."

The two men stared at each other.

Morgan smirked. "I'd apologize for what I did to you last night, but you left me no other choice."

Braemar sniffed dismissively.

"I gotta say, you are clearly the better fighter. Did they teach you that stuff in Pararescue?"

The younger man's left eyebrow lifted.

"No, huh? You learned that somewhere else along the way?" Morgan gave him a grudging nod of admiration. "You're good. I'll give you that. I was going to lose, and I didn't know what would have happened then. You might have taken my gun and shot me. Would you have done that? Shot me?"

Braemar didn't answer. Instead, he looked toward the window and the unseasonably blue sky that had arrived for the day. Morgan checked it out as well.

When he turned back to Braemar, he asked, "You don't have to answer that question. It doesn't matter, anyway. You're under arrest for the assault."

Braemar turned to him. "You broke into my house."

"What do you mean? I wasn't in your house."

"Yes, you were. You were there when I got home."

"You're mistaken. Maybe you sustained a concussion during our fight, and it messed up your sense of time. Let me tell you how this went down. I followed you, a murder suspect, to your house. When I confronted you, you became violent. You got the upper hand, took me down, assaulted me. I've got the bruises to confirm it." Morgan pointed at his face.

"That's not what happened."

"Then I was afraid you would render me unconscious and kill me with my own gun. I did the only thing I could think of at the time, which was pull your ear off."

Braemar winced.

"Once I was free from your grasp, I called for medical assistance, and you were transported here, where they reattached your ear. Everything is going to work out okay. It may take a few surgeries, but they'll make you look pretty again. You might have to grow your hair longer to cover some scars, but worse things have happened. Right?"

"You were in my house," Braemar repeated.

"You're missing the point. Do you know what Third Degree Assault is? By the look on your face, I'm assuming you don't. To make it simple, let's just call it assaulting a law enforcement officer."

"Who was in my house. *Illegally.*"

"I identified myself as a detective of the Spokane Police Department when I was at your back door."

Confusion flashed over Braemar's face. "No, you didn't. That's a lie."

"I said very loudly, and clearly, I might add, 'I'm Detective James Morgan of the Spokane Police Department.' Then you attacked me. Just like that. Bam bam. There was no time to think. It happened so fast. You were either trying to hide something or run away, I don't know, but you attacked me with such ferocity that you easily overwhelmed me. I immediately believed my life was in danger."

"No," Braemar said, shaking his head. "That's not true."

"As I was saying, Third Degree Assault, also known as assaulting a law enforcement officer, is a felony. It's so easy to prove, too. I mean, I'm a law enforcement officer. We can check that box. I've been assaulted. Check that box, too. That's it. All the elements of the crime are right there. Now, we might be able to push the assault to a higher level, like Second Degree, due to what you tried to do—in other words, kill me—but regardless, we've got Third Assault locked down." Morgan snapped his fingers. "It's a done deal. Felony."

Braemar glared at Morgan. "You're corrupt."

"I'm a cop."

They sat quietly for a moment. Both men were lost in their thoughts. However, Braemar's thoughts turned his face red, and his jaw clenched.

Morgan said, "I can see you're upset about me being inside your house."

"Yeah."

"And for tearing off your ear?"

"Obviously."

"But you didn't get bothered when I called you a murder suspect."

Braemar stared at Morgan and blinked several times.

"Just so you're aware, you don't have to say anything about the murders if you don't want to. We've got you. We've got your sister already."

"Crystal?"

"She talked."

Braemar started to say something but closed his mouth. He struggled to hide the emotions that played behind his eyes.

"I can see what you're thinking. You probably planned this scenario out, right? If either of you were ever caught, don't say anything. Don't ever say anything because it was planned so well. The problem is she wasn't built for this life. You were. I am. She wasn't."

Braemar turned toward the window.

"She started off tough. It was clear she had some coaching, but eventually, she talked. They all do except maybe you. I figure you won't say a word due to your survival training. Like, you've been through simulated torture, right? Don't they waterboard you there? After that, anything we can do to you will seem like child's play."

Beads of sweat formed above Braemar's lip.

"Except we don't do torture. We build cases, especially the detectives you're going up against. They're the best. They've got a couple of witnesses tying you to Rado Jones. I found them, just so you know. I'm sort of a bloodhound, but you probably realized that now. You were good at making sure there was no DNA tying you to his murder. You did nice work, by the way. However, with your sister cracking and our witnesses tying you to him, the dominos are falling. You can be completely uncooperative; you'll go to prison without ever saying a word in your defense."

Braemar struggled to swallow. "Bullshit."

"Maybe," Morgan said and leaned against the far wall. "And you should probably play it that way, except you didn't ask who Rado was, so I'm going with the fact that you knew him."

They sat in silence for a few seconds. It was then Morgan noticed the ticking of the wall clock. He started counting the clicks, letting it get to thirty before he spoke again.

"We found your car, by the way, parked on the opposite side of the tracks at Fourteenth and Chestnut. You had to hump it up the hill to get home, but it was a nice job hiding it. It took us a little work to locate it.

Sweet ride. I haven't had a classic like that since high school. Makes me sort of want to get one again. Did you wipe it down after Rado was in it?"

Braemar licked his lips as he thought about Morgan's words.

"It doesn't matter if you did or didn't, because we impounded it. They're pulling prints today, probably right now as we speak. They'll find Rado's prints, right? You didn't wipe it down after he was with you in that car. Seems sort of innocuous, right? Oh, wait, you didn't put him in the trunk, did you? Tell me you didn't do that. Even if you were super careful, there's always some transfer of evidence. Given your meticulous nature, I'll pretend the trunk is clean, but by the look in your eyes, we're going to find Rado's prints in the car. He touched something, a window, a handle, the dash, something. They'll find it."

"It won't mean anything."

"Sure, it will. We have your sister's taped testimony. With that, we'll have witnesses that place you with Rado, talking about the killing of the Smith couple, in your car. The noose is getting tighter. Then we walk back to the Smith couple."

"What if I tell them about you being in my house? About you lying?"

"It's your word against mine, and I'm not the guy facing murder charges. Crying about me being in your house seems like an odd deflection, don't you think?"

Casey Braemar stared at the detective.

"Do you want my opinion?"

"Not really, no."

"Tell the truth," Morgan said. "Your version of it, at least. Tell them it was all about getting back at your father. I don't know. You're a smart guy. You'll see the angle once it presents itself. If they ask about our altercation, tell the truth the way I told you. If you do that, I won't press charges on it."

"It sounds like I've got bigger problems than assaulting a cop."

Morgan laughed. "You do, for sure."

Braemar studied Morgan for a moment, then said. "Why are you here?"

"Because you killed some people, then fought with me last night."

"No, I mean right now. This isn't an interview. You just told me the detectives are on the way. So why are you here?"

Morgan nodded. "I'm here for Rado."

"The junkie? What's he matter?"

"He mattered to me," Morgan said, crossing his arms. "I owed him."

The door to the room swung open, and Quinn Delaney stepped in. Marci Burkett was on his heels. They both looked suspiciously at Morgan, who leaned against the far wall, his arms crossed over his chest.

"What's going on?" Quinn said.

"I'm here for the interview," Morgan said.

Quinn waved at Morgan to follow him outside, and he left the room with Marci by his side.

Morgan said to Braemar, "Gotta go."

As he passed the door, Morgan pulled it closed behind him. Quinn and Marci were down the hall away from the front of Braemar's room and out of earshot of Officer Sheets.

"What are you doing here? This is our interview," Quinn said as his face reddened. "We told you that on the phone."

"I know."

"Did you read him his rights?" Marci asked.

"No. We were just talking."

Quinn's face tightened. "I said you could witness it, not lead it."

"I wasn't. I was making small talk with the guy."

"With a killer? A guy who assaulted you?"

"I was building rapport."

"Rapport?" Quinn said. "Are you dense, Morgan? You aren't interviewing him. You don't need rapport."

Morgan clicked his tongue against the roof of his mouth. "You two ding-dongs are lucky you even have this guy. If it wasn't for me, you'd still be standing around holding your dicks hoping to find him."

Marci started to say something, but Morgan waved her off. "Listen," he said, "the kid thinks his sister talked."

"What?" she asked.

"You're welcome, princess. I set him up. All you gotta do is go in there and let him believe that. Walk him into it nice and slow. Especially play up the Rado Jones angle. He's locked down on that one. He knows he's done for with that murder."

Quinn and Marci glanced at each other.

"This is where you say thank you."

The two Homicide detectives said simultaneously, "No."

They then turned and headed back toward Braemar's room.

Morgan grinned. It was going to be a good day.

Chapter 46

Quinn held the door for Marci as she entered the hospital room. He pulled the door closed and joined his partner at the foot of the bed. Casey Braemar looked at them both expectantly.

"Mr. Braemar, I'm Detective Delaney. This is my partner, Detective Burkett. We'd like to talk with you."

Braemar didn't react.

"Since you're already in custody, I need to read you your rights. Were your rights read to you last night?"

Braemar's eyes moved from Quinn to the window.

Quinn pulled out a Miranda Warning card and began, "You have the right to remain silent. Anything you say, can and will be used against you in a court of law. You have the right at this time to talk to a lawyer and have him present with you while you are being questioned. If you cannot afford to hire a lawyer, one will be appointed to represent you before questioning if you wish. You can decide at any time to exercise these rights and not answer any questions or make any statements. Do you understand each of these rights I have explained to you?"

Braemar did not look at Quinn, but muttered, "Yeah."

"Having these rights in mind, do you wish to talk with me now?"

Stifling a yawn, Braemar said, "Not really."

"Not really?"

Braemar turned back to face Quinn. "I'm stuck in here after that psycho detective ripped my ear off. Now you're here to charge me with some made-up crime, right? So no, I'm not really in a mood to talk with you."

Quinn repeatedly flipped the white card over in his hand while he studied Braemar. Marci moved over to the window and looked down.

"What?" Braemar asked. "Giving me the silent treatment now?"

"You said you didn't want to talk," Quinn said. "We're respecting that."

"It's high up here," Marci said, keeping her focus outside. "We're on the seventh floor, right?"

Quinn walked over to look out the window.

"Remember the jumper?" Marci asked. "The one from the Paulsen Building? That was fifteen floors, double this. Can you imagine that fall?"

Quinn shook his head. "I can't imagine doing something like that. Sort of selfish."

Marci whistled and then smacked her hands together.

"That's not going to work," Braemar said.

"What?" Quinn asked, turning back from the window.

"Trying to disassociate me, make me feel isolated. I know the tricks that you're using."

Marci faced him and smirked. "Dude, we don't get to be in high buildings very often. Sometimes it's cool to look out a window. Don't be so narcissistic."

Quinn shook his head. "It's not narcissism. Perhaps self-absorption."

"Really?" Marci said.

"Yeah, really. They're two different things."

"No, they're not."

"They are. Narcissism is a grandiose belief in one's self. Self-absorption is being preoccupied with yourself. Two different things."

"You're making that up," Marci said. "I bet if you looked it up in a thesaurus, you'd see self-absorption listed right under narcissism."

"You're doing it again," Braemar said.

Marci turned to him. "What?"

"Now, you're trying to minimize me, to make me feel small and ineffectual."

Marci laughed. "Oh my God, you must be hell to go out with. Do you always get your feelings hurt like this?"

Braemar's face scrunched. "My feelings aren't hurt, lady. I'm just pointing out what you're doing. I'm going to see whatever you're doing and be able to counter it or withstand it."

Marci looked at her partner, and at that moment, they both knew who should lead the interview. Braemar wasn't interested in talking with Quinn, but he couldn't resist engaging with Marci. Quinn exaggeratedly rolled his eyes to let Marci know he would participate in the conversation silently. She was going to carry the weight from now on.

"See!" Braemar said, "That's what I'm talking about. The eyeroll is so obvious."

"Quit being such a dick," Marci said. "Not everything is about you. Does any woman stay with you long?"

"Now you're attacking my masculinity. The game you're playing isn't going to work."

"Geez, dude," Marci said, "you're winding up, and I'm not even asking you a question. Why don't you chill for a second and calm down?"

Braemar was breathing heavily and looking between the two detectives.

"You better?" Marci asked. "I mean, if you need another minute to get control, I can give you one."

"I'm fine," Braemar said through clenched teeth.

Marci nodded. "So last night—"

"I said I didn't want to answer any of your questions."

"Dude, I was only going to ask about your fight. We're Homicide detectives, and we couldn't care less about that assault you had with that detective, but the fight itself interests me. I'm something of a fighter myself."

"You?"

"Yeah."

"Really?" Braemar looked to Quinn.

"The guy that tore your ear off? Even he won't fight her."

Marci shrugged. "I'm nice that way."

Braemar stared at her.

"I'm always interested in meeting a fellow fighter. Where did you study?"

"What?"

"C'mon, man," Marci said, snapping her fingers, "keep up. What style?"

"Ju-jitsu."

"Who's your instructor?"

"What?"

Marci glanced at her partner. "Am I stuttering?

"I hear you fine," Quinn said.

She looked back at Braemar. "Who's your instructor?"

"I didn't have one."

A feigned look of shock passed over Marci's face. "You didn't have one? I thought you told people at that boxing gym you did."

"What?"

Marci blinked exaggeratedly several times.

Braemar's face flushed.

"You lied to them? To a gym full of boxers?"

The younger man remained silent.

A slow, mischievous smile grew on Marci's face. "So, where did you learn to fight?"

"My training," Braemar said.

"The Army, right?"

"Air Force."

"Oh," Marci said, that single word filled with disappointment.

"What?" Braemar said.

"Nothing," she said, shaking her head. "It's fine."

"What?" he repeated.

"The Air Force. You learned how to fight in *the Air Force*."

Braemar's face reddened. "I see what you're doing."

Marci chuckled. "Relax, man. I make fun of everyone's fighting skills. Don't get your panties in a bunch."

The younger man glanced at Quinn, who remained impassive. When he turned back to Marci, he said, "My head is hurting. You should leave."

"You're pussing out?" Marci turned to Quinn, a look of disbelief on her face. "This guy is already pussing out."

"No," Braemar said, "It's just that—"

"We haven't even tried interviewing you, and you're already pussing out. I would have at least thought a man as supposedly tough as you are could have made it through a little razzing before tapping out."

Braemar's face purpled.

"Am I wrong?"

Casey Braemar pursed his lips.

"You want us to leave?" Marci asked.

Braemar closed his eyes and inhaled deeply.

"Let me ask you one question. This one is bothering me and my partner. Crystal didn't have an answer for it. It really stumped her. Actually, it left her crying, so I want to know what you think."

Braemar slowly opened his eyes and relaxed. "You're messing with me."

"No. Real deal." Marci raised her hand. "Hand to God."

It took several seconds before Braemar asked, "What?"

"After all the scheming and the murders, to set the mechanisms of the blind trust into motion, why kill your grandfather? I mean, he would die soon enough, right? At that point, it would have been natural causes, and nobody would have suspected anything—one less chance of getting caught. Then the money would go to your father and your aunt. Also, were you planning to kill her? Oh, that's a second question. Sorry. Stick with the first one. Why kill your grandfather?"

Quinn saw it at once. As Marci spoke, the realization of Derwood Smith's death sunk in on Braemar.

"My grandfather is dead?"

"Duh," Marci said. "Why kill him?"

Braemar shook his head. "No. This is a mental game. You're messing with me."

Quinn pulled out his phone and stepped over to Braemar. "This," he said, "is an email from the investigating agency, the Whitman County Sheriff's Office. Your grandfather was murdered. Our initial belief is that he was suffocated to death. It's how we believe his brother Renard was murdered."

Braemar looked up at Quinn, then to Marci. "We didn't..." he said very softly.

"Well, someone did," Marci said.

"You could have faked those pictures."

"We didn't."

"You could have," Braemar whispered.

"And man did not land on the moon," Marci said. "Don't be dense, dude. Your grandfather is dead, and we're not making it up. Why would you kill him? It doesn't make sense with how bad his health is. It's overkill. Sloppy even. Especially after all the planning that you put into the other ones."

"I loved my grandfather."

Marci glanced at Quinn. "I don't know."

Braemar blurted, "Why? What did Crystal say?"

Marci turned her attention back to the injured man. "She said you two were responsible for the others, but your grandfather wasn't part of the plan. Unless you went rogue and killed him yourself. She didn't think you would do that, but we aren't so sure."

Braemar remained silent.

"It was important for her to understand why you would do it. *If* you did it. She was worried that maybe you liked it too much."

"It?"

"Killing," Marci said.

Braemar's eyes dropped while he thought.

Quinn took this as a signal to re-enter the conversation, to give Braemar the false hope of a lifeline. "If you didn't kill him, then who did?"

Braemar stared at his hands and thought. Both Quinn and Marci remained silent. The hum of fluorescent lights filled the room.

His words were so soft that both detectives initially missed them.

"What?" Marci said and leaned forward. Quinn leaned forward as well.

"I loved my grandfather."

Marci nodded. "You've said that."

"I could never hurt him."

"But the others…"

Braemar sighed and nodded. He looked up at the two detectives. "If I tell you what you want to know, you've got to promise me something."

Quinn and Marci stared at him, both knowing better than to promise a murderer anything.

"You've got to find who did this to my grandfather."

Chapter 47

Tom Jessup's brow furrowed in concentration as he reviewed the latest budget report, a task he hated, but which was unfortunately necessary. When his phone rang, he was thankful for the interruption.

He answered the call and said with a little too much enthusiasm, "Jessup."

Marci Burkett laughed on the other end of the line. "Hey, Tom."

The sheriff leaned back in his chair and looked up at the ceiling. "Hey, Marci, thank you for the interruption."

"Working on something important?"

"Budgets."

"Ugh. I forgot you're one of them. The brass."

"It's not all the glory everyone thinks it is," Jessup said. "So, are you calling to tell me we're wrapped up? That you and your partner caught the killers, and they confessed to the evils of their ways?"

"Almost."

Jessup was immediately concerned about the tone in her voice. "That doesn't sound particularly good. What's that mean, *almost*?"

"We've tied them to four killings."

"So, we're done."

"No. We've confirmed Renard Smith's death—"

Jessup's heart sank when he heard that Renard Smith was indeed murdered. Initially, he thought it was a natural death and only later suspected it might have been due to unnatural causes. He had still held hope his first hunch would have proven right.

"—Clayton and his wife, and Cadillac Jones."

"That leaves Leland and Derwood."

"It seems Leland died naturally."

"Wait. Wasn't the woman, Crystal, wasn't she already working for the attorney by then?"

"She was. Call it fate or luck. No, let's not call it luck. It was fate. Leland had a heart attack and died in his home. The siblings were already putting their plan into place, trying to figure out what they were going to do when the first brother passed. Suddenly, they had to move."

"Huh."

"That's when they killed Renard."

Jessup closed his eyes. "Yeah," he muttered.

"They didn't think they could get away with quiet deaths for both Clayton and Helen, so they went the opposite direction. They made it messy."

Jessup leaned back in his chair and looked up at the ceiling. "These kids, they graduated to killers pretty quick, didn't they?"

"We think they may have killed Ezra Baumbach's former assistant and her husband, but we're still looking into that. They died in a hiking accident. That's how Crystal got the job."

"That's more than four killings. We're up to six."

"Right," Marci said, "six."

"But what about Derwood? Why wouldn't they admit to his? He was the lynchpin to them getting the family fortune."

"According to the brother, that's not what they wanted. It seems they loved their grandfather and knew of his condition. He was going to pass soon enough. They just wanted to protect the family legacy."

Jessup dropped his chair forward. "Huh."

"We couldn't get either of them to admit they would hurt the aunt. It's possible they expected her to leave her portion of the fortune to them when she eventually passed. Who knows? We suspect there was a plan to do her, but they wouldn't cop to it. They also both denied there were plans to hurt their father. They just wanted the fortune to pass to their family, so maybe the thing about the aunt was true. Half of something is better than half of nothing. Especially of something that big. So the question remains…"

"Who killed Derwood Smith?"

***

When Tom Jessup banged on the front door of the house, there was no answer. Lupita's red Toyota wasn't in front. He walked around to the back of the house and saw no car parked there.

He looked into a window of the house. It was full of contents, but everything looked eerily still.

Jessup returned to the front of the house and stood with his hands on his hips.

Before coming to check on Lupita, he had tried phoning her, but the call had again gone straight to voicemail. Maybe something bad had happened to her. After she had called him, perhaps the people who had been inside Derwood Smith's house had grabbed her and taken her car. He still hadn't been able to talk with her and get a description of what the attackers looked like. He had put out an Attempt to Locate, but no one had found her.

He pulled out his cell phone and called her once more. This time he was greeted with a new message. "This wireless subscriber you are trying to reach is no longer receiving calls."

Jessup called the station, and Autumn answered on the first ring.

"Do me a favor and look up the legal owner of this house," Jessup said and gave her the address.

He could hear her typing on her computer. In a moment, she said, "Gilbert Hartley. He also lives in Garfield. I'll text you his address."

Jessup's phone beeped in his ear. He pulled it away and saw the address. It was only a couple of blocks from where he was. He put the phone back to his ear. "Thanks, kid."

"Need a backup unit?"

"I'm fine."

Gilbert Hartley was in his early eighties and hunched over. He wore a threadbare, blue button-up shirt, black suspenders, faded blue jeans, and brown cowboy boots. His silver hair was short and mussed, but his eyes were bright and focused.

"Yessir?" he asked as his eyes carefully assessed the uniformed man at his front door.

"I'm Sheriff Tom Jessup."

"You knocking for my vote, Sheriff? It ain't that season yet, is it?"

"No, sir."

"I don't think I voted for you last time. Does that make a difference in this conversation?"

Jessup politely smiled. "No, sir."

"All right then. How can I help?"

"Did you rent a house to Lupita DeLeon?"

Concern washed over his face. "Why? Has something happened to her? Has she done something?"

"We need to find her."

"It's something serious, isn't it?"

"Maybe. We don't know yet."

He smirked. "Is my house okay, Sheriff? Do I need to go check on it?"

"Your house is fine."

"You sure?"

"Pretty sure."

"I should go check on it just the same. I knew better than to rent to her."

"Why do you say that?"

"Because of her type."

Jessup frowned. "Her type?"

Hartley pulled back from the sheriff and studied him.

"Because she's Hispanic?" Jessup asked.

The older man's face contorted in anger. "God, no, man! I've loved me some brown girls in my time, which is why I gave the woman a chance. See? This is exactly why I didn't vote for you. Jumpin' to conclusions without askin' the right questions. I knew I had you pegged."

"I apologize, Mr. Hartley. What did you mean by her *type*?"

"I thought you, of all people, would know."

"Know what?"

"She's a felon."

"No, she's not."

Hartley dismissively shook his head. "She most certainly is."

Jessup paused for a moment and thought back to asking Autumn to run Lupita's name. He knew for certain that she confirmed that record was clean. Could Autumn have made a mistake? Or did the sheriff?

"We ran her through the system. She came back clean."

Hartley crossed his arms. "The woman is a felon. She even told me so before I ran her credit application. When she batted those big brown eyes, what was I to do?" Hartley stuck his tongue under his lip while he thought. "Hold here for a minute, and I'll get her file." He turned and walked into his house. A moment later, he returned with a manila folder and handed it to the sheriff.

Jessup opened the file and froze. The first thing he saw was a photocopy of her driver's license.

Guadalupe D. Leon.

It was her. Lupita.

The older man tapped the color picture of her license. "I got one of them fancy printer-scanners. Does a pretty nice job, huh?"

Jessup nodded absently.

She had told him her legal name was Lupita. He had assumed the correct spelling of the last name was DeLeon.

A burst of adrenaline now surged through Jessup. He flipped to the second page in the file. There was a report from a credit agency on her. Missed payments, poor credit, and a warning of a felony record. The recommendation from the agency was not to rent to her.

"Why did you ignore their recommendation?" Jessup asked.

Hartley shrugged. "There are not a lot of renters around here, Sheriff. Besides, I tol' ya. She batted those eyes at me. She must've known about my history with the brown girls. They're my weakness."

"I heard you. She pays her rent?"

The older man looked away. "Not always, no."

"But you still let her stay?"

The two men stared at each other until Hartley said, "That's a little personal, Sheriff."

Jessup handed him the file.

"If she shows up, call me."

"Yeah, Sheriff, I will."

"Even if she bats those big brown eyes at you."

Gilbert Hartley shook his head. "See? I was right for not voting for you."

***

Guadalupe Dorotea Leon was in the National Crime Information Center database, which was good for the case but bad for Jessup. She'd been under his nose the entire time. However, how often did he walk around during the day, demanding to look at the driver's licenses of every person he met? Lupita had given him a name, he ran it, and it came back matching to her description. Even the names were eerily similar. Lupita DeLeon. Guadalupe D. Leon.

He imagined she had learned of the similarity somewhere/sometime but had held off on using it until it would be necessary to escape detection.

And now she was in the wind.

After leaving Gilbert Hartley's house, Jessup called Autumn and had her run Lupita's real name. Then he asked Autumn to put an Attempt to Locate out on Guadalupe D. Leon. The ATL would alert any agencies that came in contact with her to hold her for Jessup. Autumn also contacted the various local airports in Pullman, Spokane, and the Tri-Cities.

He then asked her to cross-reference the two names in the ATL.

Jessup found a parking spot a block away from Lupita's house and waited.

It was a long shot, but he had no other play right now. He could drive around aimlessly, looking for her car. Instead, he sat still and waited.

Seconds passed into minutes, which moved into an hour. Then his phone rang. He smiled when he saw the ID screen. He hurriedly answered it. "Hey, buddy."

"Hey, Dad," William said.

"It's a little late back there, isn't it?"

"Not too bad. I was thinking about you today. Thought maybe I should check-in. It's been a while."

"It has been, but that's okay. I'm sure you're busy. What have you been up to?"

"Work mostly," William said. He sounded tired.

"Is that going okay?"

"Uh-huh, yeah, not too bad."

"Meet anyone new?"

"I meet a lot of new people, Dad."

"Yeah, I know," Jessup said softly.

"I don't have a girlfriend if that's what you're asking."

Jessup chuckled. "I wasn't asking that."

"I don't need one right now. I've got a lot going on."

"I know, pal. I know. You eating okay?"

"Yeah, I'm doing okay."

"Need me to send some money?"

"No, Dad, I'm good. I was seriously just calling to check on you. What are you doing now?"

"Sitting off a house."

"You're working?"

"Yeah. A murder case."

"A murder in Colfax?" William asked, his voice a little brighter.

"It's kind of a big one, actually."

"Wow. That's crazy."

"Yeah," Jessup said. He didn't want to talk about work with his son, but anything was better than silence.

"You're not in danger, are you?"

"No, pal, I'm good."

"That's probably funny of me to ask, but you know, I worry about you and all."

A car pulled down the street, its headlight sweeping over Jessup's truck. It suddenly stopped and backed up. As it turned around, Jessup turned on his lights and illuminated the car. The happiness he felt at that moment evaporated.

"Will?"

"Yeah?"

"I'm sorry, but I've gotta go. The person I've been waiting for just showed up."

"Oh."

"I love you."

"I love you, too. Hey, Dad?"

"Yeah?"

"Be careful."

"I will."

Jessup hung up and tucked the phone into the console next to him. His truck then leaped from its parking spot, and he activated the emergency lights.

The red, dented Toyota Camry backed up, turned around, and sped away.

The sheriff grabbed the microphone from the dashboard and keyed it. "Dispatch," Jessup said.

"Dispatch, go ahead." The night operator was on duty now.

"This is Sheriff Jessup. I'm in Garfield in pursuit of a homicide suspect. Northbound on Highway 27. Start backup."

The radio crackled to life.

The Toyota raced ahead, and Jessup's truck roared in excitement at the pursuit. A State Patrol officer jumped on the radio.

"Sheriff, this is Trooper Esser. I'm approaching Belmont now. I can deploy a spike strip."

Belmont was six and a half miles to the north of Garfield.

"Speed is approaching seventy miles per hour," Jessup advised. "If you can get the strip out, do it."

The bends of the winding road did little to slow the Toyota. Several times Jessup jammed his brakes for fear of losing control of his truck. He would catch the small car in the straightaways, but then he would lose ground in the tight curves.

As they approached the small unincorporated community of Belmont, the little car suddenly braked, the driver no doubt seeing the trooper standing near the road, his patrol car behind him. A spike strip lay across the roadway.

The Toyota's braking came too late, though. All four tires blew out almost simultaneously. As soon as the little car passed, the trooper yanked the spike strip off the road to allow Jessup to pass safely by, untouched.

The little car continued a while further as its tires disintegrated, throwing chunks of rubber along the roadway amidst sparks from the rims. When the car was almost entirely on its rims, it jerked to the shoulder. The driver's door flew open, and Lupita jumped out. She sprinted into the nearby field.

Jessup carefully drove his truck off the road and followed her. The engine of his vehicle loudly protested as it fought through the soft dirt. The four-wheel-drive kicked the loose earth high into the air as he pursued the woman deeper into the field.

Finally, Lupita slowed, turned around, and lifted her hands into the air.

Jessup stopped his truck, its high beams illuminating her in the night.

***

Guadalupe Dorotea Leon was arrested for Attempting to Elude a Police Vehicle. She initially protested, saying, "I didn't know it was you, Sheriff. I would have stopped."

Even though Lupita nervously chattered and asked questions, Jessup kept his mouth shut as he secured the handcuffs and patted her down, searching for a weapon. There was an argument for her to avoid the Class C felony of eluding since Jessup was not in uniform, and that was an element of the crime per the state code. A prosecutor could drop it to the much broader Failure to Obey a Police Officer, but Jessup didn't really care about either charge.

His mind was whirring. Lupita had run from him, and he needed to get prepared for a line of questioning he had not expected to have with her only a day before.

When he completed his search of her, he sat Lupita in the backseat of his truck.

"Sheriff?" she asked.

Jessup didn't verbally respond, just looked at her.

"Why are you doing this?" she asked, her face full of contrived innocence.

"You ran from me."

"But I didn't know it was you. I was scared."

"Then who did you think I was? Why would you speed away, racing through town, putting people at risk?"

Lupita stared at him.

"That's what I thought."

He swung the door closed.

"Wait!" Lupita yelled through the window. "I thought it was Border Patrol. ICE!"

Jessup walked over to Lupita's vehicle on the shoulder of the road. Trooper Esser stood near the car.

"Sheriff," he said with a nod. "Need any help?"

"Hang out for a minute. Make sure she doesn't do anything foolish while I search her rig."

Esser nodded and headed over to Jessup's truck.

The sheriff opened Lupita's car and began the search. The interior was dirty. It surprised him that a housekeeper would keep a car this dirty.

He paused then. She was not a housekeeper. She had been at Derwood Smith's under false pretenses. The profession was an illusion, a sham, to get into his house.

Why did she want to get close to him? he wondered.

He moved empty soda cans, hamburger wrappers, and old mail out of the way. He found a partially smoked marijuana joint and ignored it. The laws had long been changed since his days as a young officer, and unless he wanted to go through the hassle of proving she was driving under the influence, it was a waste of time and mental energy.

The backseat provided more of the same flotsam and jetsam of a hastily lived life. There were more burger wrappers, unopened mail addressed to Guadalupe Leon, empty soda cans, and an empty box of Cheez-its. Behind the passenger's seat was a briefcase. It was worn leather with a brass plate near the handle. The initials DXS was engraved into the brass. Derwood X. Smith. Jessup tried to remember what Derwood's middle name was. Had he ever learned it?

He then stepped back, removed his phone, and took a photo of the briefcase.

He walked back over to his truck and opened the passenger door. As he reached into the glove box, Lupita said, "Sheriff, that is not mine. Mr. Smith, he asked me to keep it safe from his daughter. He was worried she would take it from him."

Jessup removed a pair of latex gloves and shut the door. He motioned for Trooper Esser to follow and headed back toward Lupita's car. Jessup pulled out his notebook and recorded the statement Lupita had just made.

Esser waited for Jessup to stop writing to ask, "What did you find?"

He walked to the rear passenger door and reopened it. "That briefcase. The initials on it are for a murder victim in my county. The woman was in his employ. She just said he gave it to her."

"You need a statement from me on this?"

"Let's see what's inside first, but she seemed pretty upset that I found it."

Jessup lifted the heavy briefcase onto the trunk of the car and opened it. He stepped back, his mouth dropping.

"Wow," Trooper Esser said.

"Yeah."

Inside the briefcase were a couple of stacks of bills and numerous small bars of gold.

The sheriff pulled his cell phone from his back pocket and took another photograph.

"She's a murder suspect, right? Is that your motive?"

Jessup glanced at the trooper. "That's the motive."

With a sigh, Jessup called dispatch and requested one of his deputies respond to his location. Each deputy had a camera in their vehicle so they could photograph the scene of any crime. Jessup had a camera in his truck as well, but he decided one more witness to this event would be better.

He also requested dispatch start a tow truck to their location. They would impound Lupita's vehicle as evidence and search it more closely. He would also get a search warrant for the car. Recent legal challenges had changed the law for searches of vehicles following arrest, and officers were not allowed to search the trunk immediately. He wanted to know if there was anything hidden there. The same laws applied to items like the briefcase, but due to the initials on the case as well as Lupita's statement, Jessup felt more than confident opening it up.

Trooper Esser ran back to his car and got a coat as the night air had turned chilly. When he returned to the scene, Jessup opened the rear door to his truck. Lupita turned to face him, tears running down her face.

"You're under arrest for Attempting to Elude a Police Vehicle. I need to read you your rights."

Lupita nodded.

Jessup recited the Miranda Warning from memory. When he was done, he asked, "Do you understand these rights?"

She nodded again.

"Yes or no," Jessup said softly.

"Yes, uh-huh."

Jessup's eyes shifted to Esser, who nodded he'd heard her response.

Then Jessup asked, "Are you willing to waive these rights to answer my questions?"

Lupita lifted her head and looked back at her car. A row of three cars slowly drove by on the highway, followed by a noisy semi-truck.

The sheriff began to repeat his question, "Are you willing to—" but Lupita interrupted.

"Yes," she said.

With his peripheral vision, Jessup noticed Esser's trooper hat bobbing up and down.

Jessup placed his hand on the open door and casually leaned down, trying to take on an air of familiarity. He knew it was impossible to do since Lupita was in handcuffs, in the back of a police vehicle, in the middle of a field, in the darkness of night. Relaxing would be near impossible.

"Do you remember when we first met?"

She nodded.

"You told me your name was Lupita DeLeon."

She scrunched her face. "No, I didn't."

"I specifically asked if Lupita was short for Guadalupe, and you said it wasn't."

She turned away.

"You're not Lupita DeLeon. You're Guadalupe Dorotea Leon. I'm guessing that somewhere along the line, a mix-up occurred with Lupita DeLeon and Lupita D period Leon. Maybe it was a cop. Maybe it was a credit check. Who knows? But that's when you realized there was someone out there with a very similar name to yours."

Lupita stared straight ahead.

"You're not in trouble for playing the name game, Lupita. I just want to know."

She stared straight ahead.

"Was it during a credit check that someone ran for you?"

Her eyes shifted to the sheriff.

"That was it, huh? The check showed potential other names used."

Lupita looked away.

"You used it then and got away with, huh? Did you know that you and the real Lupita were so close in age? That was just luck, huh? How long have you been using her name?"

Jessup glanced at the trooper, who rolled his eyes.

"Maybe it was a name you could count on to keep you out of trouble. Nice and clean."

Lupita's jaw flexed then. He'd hit a nerve.

"How did you meet Derwood Smith?"

The flexing stopped.

"He wouldn't have hired you, but he hired Lupita. He was certainly fond of her."

She turned and looked directly at Jessup. "You wanna know how I got a job cleaning a rich man's house?"

"How did you know he was rich?"

"How many poor people do you know hire a housekeeper?"

Jessup watched her for a moment. "Did he put an advertisement in the newspaper?"

She faced forward, her jaw flexing.

"He didn't run a background check?"

She shrugged. "He didn't have me fill out no paperwork."

"What did you do?"

"I showed up and gave him my name."

"Did you go through the gate?"

"Yes."

"He let you in?"

"Yes."

"Was his daughter there?"

"No."

"What did you tell him when you met?"

"My name."

"Your real name?"

"Yes."

The way she said it was different from the previous affirmations, with more force and conviction, as if that would show him it was the truth. He didn't believe it.

"How quickly did you start working for him?"

"A couple days."

"Why did he need a housekeeper?"

"The old one moved away."

"Where did she move to?"

"I don't know. She moved, and he needed some help. He never talked to me about it. He wanted me to cook and clean. I said I could do it, and he hired me."

"Can you cook?"

"Are you kidding?"

"Was the plan to rob him all along?"

Lupita's jaw flexed again.

"You were there for how long?"

She opened her mouth to say something, then stopped.

"Why's it matter how long you were there?"

"About a year," she muttered.

"Why wait so long?"

"It wasn't hard work. I got him food occasionally. Cleaned up around the couple of rooms he used. That was it. He would let me sit and read until he rang for me. I've had worse jobs."

"Then why kill him?"

Lupita didn't look at Jessup. "I did not kill him."

"He was suffocated with his pillow."

"I did not do that."

"You have a briefcase full of cash and gold. You reported several people had broken into his house but then refused to return my calls."

Lupita turned to stare at the sheriff now.

"You knew the code to his safe. He told me he'd been buying gold lately. Had you been driving him to buy it?"

She looked away again.

"He couldn't drive his car, and his daughter wasn't taking him. You were. You would have known about the cash and the gold. You would have known about its hiding place."

Lupita lowered her head and placed her forehead against the back of the driver's seat.

"And the way the house had been tossed and disrupted, it was too… organized. Like it was messed up by someone who would have to clean it again."

She turned to look at Jessup, keeping her head touching the seat in front of her.

"Nothing was broken. It was like the person who wanted it to look like a break-in knew how much work it would take to clean the house back up."

Lupita rolled her head back into position and stared at her feet.

"You did it, Lupita. You knew where the money was, how much was there, and how easily you could take it. All you had to do was get Derwood Smith out of the way."

She sat upright and turned to him. "I admit I stole the money. I took it, as you say, but I didn't kill him. He was already dead. He was dead when I got there."

"He was dead when you got there?"

"Yes."

"What did you do?"

Lupita thought about it. "I messed up the house to make it look like a burglary. Then I took the money and left." She nodded when she was done. "Yes," she said, "that is what I did."

"Why?"

"Huh?"

"If he was already dead when you got there, why did you call us and tell us someone was breaking in? You could have taken the money and left. Or you could have taken the money and called us. Or you could have called us and then come back later for the money. Don't you see? The story you're trying to tell doesn't make sense."

Lupita opened her mouth to say something but stopped. She glanced over to Trooper Esser, then back to Jessup. "The daughter did it."

"She didn't do it. She has an alibi. You did it."

"You've already made up your mind," Lupita said. "I can see what you're doing. You're a racist."

Jessup said, "Accusing me of racism won't get you a different outcome. You're under arrest for the murder of Derwood Smith." He carefully shut the door.

Trooper Esser shook his head when they made eye contact. "The last bastion of hope for the guilty."

Jessup raised his eyebrows.

Esser said, "Sling mud at your accuser and see if it sticks."

A patrol car pulled up on the scene, its tires crunching the roadside gravel. Jessup wasn't sure which of his deputies would be behind the wheel, but he was happy he could pass processing the vehicle to them and take Lupita back to the jail for booking.

He looked up into the dark sky and saw a multitude of stars. For a moment, he wished he knew more than the Big Dipper.

Chapter 48

Marci Burkett and Quinn Delaney were seated at the Harvester Diner in Spangle, a small community located just off U.S. 195. It was a Saturday and their day off. They weren't working a case.

Instead, they were eating breakfast and drinking coffee. Quinn was eating a short stack of pancakes and drinking black coffee. Marci's breakfast consisted of two hardboiled eggs, a bowl of fruit, and two pieces of heavily buttered toast. She opted for hot chocolate that morning.

"How's the boyfriend?" Quinn asked, sticking a bite of pancake into his mouth.

"None of your business."

"What's wrong?"

"Nothing. It's casual. We're not exactly full time or exclusive."

"I don't know what that means."

"That makes two of us," she said, "so let it go."

"I worry about you," Quinn persisted. "You're my work-wife, so I want to know how things are going in your personal life."

Marci paused, her toast hovering in front of her face. She slowly closed her open mouth and set the piece of toast on her plate. After wiping her hands, she said with exaggeration, "Excuse me?"

Quinn smiled. "You heard me."

"Pretend I didn't. Say it again."

He looked at his plate and cut his pancakes, even though they were already bite-sized.

"Say it," Marci said.

"No."

"Are you chicken?"

"Nuh-uh."

"Then say it."

Quinn put down his knife and fork and smiled at Marci. He took a deep breath and slowly said, "Work-wife."

Marci pointed her finger at him and whispered through clenched teeth, "Don't. Ever. Say. That. Again."

"We spend more time together than most spouses do."

"Stop it."

"You might as well admit I'm your work-husband. I'm a good provider. I carry my weight, don't I?"

"Knock it off, Delaney."

"We should have some sort of ceremony, don't you think? Maybe hold it on our anniversary."

Marci's face reddened, and she silently fumed at her partner.

Quinn remained still for as long as he could before bursting into laughter.

Marci turned away, her face relaxing. Then a small smile formed, and she shook her head. "Why do you do that?"

"Tease you?"

"It winds me up."

"I know, but I get a perverse sense of enjoyment out of it."

Marci nodded and stuck a piece of cantaloupe in her mouth.

The door to the diner opened, and Sheriff Tom Jessup walked in. He was in plainclothes—blue jeans, a black T-shirt, and a black Carhartt jacket. On his head was a green John Deere baseball hat. If someone didn't know Jessup's profession, they might have guessed him to be a local farmer.

Spangle was between Colfax and Spokane and had been a convenient meeting point for the three of them. Jessup had asked them to meet for coffee.

The sheriff slid into the booth as an elderly waitress approached.

"Having breakfast?" she asked.

"Just coffee," Jessup said. To Quinn and Marci, "Morning, do-gooders."

"Do-gooders?" Quinn asked.

Jessup smiled. "Better than ne'er-do-wells."

"You're in a good mood."

"What's not to be happy about? We caught the bad guys."

"There will always be more bad guys," Marci said, then took a bite of a hardboiled egg.

"Don't you celebrate your wins?"

Marci and Quinn eyed each other before shrugging.

"Really?" Jessup said. The waitress set a cup of black coffee in front of the sheriff. He wrapped his hand around it. "You should take a moment to appreciate your wins. Enjoy the moment."

Quinn leaned back in his chair and crossed his arms. "I think we do."

"No," Marci said through a mouthful of food. "We don't. We never do."

"Never?" Quinn asked, thinking about Marci's words. "We never celebrate a win?"

Marci swallowed. "We close a case and move on. You and me, we've never once had a celebratory meal over a case."

"That doesn't seem right, does it?"

"No, it doesn't," Marci said. "I wonder why that is."

Jessup sipped his coffee and watched their interaction, confusion clear on his face. He asked, "So, prosecutors are moving forward with the Braemar cases?"

Quinn nodded. "Everything looks strong. Not sure how quickly we'll get to trial, but we feel good. What about Lupita's? Everything good?"

Jessup nodded. "Yeah. We're fine. She signed a confession."

"She did?" Marci asked.

The sheriff nodded. "After we arrested her, it took some additional talking, but she finally admitted to killing Derwood."

Quinn and Marci nodded, simultaneously saying, "Congrats."

Jessup lifted his coffee in a salute.

"Have you talked with the daughter?" Quinn asked. "What's her name? Adeline?"

"Yeah," Jessup said. "She's a mess. Father's dead. Niece and nephew are in jail."

"The trust money is going to feel like blood money now," Marci said.

The sheriff set his mug on the table. "She said pretty much the same thing. What about her brother? You talk with him?"

"He's taking it surprisingly well," Quinn said.

Jessup raised his eyebrows.

"He wasn't broken about the old man's death."

"Interesting," Jessup said.

Quinn tapped the side of his head. "The head injury mixed with some bad blood. Anyway, when we told him, he didn't bat an eye. His first question after learning about the fate of his son and daughter was, who's going to help me now?"

"Huh."

Marci interjected then. "That lasted only about a minute until he learned about the trust. Everything seemed to fall into place for him then. I think he's planning his new life with a buttload of money. Even though he's got the brain injury, it's not enough to stop the greed from kicking in."

"He didn't care his kids were going to jail?" Jessup asked.

"Not really," Marci said.

"People," Jessup said. "Just when you think they can't let you down any further."

"There's always a new low for them to sink to," Quinn said. "We just have to step back and let them show us how far they can go."

Marci's face scrunched. "Damn, dude."

Jessup smiled as he watched the detectives.

"I'm only telling the truth," Quinn said.

"But you're so damn pessimistic," Marci said. "You need to get a girlfriend."

Jessup said, "Oh."

Both detectives looked at him.

"What?" Marci asked.

"I thought you were his girlfriend."

Marci pointed her finger at him. "Don't you start, Tom!"

Did You Like the Book?

I love when friends and family recommend a book for me. I'll often give it a read just because the recommendation came from someone I trusted. That's probably how we all are.

If you enjoyed this story, I'd truly appreciate it if you would tell your friends and family or leave a review at where you got the book.

All writers need feedback on their work—not only to help other readers discover them, but so they know they're delivering the goods with their stories.

Thanks for reading and I hope to see you again!

About the Author

Colin Conway is the creator of the 509 Crime Stories, a series of novels set in Eastern Washington with revolving lead characters. They are standalone tales and can be read in any order.

He also created the Cozy Up series which pushes the envelope of the cozy genre. Libby Klein, author of the Poppy McAllister series, says *Cozy Up to Death* is "Not your grandma's cozy."

Colin co-authored the Charlie-316 series. The first novel in the series, *Charlie-316*, is a political/crime thriller that has been described as "riveting and compulsively readable," "the real deal," and "the ultimate ride-along."

He served in the U.S. Army and later was an officer of the Spokane Police Department. He has owned a laundromat, invested in a bar, and run a karate school. Besides writing crime fiction, he is a commercial real estate broker.

Colin lives with his beautiful girlfriend, three wonderful children, and a codependent Vizsla that rules their world.

Find out more about Colin at colinconway.com.

www.ingramcontent.com/pod-product-compliance
Lightning Source LLC
Chambersburg PA
CBHW022017310726
48972CB00006B/1693